Also by David Funk

On the Banks of the Irtysh River
The Last Train to Leningrad

Under Siberian Skies

A Novel

By David Funk

This is a work of fiction based on actual historical events. The characters are all products of my imagination. Any resemblance to real people is entirely coincidental.

Acknowledgements

The publication of this novel has truly been a family affair. I owe a debt of gratitude to my daughter, Angela Funk, and to my brothers Bob Funk and Tony Funk. Thank you for your comments, your red ink, and your suggestions that caught my errors and omissions and improved the story at many turns. My deepest gratitude goes to my wife, Shirley, who played her own editing role, and encouraged me every step of the way.

"It always seems impossible until it's done."
Nelson Mandela

"No one leaves home
unless home is the mouth of a shark."
Warsan Shire

Prologue

During the warming days of an eastern Siberian spring, the Mennonite village of Alexandrovka rose from the black, virgin soil.

Strengthened by a desperate optimism, men, women, and children worked side-by-side to cut the lush, waist-high steppe grasses. Under the vast Siberian sky they raked and dried the grass and forked it into huge piles that would become next winter's livestock fodder. They yoked their strong horses and plowed the bared earth in long straight furrows. With spades they cut the upturned sod into the lengths they desired.

Amongst the swaying pine and larch trees at the edge of the nearby forest, golden-eyed daisies watched these strange developments, their keen eyes dancing. Joyful blue columbines waved in the breezes to anyone who would pause long enough to take notice.

Walls appeared as the sods were piled one upon the other. Daisies and columbine were pushed aside as sharpened axes loudly felled specially chosen pines. The trees were stripped of their branches and laid side-by-side along ridgepoles set atop the earthen walls. Overlapping sods carefully laid upon the logs became roofs for shelter from sun and rain. Windows were installed and the dirt floors were swept clean. Belongings were carried from tents and wagons into these crude dwellings. More than one grateful pioneer carved the year 1927 on the lintel of their doorway.

Their temporary shelters built, the determined settlers got down to the serious business of working the soil. They planted crops with seeds brought from places thousands of kilometers distant: Omsk and Slavgorod in west Siberia, and farms in far-off south Russia. While they waited for nature to bring them her bounty, they returned to the forests to choose the logs that they cut into boards. They began in earnest to build the houses in which to raise their children and grandchildren.

As they worked, the pioneers occasionally paused and wiped their sweating brows. They peered into the far-flung steppe. Their gaze reached past brush-filled gullies scarring the plain like splits in dried pinewood and beyond the wide Amur River flowing unseen twenty kilometers away. The remote mountains of China shimmered blue in the distant haze.

In the hopeful certainty of their faith, the settlers thanked God for giving them this beautiful land. It was a place where they would start afresh. It was a place as far from Moscow as it was possible for them to go, a refuge far from the oppressive communist interference that characterized life in the Union of Soviet Socialist Republics.

Alexandrovka thrived.

Unfortunately, the local soviet committee took notice. The secret police opened new files. In accordance with the will of its Leader the committee organized the pioneers and collectivized their villages, imposing the communist will upon them. Threats of imprisonment discouraged those who objected from voicing their concerns.

And then one frigid December night three years after they'd arrived, while the sleeping pines and larches shivered in the dim light of a quarter moon and the snow-covered columbine and daisies dreamed of spring's resurrection, Alexandrovka was quietly abandoned. It was given over to the snow, the cold, the wind, and the wolves. It was left to anyone who might consider it good fortune to find a village with streets empty of people, furnished houses vacant, wood fires cooling, and solid barns, their doors left wide open, with clucking hens warming eggs, snuffling pigs nosing their troughs, and lowing cattle impatient to be fed and milked.

September 1928

When Jacob Enns first stepped into the Alexandrovka collective manager's office, he was reminded of children he once taught. He remembered the look of trepidation on their faces as they walked into his class on the first day of school. He felt like one of those boys, twelve years old and insecure, unsure of what might be asked of him. He remembered the time his instructor had had him bend over in front of the class for an innocent misdemeanor and had caned him while one or two of his classmates quietly snickered behind their fingers.

The office was in the heart of the village of Alexandrovka, in its newly constructed flourmill. The office was not large. If it were a bedroom, Jacob thought, it would comfortably hold no more than a double bed and a small bureau. The walls were constructed of rough boards nailed horizontally. The same boards covered the floor.

Jacob stood rooted in the doorway. His eyes were drawn to the black and white portrait of the General Secretary of the Central Committee of the Communist Party of the Soviet Union, Joseph Stalin. The man stared at him from the center of the opposite wall. His face inside the frame made an attempt to appear paternal, friendly even, but succeeded only in presenting a look of smug arrogance. Jacob was struck by the thought that the Supreme Leader wished to be perceived as Uncle Joe, kindly offering his warm all-powerful embrace to Russia's millions like a mother hen protecting and warming her brood under her wings. But Jacob knew Stalin's embrace inevitably crushed all it encompassed. It was slowly squeezing the life-blood from his country and pulverizing the bones of its citizens.

A whistling sound wormed its way into Jacob's consciousness. With an effort, he broke Stalin's stare. In the center of the room was a potbellied stove with a small iron cook top. A kettle was lustily singing upon it; steam billowed from its spout. As it rose, it wreathed the black stovepipe that reached up toward the low ceiling. Jacob wondered, with the amount of steam already in the air, whether it might not begin to rain. The thought almost made him smile.

To Jacob's right, the manager, Abram Siemens sat at his desk on a straight-backed wooden chair. The desk, Jacob noted, was makeshift. He saw it was made by laying half of a flat-paneled door atop two stacks of narrow wooden boxes. Probably the top half, Jacob thought; there was no evidence of a hole where a doorknob would have been. There were a few papers and pencils scattered about on the desktop. A black fountain pen stood in a holder beside a half-full inkwell.

Abram looked up from his work. He saw Jacob standing slightly stooped with delicate hands hanging limply by his sides. Not the hands of a farmer, he decided, and the posture of one who carried the weight of the world upon his back.

Abram smiled. "You must be Jacob."

"Yes."

"Welcome, Jacob. I've been expecting you. I'll be with you in a moment. Please, take a seat."

Abram gestured to Jacob's left where he saw a desk and chair identical to the one at which Abram sat. There's the other half of the door, Jacob thought, glancing at the small desk and seeing a small hole cut close to one corner.

"Grab that chair, won't you, and bring it over here."

Jacob set his chair down in front of Abram's desk. Before he could sit, Abram stood and shook his hand.

Jacob's grip, Abram noted with satisfaction, was firm. Looking more closely, he saw a man in his late twenties, slightly built, fair-haired with a receding hairline. As Jacob had gone for the chair, Abram had noticed he was balding on the back of his head—a bit early for a man his age, he had thought.

Abram Siemens was a big, broad shouldered man. When he stood to shake Jacob's hand, Jacob had had to look up to meet his grey eyes. Though Abram was manager of the collective, Jacob saw he was lean and fit. The palm of his hand was rough and calloused. Not the hands of an office worker, Jacob observed.

When they were both seated, Jacob glanced back at the portrait on the wall. Irrational though the feeling was, it made him feel very uncomfortable.

Following Jacob's gaze, Abram commented drily, "The comrades in the local soviet insisted on it. As patriotic citizens, we gladly hang the portrait of our Glorious Leader in a prominent location in our office."

Jacob missed the hint of sarcasm and could think of no suitable response. He was unwilling to speak the expected words of affirmation. Instead, he began a conversation that was much less threatening. "My family and I have only been in Alexandrovka for a couple of months. I understand the village has recently been organized into a collective."

Jacob tried to keep his voice calm and noncommittal. He did not want to appear to have an opinion about the reorganization that had taken place. He had learned the hard way that holding contrary opinions in the Soviet Union was dangerous.

"Yes," replied Abram. "We were collectivized about a month ago. But let's leave that discussion for another time. Would you like some tea? I was just about to make some."

"Yes, thank you."

Abram poured two cups of tea. "Sugar?" he asked.

Jacob shook his head, no. He was surprised at the offer. Sugar was hard to come by. How was it Abram had some?

Abram blew on his tea and sipped it delicately. "Hmm, hot." He smacked his lips and leaned back in his chair.

"I'm glad you've come, Jacob. Tell me about yourself."

"Well," Jacob began, "I grew up in the Ukraine. As a student, I always enjoyed school. Becoming a teacher seemed a natural fit for me." His voice drifted into silence. He had no desire to go into the details of his life with this man about whom he knew so little.

Seeing Jacob's hesitation, Abram smiled an encouragement, "Yes, you're a teacher."

"Yes. I love teaching, seeing the light go on in a child's eyes when she finally understands a new concept, having meaningful conversations about things and hearing the child's perspective. They're so wise."

Jacob's eyes had grown bright as he spoke. Abram watched him come alive and smiled thinking, he is probably a very good teacher. But he did not comment. Instead, he said, "I heard about that business at the school. I was very sorry about it. But such is life in our brave new world."

Jacob's eyes darkened. He nodded his appreciation for Abram's sentiment. His brown eyes were once again wary. Not knowing if he could trust the collective's manager he said nothing. After all, he thought, a man in Abram's position of responsibility had to be sympathetic to the communists and their misguided ideology. Why else would they accept his appointment? How else would they trust him?

After a moment, Abram continued, "I'm going to be honest with you, Jacob. Like you, we all moved here thinking we could begin a new life without interference from Moscow. After all, Moscow is thousands of kilometers away. Who are we that they should notice us so they could bend us to their will? But, we were wrong and we were naïve to have thought so. We should have known it was not to be. God knows they've broken every promise they ever made to us. Why should it be any different here?" He laughed but it came out as a grunt. "Free land! You'll be left alone! No taxes! Hah! We live at the whim of the Soviet apparatus like chickens in a henhouse pecking about in the dirt while outside the hungry farmer's wife sharpens her ax. Our blood runs in our veins only to feed our General Secretary's vision."

Jacob straightened his back uncomfortably and pulled his feet closer to the chair.

Siemens chuckled without humor. "I apologize." He paused. "I should not have voiced such troubling, counterrevolutionary thoughts." He emphasized the word counterrevolutionary. "The walls have ears and I suspect that we may have one or two collaborators among us. That fellow who replaced you at the school, for instance; not to be trusted. If the secret police are his friends, as we suspect, you know there will be strings attached. Unless we can somehow convince him otherwise, he'll be dancing like Pinocchio in Stromboli's puppet show when the time comes.

"But, you did not hear that from me, though I know you can be trusted. You see, Comrade Yevchenko of the GPU, our Joint State Political Directorate, was kind enough to tell me your story. You've come from Omsk in west Sibeeria where you were dismissed for insubordination and unspecified crimes against the state."

Jacob nodded cautiously.

"You're lucky you weren't arrested and sent to prison."

Jacob face reddened. He wondered if that might not still happen, a knock on his door one night, a ride to a police station.

Abram saw Jacob's discomfort and sought to reassure him. "Don't worry, Jacob. My conclusions about your character are diametrically opposed to those of the colonel's."

These were reassuring words. Jacob felt his carefully constructed wall of self-preservation open ever so slightly.

Siemens' voice softened. "We'll have plenty of opportunities to grumble about the state of our nation some other time. Right now, I believe, you are in need of work."

Abram looked down at a paper he held in his hands. For a moment he seemed distracted, his concentration wavering like wind-buffeted snowflakes. He grimaced and put the paper down. Another government demand to be met. He'd deal with it later. Raising his gaze to look at Jacob, Abram saw sparks of hope in his eyes.

"So, you're a teacher. As it turns out, the secret police have seen to it that we don't have a classroom for you. But I suppose keeping books and accounts straight won't be too difficult for you?"

Jacob smiled hesitantly.

"As it happens, Jacob, I am in need of an assistant."

Jacob Enns

Jacob stepped outside and closed the door quietly behind him. He breathed deeply, savoring the feelings of relief that were washing over him. He had a job.

Standing in the sunshine on the office's stoop, Jacob surveyed the village of Alexandrovka. Compared to Omsk with its magnificent shopping districts and cathedrals, it had little to recommend it. Instead, he saw a collection of clapboard homesteads clustered along a broad, rutted dirt track. Directly in front of him, the road widened so that it presented a sort of public square. But, rather than an ornate fountain at its center around which the community could gather—as one might expect to see in the city—there was simply more potholed dirt with the occasional stubborn weed struggling to raise its bruised head.

Jacob shook his head in disbelief thinking, what are we doing here, anyway? The city was where he belonged; it was where he felt most comfortable. He had spent his childhood in a small village in south Russia and had done his schooling in a larger town. But moving to the city had been a revelation. Omsk had been wonderful. Even living across the Irtysh River in the smaller center of Novo Omsk had been fine. Any time he and his wife, Naomi, had wished, they had taken the ferry across the river to the city to see its amazing electric lights and endlessly interesting shops. In winter, when the Irtysh froze, the crossing had been even easier. No waiting for the ferry, just bundle up and go.

Still, Jacob reminded himself, he and Naomi with their three-year-old son, Joseph, had jumped at the opportunity to move to Alexandrovka. In the spring, he had received an invitation to teach at the primary school being established in the village. The offer was a godsend. Only weeks before he had lost his teaching position at the Mennonite school in Novo Omsk. Government officials had been pressuring him to help root out counterrevolutionary behavior in the community by asking his students if their parents prayed, read the Bible, or spoke about

God at home. Jacob had already compromised his principles by obeying the order to end religious instruction at school. For refusing the directive to become an inquisitor of children, he was fired. The invitation to teach in Alexandrovka offered the hope of a new beginning.

When his family arrived in Alexandrovka in August, Jacob had immediately wanted to see his new school. He was surprised to find that his classroom was simply a room set aside for that purpose in a newly constructed house. He met the home's owner who told him to keep the noise from the children at a reasonable level. Jacob wondered at the wisdom of the school's location, but was determined to make the best of it.

Once his family was settled in their small two-room home— front room for cooking, eating, visiting; back room for sleeping— Jacob spent a week in the classroom. He arranged tables and chairs, familiarized himself with the few books provided, and wrote lessons with which to challenge the children. He loved teaching and he loved children. He would make his classroom an inviting and interesting learning center.

At last the new school year began. But, no sooner had lessons started than an officer of the GPU appeared in the classroom. The secret police had an office in the nearby village of Konstantinovka, a kilometer or so south of Alexandrovka. With him, the officer brought a teacher, Gerhard Wieler. Jacob was informed that Wieler would be replacing him immediately. In vain, Jacob argued for his position. The officer quickly made it clear that educating the innocent minds of the village children was not to be left to one who had been dismissed from his position elsewhere for behavior judged to be subversive. Jacob was stunned news of his dismissal in Omsk had followed him so swiftly. He was escorted from the school property and warned never to return.

Jacob had walked home in a daze. He felt disconnected from his body. His thoughts refused to formulate. He found he had no peripheral vision; everything around him was a blur. It wasn't until he had reached the other end of the village that he realized he had walked by the gate to his house. In a state of utter confusion, he stumbled back to his home.

When Jacob stepped into the house, Naomi didn't need to hear any words to know with certainty something terrible had happened. His face told her more than she wanted to know; she had seen that look before. Naomi helped Jacob remove his coat and boots. Jacob collapsed into a chair at their table. He stared at his trembling hands while she made tea. When finally he could speak, Naomi's eyes grew large with fear at his news. While Jacob sat and wept, she stood beside him, holding his head to her breast, caressing his hair.

"What will become of us?" Jacob had cried. "We used all the money we saved in Novo Omsk to travel to this godforsaken village." His voice had been desperate. "We have nothing, Naomi, nothing! With no work, how will we survive? I'm a teacher, not a farmer. I studied for years in order to shape young minds. I don't know the first thing about cows or chickens or growing wheat or barley."

The laughter of nearby children brought him out of his reverie. That was then; this was now. Jacob smiled. I guess I won't be reduced to shoveling manure for some farmer after all, he thought. A bookkeeper. I can do that. And Abram Siemens seems like a good man to work for.

Jacob took a deep breath. The air was warm but he caught the scent of drying leaves and of straw piled in farmyards along the street. It smelled like autumn. Winter was coming. He and his family would be fine. Jacob stepped into the street and headed home, whispering a prayer of thanksgiving.

As it sometimes occurs between those who are fortunate enough to find a kindred spirit, it did not take long for Jacob and Abram to form a firm bond of friendship. Not that they agreed on everything. But a deep sense of mutual trust and respect grew between them. There was something in the character of each that the other found compelling. Jacob was moved by Abram's sense of certainty and decisiveness, for he himself was often indecisive and uncertain. Abram was drawn to Jacob's questioning and thoughtful nature, for though he presented himself as confident and single-minded, he was not always so.

One quiet autumn afternoon when they found themselves with little work to do, Abram told Jacob the story of Alexandrovka's beginning. "I lived in Orloff, in the Slavgorod colony," he began. "That's just over five hundred kilometers east of Omsk in west Siberia."

Jacob nodded. He was familiar with the Slavgorod colony. He had relatives there.

"We homesteaded there in 1908. We did well. The soil is rich. We worked hard. God rewarded our efforts with good crops and high prices. Then came the revolution in 1917 and the civil war swept through our area in 1919. The Bolsheviks were not to be stopped and the monarchists were weakened by their own corruption. Once the Reds had defeated the Whites, they turned their attention on us."

Abram recounted the meeting that set his and other families on their journey to Alexandrovka. It had been held the year before, on a pleasant spring Saturday evening. A group of men and women representing more than forty families had gathered in the Mennonite church in the village of Orloff. They had traveled to the meeting from small villages in every corner of the Slavgorod colony. The building was a simple wood structure with benches on either side of an aisle leading to the raised platform from which Abram addressed the assembly. As was the custom the women sat across the aisle from the men, their faces lined with concern for the life-changing decision being mulled over.

The mood of the meeting had alternated between gloom and hope. It was a mere twenty years since many of them had come to western Siberia from German Mennonite colonies in south Russia. They had found the fertile farmland they needed and had established the Slavgorod settlements. Many of those at the meeting had helped build the villages that, until recently, had prospered.

And now it was time to move again. No sooner had Abram carefully laid out the obstacles facing their people in Slavgorod and his plan for their future in a new location than a farmer rose to his feet. "I will not be intimidated by the communists. How dare they take away our farms and form them into a collective! There must be something we can do to stop them. Don't they realize we are the best farmers they have? Why can't they leave us alone?" His voice had risen as the emotion rose high into his throat.

A speaker recounted how, ever since the Bolshevik revolution, collective farms, or *kolkhozy*, had been established all over the country. It had started in European Russia and the Ukraine, but now western Siberia was being organized according to the communist ideology. More than that, the communist war against the wealthy, the successful, and the religious was threatening every facet of their lives.

Another speaker rose to his feet. Abram wasn't sure from which village he had come. "They've arrested our minister. They've put a lock on our church. They plan to use it as a granary. They are mad, these people!" His voice was filled with disbelief and anger.

Before he had taken his seat, another man rose. "In our village they have confiscated the farm of Isaac Suderman. He worked hard for his wealth. Now he and his family have been put out onto the street with nothing but the clothes on their backs. For no reason!"

Abram had heard of Isaac Suderman's misfortune. Nor was it an isolated case. He was himself a successful farmer, a big man made strong by years of working on the land. He had wondered if the secret police have plans to come after him. Was his name on a list in some GPU office?

Someone shouted, "If we speak up we face arrest! What can we do?"

Abram looked over the agitated crowd. They were angry because of an increasingly intolerable present, yet fearful of an uncertain future in a land with a malevolent government. They needed guidance and wisdom.

A red-bearded farmer had voiced what everyone was thinking. "We've worked hard to sink roots into the land here. And now we're talking about starting over from scratch again. I don't know if I have the energy." He had looked for agreement from the men sitting on either side of him. Numerous heads nodded. "Not that I'm afraid of hard work," continued the speaker, "but what's the guarantee that the government won't interfere with us again?"

Abram's resolve had hardened. Holding up the signed contract with the government, he renewed his effort to convince his audience. "I believe God has provided this opportunity for us. This Privilegium, this document from the autonomous government of the Eastern Republic of the Amur Region, guarantees us fifteen hectares of free land for every member of a family, children included." He had looked at a friend, Johan Loewen, in the assembly. "Think of it, Johan. You have six children. With yourself and your wife, that is 120 hectares. I've seen the land. It is flat and the soil is perfect for the crops we farm. And, they are offering each family 400 rubles to help us get established." Abram had raised his voice and waved the papers in the air. "They promise no taxes for three years. They're cutting the rate for transporting our goods on the train so we can bring along our livestock, our farming machinery, our household furniture and everything else we need to begin our lives there. They are serious about wanting new settlements on their sparsely populated eastern steppe."

Abram paused as the men and women in the congregation murmured amongst themselves. "Can we trust them? Will they keep their promises?" It was a moment before he continued. "I don't know. But, for myself, with God's help, I am prepared to take that chance. Perhaps this place in the east is where we can escape the attention of the communists. In this country, it is about as far away from Moscow as one can get. What could be better than that?"

There had been muted laughter at his attempted levity.

"And so, Jacob, that spring, along with dozens of other families, we moved from the Slavgorod colony to this uninhabited steppe. We established this village, Alexandrovka. Families—all German and mostly Mennonite—from villages in Ukraine and west Siberia soon joined us. Other villages appeared on the steppe nearby, built by other equally ambitious pioneers: villages like Halbstadt, Friedensdorf, and one with the unlikely name of someone's dream, New York."

"I think going to America is everyone's dream," concluded Jacob.

Abram continued. "A year later, in the summer of 1928, in keeping with its drive to industrialize farming in the Soviet Union, farm managers appeared in Alexandrovka and the neighboring villages. The local soviet council proclaimed the four villages in our area a *kolkhoz*, a collectivized farm. They named the collective after our village, Alexandrovka. We were told we would now be sharing everything with the people in the villages of Halbstadt, Friedensdorf, and New York: machinery, manpower and expertise. We had no choice but to cooperate. Anyone refusing to cooperate would be declared counterrevolutionary and handed over to the GPU. Some of our most successful farmers were labeled *kulaks*. They were stripped of all their possessions and human rights. Excessive, compulsory taxation of crops under the guise of volunteerism was immediately enforced.

"To my surprise, in a meeting at which the new collective's governing council was elected, I was named the collective's manager. I was given an office here in the flourmill. When I complained the job was too big, the council agreed to provide an assistant. So, here we are."

Abram chuckled, though Jacob didn't find any humor in what he had just been told. It never ceased to amaze him how the communists, with the stroke of a pen and the threat of force, dared to turn people's lives completely upside down. Or end them. Prison, exile, execution he knew had become common punishments since the revolution. No different than under the Tsar, he thought, though perhaps even more viciously practiced.

Abram continued. "You can imagine how upset we were, being told our farms no longer belonged to us. The gall of the government." Abram shook his head as the emotion hit him afresh. "There was no question of resisting. They were making of us a collective and a collective we became. We decided to take the Christian path and farm for the communists 'as unto the Lord.' We would do our best work even though we were servants of a harsh taskmaster. Like the Israelites of old, we are helping to build Pharaoh's pyramids." Abram chucked again. "And of course, we are still good capitalists. They agreed that we can sell anything extra we have left after paying our taxes and setting aside what we need for next year's planting. We look after their demands and are allowed to keep a small piece of the pie."

"I remember a conversation I had with my assistant at the time, Ludwig Hostetler, the fellow you replaced," Abram continued. "We were here in the office talking like you and I are now. 'We'll show those Bolsheviks how Germans farm,' I said to him. 'We will give them nothing to complain about.'"

"I'll never forget what Ludwig said. 'Oh, they'll complain,' he smiled with his usual acerbic tone. 'There is no keeping those boys happy. If God Himself were to stand before our GPU brothers, they would demand to know from Him why crop production is not double what it is. They'd finger their pistols and ask the Almighty who's in charge and browbeat the poor soul without so much as blinking.'"

"So, I said, '"we won't give them an excuse to interrogate God, will we.'"

"And, indeed, we have not," said Abram as he concluded the story for Jacob. "Our harvest this year has been bounteous. In a month or so, our grain taxes will all be paid in full. Hopefully, the collective's soviet overseers will be impressed."

And so it would be. A beaming Colonel Yevchenko, the commander of the regional GPU, the secret police headquartered in nearby Konstantinovka, would enthuse during one of his frequent visits to the Alexandrovka collective's office, "Our first harvest and you are proving that Alexandrovka is a perfect example of how a soviet collective should operate. Moscow applauds your efforts."

As a reward for their diligence and honest hard work, the grain quotas required of the farmers of the Alexandrovka collective for the following year, 1929 would be increased by fifty per cent.

October 1928

One bright autumn afternoon, Ludwig Hostetler stopped at the collective office. He poked his head in the door and offered a cheery, "Good afternoon, gentlemen!"

"Come in," said Abram. "It's good to see you, Ludwig. You've met my new assistant, Jacob Enns?"

Jacob and Ludwig shook hands.

"I can't stay," said Ludwig. "There's a wagon loaded with grain down the road. Axel broke. My services are needed." His face was warmed by a wide smile.

Abram grinned. There was a light in Ludwig's eyes he hadn't seen before.

"What is it Ludwig?"

"Anna has given birth to our third child. Last night. A son! A brother for Margaret and Judith."

"Yes, of course. I knew she was expecting," said Abram. "And here he is. Congratulations! May God bless your little one with good health."

Jacob rose from behind his desk to shake Ludwig's hand again. "What a joy your family has received, Ludwig! Congratulations."

Ludwig beamed. "We have named him after my father, Peter. Peter Ludwig Hostetler."

"A fine name," pronounced Abram.

The three men looked at each other, sharing the happiness of Ludwig's announcement. Abram said, "Well, be off with you. You need to finish your work so you can go home to be with your family. And, it looks like it might rain. You don't want that grain to get wet."

"Yes, you're right! I'll be seeing you then," Ludwig boomed with a wave.

"There goes a happy man," Abram said with a chuckle. "And he's a good man. I told you Ludwig was my assistant for a month when the office first opened, didn't I? You replaced him."

"Yes, you mentioned him. What happened?"

Just then, the kettle started to whistle. Jacob made tea. He poured a cup and gave it to Abram. It seemed their desks were seldom without a steaming cup resting among the papers. To cool the tea more quickly, Abram poured some of it into his saucer and sipped it tentatively. With a sigh, he put his cup and saucer on his desk.

"Ludwig wasn't cut out for office work. I've no idea why the council chose him in the first place."

Abram recalled his conversations with Ludwig during his short time in the office. With a smile he told Jacob.

"They didn't even ask my opinion," Ludwig had complained shortly after he was assigned to the office. "They didn't ask anybody what I do around in the village. They're as daft as a blind bull. I feel like a screw trying to fit into a hole with the wrong thread. I'm just not meant to do office work. No matter how hard I try, it's impossible to keep the letters of the words I'm supposed to be reading from swimming off the page."

And, indeed, the letters were more difficult for him to catch than the fleas on his favorite dog's belly, scurrying amongst the hairs, always moving when he was just about to pinch them. His wife knew Ludwig had difficulty with reading. They had talked about it early in their marriage and had reached a comfortable arrangement. It is she who led the family in Bible reading each evening before bed.

One cloudy September morning after a month at his new job in the flourmill office, Ludwig had approached his boss. He had stood before Abram's desk. His hat was held firmly in his two hands. He had nervously cleared his throat of imagined phlegm while Abram finished jotting a note.

When his boss had finally looked up, Ludwig had begun.

"Abram," Ludwig said, avoiding his boss's eyes. He was staring sorrowfully at Abram's brown mustache growing thick and bushy directly out from his nostrils. "I'm not suited for this work. I've been in this office for four weeks now, and I just can't get the hang of things. Perhaps I need new spectacles." Ludwig had taken off his glasses and gazed myopically at them, as if to prove they were deficient. He was too embarrassed to address the issue of his illiteracy. When Abram said nothing, Ludwig had hesitated. He had replaced his spectacles on the bridge of his long nose.

Ludwig had gathered his courage and said, "The truth is, I need to work with my hands. Give me a hammer or a saw. Show me a broken piece of machinery and I'll repair it as quickly as you like. I need a solid wrench in my hands. This book work, it's not for me."

Siemens had seen the validity of Ludwig's plea. He, too, had increasingly grown frustrated by Ludwig's lack of progress in maintaining accurate records in the office. He knew Ludwig's skills as a mechanic were being wasted.

"I understand. I'll see what I can do," he had answered.

A week later, Ludwig was assigned to repair farm equipment in the collective's machine shop.

"He's a good man," Abram said. "His skills were wasted in here. Since he was put in charge of repairing our farming equipment, breakdowns have been fixed in half the time it was taking before. The collective is far better served by having him do what he excels at."

"Would that we were all as fortunate," mumbled Jacob under his breath.

November 1928

On another occasion, when the work was slow, Jacob asked Abram a question that was nagging him. "You told me once that you believed God led you to this place. Do you still believe that?"

"Yes." There was no hesitation in Abram's response, but he paused before he continued. Lost in thought, he steepled his fingers and tapped his thumbs together a few times. "Even so, I cannot now see what His purpose was. I was so certain coming here would be God's answer to so many of our problems. But, does it matter that I cannot see God's design, His plan? The important thing is to remember we are always in His hands."

Jacob was quiet for a moment. He wasn't sure he wanted to talk about what came to mind, but he found himself speaking anyway.

"Let me tell you my story. I grew up near Margenau, in the Molotschna. My father was a lay minister. We had a good life. My father was respected in the community. He preached about a God who keeps safe those who put their faith in him. Despite all that and despite all of his prayers and my mother's and mine, my father died of typhus during the civil war. My mother, brother, and sisters starved to death in the great famine in the early 1920s. My brother was ten, my sisters, eight and six. They were children." Jacob's mouth was suddenly dry. Suppressed emotions were sweeping over him. He was having trouble forming the words. "My uncle was killed by Nestor Makhno's anarchists when they invaded Eichenfeld. He was one of 136 innocent men and women who were murdered that day in October, nine years ago. My cousins witnessed his murder. As gruesome as this sounds, what my family has been through is a mere drop in the bucket of suffering people in this country have endured over the past decade."

Jacob paused. Like a raging grass fire, the memories swept over him; he felt himself suffocating in its smoke. "I do not believe what happened to them and to so many of us was part of any grand, divine plan. What we suffer is not because God wills it or allows it. If it were, what kind of heartless god would I believe in? There is no reason behind what we have suffered. The simple truth is we are living in a place where evil things happen to many people. To most of us, in fact."

Abram wasn't convinced. "But do you not believe that God actively intercedes in the events in which we find ourselves? Surely he kept safe those who were uninjured, those who lived. Do you think him to be absent, leaving us to suffer whatever befalls us, with no redeeming purpose behind what we experience?"

"How can you say that God had a hand in keeping safe those who survived when He did not keep safe those who died?" The idea was incomprehensible to Jacob. After a moment he said, "I can understand why those who survived say that it was as a result of the grace of God in their lives. But I don't believe that God magically changes the tragic circumstances in which we sometimes find ourselves. To live is to endure the consequences of our own actions and the actions of others. When evil visits us, some survive; some do not."

Abram didn't know how to respond to what he considered to be Jacob's cynicism. He was well aware of the atrocities that had taken place since the Bolsheviks had won power in 1917 and continued to occur throughout the Soviet Union. Everyone knew about the horror of Eichenfeld. There had been many other similar stories. But he had always been comforted by the notion there was purpose behind the suffering. "You would agree that miracles do occur, though, wouldn't you? The Bible is full of accounts of miracles. Have you experienced no miracles in your life?"

Jacob frowned. "I've heard people say they've experienced a miracle. A miraculous healing; a relative somehow miraculously finding their way home after escaping from the gulag. I don't know. Who am I to say they are mistaken?"

Jacob chuckled. "I suppose the fact that after all my wife and I have been through together, she is still with me and loves me is a miracle." He paused. "Naomi and I are quite different. If I were a horse and she the driver of the wagon I was pulling, there would be much snapping of the whip. You see, I am the relaxed type and would often be content simply reading a good book. She, on the other hand, likes to keep moving to get things done. If she were a horse and I the driver, there would be much tugging on the reins, though perhaps with much less success than she would have with her whip." Jacob chuckled. "It works best when we pull side by side, though not without the occasional misstep and jostling to be sure."

"It sounds like you are a perfectly normal married couple," smiled Abram.

Both men were silent for a time, lost in their own thoughts, before Jacob continued. "This is what I believe. I have come to believe that the God of the Bible is a suffering God. What else can we conclude when we see His Son hanging on a cross? I find comfort in the realization Jesus participated in our suffering. God suffers with us; his Spirit indwells us and shares in our pain. And if we become aware of Him, His presence can give us strength and comfort. That is how God is present with us. It is the way he expresses his love for us in the here and now, and that is in itself miraculous.

"But more than that, God also comes to us in the tangible form of his people. It was when others shared food they could not spare with my family when we were starving that God became real to me. It was when sisters from the church came to help nurse my father when my mother was too exhausted to get out of bed that I saw God's love in action. It was when our neighbors took me in to live with them after my family was gone that the love of God became most clear to me and I saw his divine activity coming through them into my life. This is another miracle, that in this world filled with pain, where everyone suffers in their own way, there are those who are willing to come alongside us and share our pain. How else could we endure it?" He paused. "That is the only way I can make sense of things. There is no divine purpose behind suffering. But good can come from suffering when it provides us the opportunity to love others as Jesus loved us. And as we act on that love, we become more like him."

Abram looked at Jacob thoughtfully. "Well," he spoke slowly, "perhaps you have opened my eyes to a new way of seeing things."

For a few minutes the two men sat in silence, thinking about questions the answers to which were beyond comprehension.

The monochrome General Secretary of the Central Committee of the Communist Party of the Soviet Union hanging on the wall behind their desks glowered down on them disapprovingly while they discussed the uncertainties of their faith. For him all things were completely black and white.

December 1928

Jacob Enns moved the heated brick on the floorboards of the sleigh, trying to reposition it between his feet. It was steadily losing its heat and he wanted to take advantage of its last bit of warmth. He was returning to Alexandrovka after spending the afternoon in Konstantinovka where he had been summoned to explain some innovations he had introduced into the collective's bookkeeping methods.

Jacob's mistake had been that he hadn't sought approval for the changes before he implemented them. Colonel Yevchenko was immediately suspicious. Jacob had had to explain his methodology to him and a member of the local soviet. He could tell neither had understood his rationale and in the end he had been told to return to the accepted method of recordkeeping.

Disheartened, Jacob decided to take a road that followed the Amur River for a while before turning northward toward Alexandrovka. As he gazed across the frozen river at its distant southern bank, he tried to imagine what it was like for the Chinese peasants who lived there. Are they as beaten down by their government as we are, he wondered?

The long, straight track upon which Jacob traveled was no more than a trail of ruts cut in the snow on the Amur River's bank. Occasionally the road gently dipped or crested. At other places it veered slowly to the left or right as it followed the course of the river.

The cold was numbing. The brick by Jacob's feet was no longer of much use. Every so often, a gust of wind deepened the chill even further. With each breath, the vapor Jacob expelled condensed in an icy cloud about his face. His mustache had developed a row of small icicles. He could feel them pressing against his lips. The moisture in his eyes, always on the brink of freezing, threatened to stick his lids together.

The late afternoon sun was rapidly sinking, as if ashamed of its inability to warm the land in the face of winter's frigid sting.

As he glanced at the Amur River on his left, Jacob could see the river was solidly frozen over. It looked rugged and forbidding, with blocks of ice everywhere thrust up against each other in random pyramids and humps like beaver lodges. The massive chunks had been built up by the action of the fast moving water beneath. Sitting on the seat of his sleigh, wrapped in his sheep's wool coat and with his woolen hat pulled tightly over his ears, Jacob was impatient to get home.

"How cold is it?" he asked his horse pulling his sleigh. "Minus thirty? Minus forty?"

His horse flicked its ears at the sound of his voice. Its head bobbed up and down in time with its plodding steps. Jacob flicked the reins over the horse's back. "Move along, old girl. I want to be home before supper."

With little else to do Jacob's mind began to wander. It would be Christmas in a couple of weeks. He needed to spend some time whittling the little horse he planned to give Joseph as a gift. The body was almost complete. He would need to ask Naomi for some yarn for the mane, the tail and the pull string. And there was the base and the wheels to carve as well.

Naomi. Jacob remembered the first time he noticed her. A group of young people had decided to spend a summer evening on the banks of the Kusushan River, a tributary of the Molotschna River that had given their colony its name. It was a perfect evening to be out. The westering sun still warmed the air, but the intense heat of the day had lifted. A comfortable breeze kept the flies and mosquitoes at bay. Doves were calling to each other in the willows on the riverbank. For a time he had watched a hungry heron patiently stalking frogs that croaked among the tall, swaying bulrushes.

Someone had brought along a guitar. He was strumming a Russian folksong. The song spoke of longing and of love. Naomi began to sing along. Listening as he lounged on the grassy bank, Jacob was immediately captivated. Though they had known each other since childhood, it was as if he was seeing her for the first time. Her long hair was the color of cherry wood. Her bright eyes were as blue as the sky at dawn. Her beauty dizzied him.

Naomi's face shone in the glow of the setting sun. As she sang the slow Russian lullaby, her lips drew him in as surely as a trout caught on a fisherman's line. He could not tear his eyes away as they puckered and moved to form each new consonant. As her lips parted while taking a breath, he felt himself snared, entangled. The sound of her voice was delicate and alluring. He yearned to kiss her, to run his finger along the soft line of her chin. Yes, Jacob thought, had she been a siren, he would quite happily have driven his ship onto any jagged rocks to possess her.

Jacob shook his head and smiled. Their courtship had begun soon after. He was still amazed Naomi had accepted his advances. She had waited for him and when he had finished his teacher training, her father had allowed them to marry.

And they had been blessed with a son. Joseph would be four years old next April. He was small for his age, but clever. Jacob smiled as he thought of his son and his vivid imagination that enlivened all of his play.

"I am a fortunate man," Jacob mumbled.

Hearing his master's voice, the horse flicked its ears. Its pace quickened as the thought of home brought strength to its efforts.

In the distance, Jacob saw a sleigh coming toward him. It was piled high with shapes he decided must be household goods. As the sleigh drew closer, he noticed a second sleigh behind it. Riding on each sleigh were a man and a woman with a few children lodged firmly among the tied down bundles.

"More families," mumbled Jacob.

He pulled the icicles from his mustache and drew his scarf closer over his mouth.

As the wagons drew near, Jacob made room on the roadway for them to get by. For a moment, time slowed. The only sound was the snorting of horses' breath, the creak of leather harnesses, the soft crunch of snow compressing. As they passed him, Jacob nodded in greeting. The men driving each wagon nodded cautiously in return. Wrapped as they were to stay warm, the women and children looked out at him, past the edges of wool scarves and blankets, with eyes that betrayed fear and apprehension.

When they were by, Jacob looked back at the retreating sleighs. His glance was met by suspicious faces turned his way and slowly growing smaller. Jacob recognized none of them.

"God be with you," Jacob breathed.

He remembered passing the tower where guards were on the lookout for people, he was sure, just like these. It was perhaps half a kilometer behind him. He judged that he was about halfway between it and the next tower. Another border guard on horseback had passed him going in the opposite direction, maybe ten minutes ago. That guard would surely have also passed these two sleighs.

Jacob had a gut feeling these people were not from any of the villages close by. From the look of them, he guessed they were coming from Blagoveshchensk. They had probably come to the city from somewhere else far, far away, he thought. As soon as they felt it was safe, the men would turn their horses toward the river. They would take their sleighs down the slippery slope onto the ice, praying the sleighs would not upset, praying they would not break, praying no border guards would see or hear them. They would lead their horses around the river's obstacles: endless jagged piles of ice blocks, pools of open water where the river was too swift to freeze, blankets of snow hiding crevices in the ice. There would be no turning back. For hours they would endure the cold and the danger until they were captured, or shot, or had reached the far bank of the river and safety in China.

For over a year now, more and more people— individuals, families, small groups—had been escaping to China in this way. He had heard the stories. So had the soviets, and the border guards were becoming ever more numerous and more vigilant.

Jacob took a final look at the Amur River as the road curved away from its banks. He noticed tendrils of ice fog slowly rising above its frozen surface. Jacob flicked the reins to encourage his horse. A warm house and supper awaited him. It would be an hour or two yet before he would be able to make out the smoke from the chimneys of Alexandrovka rising above the frozen roofs. Behind him, the relentless waters of the Amur gurgled and bucked as they continued the futile struggle to be freed from the ice that encrusted its surface.

Jacob warmed himself by the stove while Joseph sat on his lap, happy to cuddle with his daddy. Naomi was putting their supper on the table.

"I saw some more people along the river today. Not locals. I'm sure they were from the city. They had seemed so tense and suspicious as they passed me. I'm sure their intention was to cross the river into China."

"They must be desperate to attempt such a dangerous crossing," said Naomi.

For a moment Jacob was lost in thought, recalling what he had learned about the Amur River as he was preparing for his family's move to eastern Siberia.

The Amur River; the blessing and the curse of all who lived along its banks and in the plains and valleys it drained. The home of giant Kaluga sturgeon that grew to weigh more than a thousand kilograms during their fifty-five years of life. Home to a myriad other fish: the 150 pound Siberian taimen, pike, carp, salmon, burbot, broadhead, keta.

"Did you know that in Chinese mythology, a river is sacred? They call our river the Dragon of the North, the Heilong Jiang, the black dragon. It is the black dragon because black is the king of the Chinese hierarchy of colors, though they think of it as actually no color at all. They consider black to be the color of water and the color of heaven. And to the Chinese, the Dragon is the symbol of imperial, omnipotent power."

"So they worship the river?" asked Naomi, a little skeptical.

"In a manner of speaking. They worship the Dragon that is the river. They believe he controls the weather and as a consequence, their fate. He provides the rain to water their crops when their meager sacrifices are acceptable, in which case they prosper. Should their sacrifices not be accepted, they believe the Dragon withholds the rain and their crops wither in drought, or he sends floods that wash them away.

Naomi frowned. "That must leave the farmers feeling pretty helpless, being at the mercy of their dragon river god." She paused. "Come to think of it, that sounds not so very different from what some of our people believe. The farmers pray and God does what he wills. He blesses with a good crop or he doesn't. Gods with different names, but either way, the god is in control."

Jacob thought for a moment. "I suppose you're right, though I've never made that connection before.

"The Amur got its name from the Russians after they gained control of the lands on its north bank less than a hundred years ago. Until then the Chinese communities thrived on both of its banks. When the Russians took over the north bank, they forced the Chinese who lived there to move to the other side of the river. Did you know the Amur flows over 4400 kilometers from Mongolia to the Strait of Tartary northeast of here, by Sakhalin Island? It's a long river! Along most of its length it forms the border between Russia and China. People have been trading across it for centuries using boats in summer and horses and sleighs over the ice in winter."

"I thought the border is closed," said Naomi.

"It is. Or at least it's supposed to be. But determined people always find a way. Abram Siemens was telling me the other day that a lot of traders have simply become smugglers. They watch the routines of the soviet border guards who patrol the banks on our side of the river, learn how to evade them, and continue their traffic from north to south and back again. They also know the river, where it's safest to cross. They're smuggling the same goods they've always traded—silk, porcelain, and kitchen cutlery among other things—but they've added a new one. Some Chinese are smuggling people across the river to China. The tougher things are getting over here, the more people are desperate enough to try it."

Naomi had heard some of the stories of people attempting the crossing. She wondered, how desperate must people be to place their lives into the hands of Chinese human traffickers? Who knew if they could be trusted?

Jacob broke Naomi's reverie. "Those families I saw on my way home today. I hope they make it."

Naomi sat down. Steam rose from the bowl of borscht she'd placed in the middle of the table. "Let us pray that God will give them strength for what lies before them," she said.

September 1929

Eight months passed as the routines of life in Alexandrovka carried on. After another frigid winter and wet spring, the cycle of farming followed its unbending course. Under Siemens' diligent leadership the collective's crops were planted and cared for. The summer was hot and the rains fell when they were most needed. The green fields flourished. Ripening heads of grain swelled on their stalks, foretelling the yeast-risen bread they would become. September was dry and the crops turned golden. More than one farmer looked with pride and gratitude at the bounty their collaboration with nature had produced. If the frosts held off until all the harvest was taken in, their hopes would be fulfilled. They would be able to deliver all of the government's excessive grain requisitions with plenty to spare for their own needs.

Jacob admired the farmers' handiwork any time he had occasion to leave the village and travel along the country roads. He appreciated the beauty of the waving fields, but was equally grateful that he had been spared the need to labor in them. More than once Jacob was heard to say, "I could never be a farmer. I would hate to always be dependent upon the weather. There are too many uncertainties in farming. I would be a nervous wreck." He asked the farmers, "How do you do it? How can you live with the unpredictability? You put seeds in the ground and you hope and pray for the ideal conditions that will cause it to sprout and grow. And for months, when your crop is growing, you search the skies for hail that can pummel the fragile plants to bits in minutes. In spring and summer you pray for rain, while in fall you fear it for the mold and disease the dampness can bring." The farmers would answer with a shrug and a smile.

Jacob enjoyed his work in the collective office. He liked the challenge of balancing numbers, the tactile feel of a pen between his fingers, the certainty of ink on paper. He also took joy in the weekends when, unlike the farmers whose work never seemed to end, his work was left behind and he could give his full attention to his family.

After a week in which, for some reason the days had dragged and seemed endless, Friday finally arrived. Jacob was looking forward to a couple of days at home. There were chores to be done. The roof had leaked during a recent rainstorm. He would need to find where the rain was getting in and repair it. There was wood to be chopped in preparation for the coming winter. Regardless of the work needing to be done, he would be able to spend the time with Naomi and Joseph. Family time was precious to Jacob. And, finished or not, the chores would be forgotten on Sunday. Sunday was a day for rest and worship with their community of faith.

Late in the morning that Friday, one of the collective's communist party overseers made a brief stop. He was polite and jovial, happy to be visiting the region's model collective.

He shook hands with Abram. "I passed some of your fields on the way over," the grey-bearded, thick jowled man said. "I couldn't help noticing how full the crops look. You have done well again this year. Very impressive! Very impressive!"

Abram smiled. "Yes, thank you. Another couple of weeks and the harvest will be done. So far, the yield is looking very good. With God's help, we expect we will exceed our quotas."

The overseer grinned uncomfortably.

"I expect the bounty of your crop has more to do with your farming expertise than anything else. Still, if you think your God is helping you, who am I to argue. The results are what we're interested in. You can attribute your success to whomever you like, though in future you may want to amend your enthusiasm for your God. Comrade Stalin takes a dim view of religion."

The overseer glanced at Jacob seated at his desk. "Well, I cannot stay. I've simply come to deliver this to you." He handed an envelope to Abram.

After the man left, Abram opened the envelope and slid out the paper it contained. Busy with his own work, Jacob was unaware of the length of time Abram took to read and reread the letter. Once he was sure he understood the words on the page, Abram called, "Jacob. Come over here a moment, would you?"

When Jacob stood in front of his boss's desk, Abram held out the piece of paper.

"Read this and tell me what you think."

Jacob took the paper to his desk, sat down and began to read. It was a decree from the Council of People's Commissars dated August 26, 1929.

Jacob said, "August 26. That's only a couple of weeks ago. Someone must think this letter awfully important for it to make it here that quickly." Typically, communication with Moscow was painfully slow.

Jacob read on. As he came to the end of the letter, he looked up. Abram was watching him. Jacob refocused his attention on the paper. He reread the black letters printed on it, his eyes darting back and forth along their length. His fingers began to tremble. He dropped the letter onto his desk and leaned back in his chair.

"They can't be serious!" Jacob exploded into the ceiling. He threw a look at Abram. "They can't be serious! Do they think they are God that they can alter time?"

Jacob picked up the letter and, in disbelief, read it for the third time. "They are changing the length of the week?" His eyes swept back and forth on the page. "As of October 1, our weeks will be five days instead of seven? Weekends are done away with? Sunday is abolished?" He began to read aloud, "Days will be assigned colors, red, green, and blue. Work will continue twenty-four hours a day every day of the five-day week." Jacob could not fathom the sheer audacity of the order.

"It's their *nepreryvka*, their 'uninterrupted' week," said Abram quietly. Jacob could not tell if the tone of Abram's voice signaled resignation or defiance. "I'd heard rumors that they were considering it. We are all to be assigned a color. Husbands and wives must be assigned different colors. Our color will determine the days and shifts we work." He laughed as he recited, "Discretion may be used when assigning colors to the children."

"But that means families will be split apart," sputtered Jacob. He thought of Naomi and Joseph. Naomi would be at work in the collective's fields, probably harvesting potatoes, or carrots, maybe cabbage. Joseph would be playing with other children at the home of a neighbor. "If Sunday is abolished and we're to work every day, how will we be able to have any church services? It will be impossible to get everyone together. We'll all be working on three different schedules. Why are they doing this?"

"It's all about their notion of efficiency, Jacob. They want to increase production. And, if that means the end of our religious activity, they'll think it so much the better."

Jacob shook his head in disgust.

Abram's tone lightened. "We have one saving grace. You seem to have missed one important sentence. The new calendar does not apply to the collectives. The directive is aimed primarily at factories, stores and government workers."

Jacob laughed with relief. "If it doesn't apply to us, why'd they bother to tell us about it?"

"Perhaps they want us to realize how good we've got it compared to the workers in the cities. Or maybe they're biding their time before they thrust it on us."

Abram frowned. The lengths to which the communist party would go to control the population that served it disturbed him. He stood and walked to Jacob's desk. Picking up the paper, he held it lightly as if to protect his fingers from being burnt. "Until I am told otherwise, we'll ignore this bit of meddling communist propaganda."

Jacob was almost sure he heard a snicker coming from the direction of the portrait of Joseph Stalin, the General Secretary of the Central Committee of the Communist Party of the Soviet Union. From his place of honor on the office wall, the malevolent dictator maligned through his gap-toothed grin, "Your eyes haven't begun to see, your ears haven't heard, nor has your mind imagined the half of what I've prepared for you."

November 1929

Jacob woke with a start. His dreams had been troubling and for a moment he sought to find the link that might provide a clue to their meaning. He gave up as the images quickly blurred and were gone.

Lying snugly beside him under their eiderdown quilt, Naomi stirred in her sleep and then lay still. Looking toward the window, Jacob saw the vapor from his breath illuminated in the half-light of a November morning. The fire had gone out. Jacob got up and shivered as he threw some wood into the stove. Seeing Joseph still asleep under his blankets, Jacob crawled back into bed. He tried to warm his cold feet against Naomi's. She kicked his feet away and burrowed deeper under the quilt.

When Jacob finally stuck his nose out the door that morning, he saw that a cold front had blown in overnight. Low in the crisp, pale sky, sundogs followed the course of the morning sun as it struggled to gain altitude. The day before had been warm for the season. The collected snow had melted and the ground in places had been turned to porridge. Because of this night's frost, those spots had frozen. Now translucent crystalline structures protruded from the ground where once there had been mud. As soon as breakfast was finished, young Joseph pulled on his boots and gloves and made it his business to crush the ice-plated puddles and soon the ruins of miniature crystal castles littered his front yard.

Fieldwork was completed for the year so Naomi was able to stay home with Joseph. She looked forward to a quiet day. There were buns to be baked and there was a pile of darning to be done. Winter had arrived and socks with holes could lead to frostbitten toes. She kissed Jacob as he left for work.

In the afternoon while sitting at his desk in the collective's office, Jacob greeted a visitor. Dietrich Reimer, a farmer from one of the other villages in the collective, stepped into the office, slamming the door behind him.

"Well, Dietrich," said Jacob after shaking his hand. "From the grin on your face, I'd say you didn't come here to talk about the weather. Come, out with it. I have a feeling what you are about to tell me is going to be good and the Lord knows, there is ever a shortage of good news!"

Dietrich laughed and told Jacob his story. He had electrifying news. Exit visas were being issued to people of German descent who had gathered in Moscow. "Our people! Mennonites!" Dietrich crowed.

Jacob put down his pen and was inclined to scoff at the very notion that Stalin would allow anyone to leave his socialist workers' paradise. No exit visas had been issued for months. Many had tried repeatedly. Everyone knew all requests to emigrate were being denied. However, Dietrich pulled from his pocket and showed Jacob a letter from a family member who had written from Moscow encouraging him to come. The writer rejoiced in the fact his family had been granted the precious exit visas. Furthermore, he noted, trains of fortunate emigrants had already departed for the border. Germany had opened its doors and was prepared to welcome the refugees.

"It is true!" avowed Jacob's friend, in a hushed voice that caressed the wooden walls and knocked the startled portrait of the General Secretary of the Central Committee of the Communist Party of the Soviet Union off-kilter.

"It's astonishing!" Jacob exclaimed. "Think of it! At this very moment, while we're talking here in Alexandrovka, our people are riding on trains leaving Moscow and the Soviet Union! Heading to Germany!" He could hardly take it in.

Glancing at the portrait of the General Secretary, Jacob noticed the startled look had been replaced by a disapproving frown. The thought had suddenly occurred to the Dictator that he might have misjudged the situation. Had the permission to leave given to the few been an invitation to the many to try for the same?

Reimer nodded eagerly. "My uncle says there are hundreds of people arriving in Moscow every day. There are thousands of them there already. They are all pressuring the government to let them leave the country. It's our only hope. I know it's a faint hope, but we've got to try," he said. "My wife is preparing food for the journey. We are leaving tomorrow. You should consider it, too."

After his friend left, it did not take Jacob long to decide. Abram Siemens was visiting Halbstadt, another village in the collective and would not return that day. There was nothing on Jacob's desk that could not be looked after on the morrow. He grabbed his coat and boots, pulled the flaps on his sheepskin hat down over his ears, and made his way outside. Closing the door behind him, he hurried down the steps. He kicked at pebbles in his path as he strode along, considering the implications of what he had been told. The fog of his breath formed a translucent scarf that wrapped itself around his neck.

When Jacob stepped inside their door, Naomi was surprised to see him home so early. "Oh!" she squeaked. "You've given me a fright." Her back had been to the door and she had been concentrating on kneading some dough for a batch of buns. "Why are you home so early? What has happened?" she asked nervously.

Working hours in the village were strictly observed; it was one of Abram Siemens' rules meant to impress upon the collective's communist overseers their loyalty to the state. 'Loyalty will have its rewards' was one of his favorite mantras. Jacob never came home until after the clock had cleared the way.

"Is something wrong?"

"Nothing is wrong, my dear," Jacob reassured Naomi. The audacity of what he was about to propose made him nervous. He hoped she didn't hear fear in his voice.

Just then, Joseph came into the house.

"Close the door, son," said Jacob. "We don't want to let the cold in. And take off your boots." He tousled his son's hair, picked him up, and tickled him. Joseph burst into giggles.

After Naomi had pinched off the dough into buns and set them aside to rise under a clean towel, Jacob said, "Sit down, Naomi. I have something to tell you."

Naomi sat on one side of the table. Jacob sat on the bench across from her. While Joseph played on their bed nearby, imagining flying horses and daring exploits, Jacob explained what he had learned and made his daring proposal. "I think we should go to Moscow. This is our chance to emigrate."

Stunned by what her husband suggested, it was a few moments before Naomi could respond. "You want to leave everything we have here—which isn't much I grant you—to go to Moscow in the hope we'll be allowed to emigrate? Listen to yourself! Do you know what you're saying? Do you know what you're asking?"

Jacob repeated his arguments. Naomi listened, her mind racing.

"I don't know, Jacob. It's a huge risk. What if we're denied? Then what?"

"Then we come back here, I guess," said Jacob calmly.

"I'm going to need to think about it. Right now I have to finish the baking. We can talk about it again later."

Hours later, dinner cleared away, Naomi and Jacob sat down at the table and sipped cups of hot water. Naomi cleared her throat. "If it were just us," she said, putting her thoughts into words, "we could make do here. But who knows what the future will bring for Joseph? The government is always tightening its rope around our necks: we cannot work without interference, we cannot say what we think, and we cannot even think what we like or believe what we wish. The communists do nothing but take from us and take from us, and I am convinced they will continue to do this until we have nothing left to give. And then they will ask for more." Her voice shook with emotion. "For myself, perhaps I could endure. But not Joseph. He must have a better future."

Jacob and Naomi held hands across the table. "So, you agree that we should go to Moscow?" asked Jacob tentatively."

Naomi nodded.

Like the danger of a house fire is found in every lit candle, the fear of failure flickered behind Jacob and Naomi's decision to leave Alexandrovka. But they gave the thought no room to grow. They knew the risk they were taking in leaving everything behind on the faint hope the government would allow them to leave the national prison it had created. If they allowed themselves to dwell on it, the candle would ignite the table and with it the curtains, and soon the whole house would fall into ashes.

Naomi had tears in her eyes as she looked resolutely at Jacob. "Once we've started, there is no turning back," she said.

Jacob set his jaw and slowly nodded his head.

They immediately set to work making preparations for the journey. Naomi began mixing more ingredients while Jacob built up the fire in the oven. They would need a lot more buns to sustain them on the 8000-kilometer train ride to Moscow.

When Jacob Enns told Abram Siemens he was taking his family to Moscow in the hope of being allowed to emigrate, Abram was not surprised. Dietrich Reimer hadn't been the only person trumpeting the news of the possibility of escape from their Soviet shackles, nor was Jacob the only person with whom Dietrich had shared his exciting news.

Abram looked thoughtful. "The reality of life in this country is causing more and more of us to want to get out. Moscow has opened the door and allowed a few to leave. Who knows for how long that door will remain open? I find it hard to believe that it would for any length of time. Nevertheless, some must try. People are becoming desperate and their desperation is driving them to become more creative. Many are taking great risks. Some are leaving everything in favor of rattling the gates of Moscow. Others plan their escape right here, across the river.

"Yesterday in Halbstadt I was told about a woman, I forget her name, who attempted an escape as brazen as one could dare. Last December, as soon as the ice on the Amur was strong enough to bear their weight, she instructed her children to play out on the ice while she watched them from the bank. When the border guard came by on his patrol, he asked the woman what she was doing loitering by the river. She was cheeky and asked him what he thought she was doing. While the guard had the dignity to look foolish she said, 'Of course I'm watching my kids play. You never know what will happen; they may stray out too far. A mother must care for her children.'

"Well, over the course of a few weeks, the woman and her children regularly went down to the river. Each time they went, she instructed her children to play further out on the ice. I guess the border guard thought nothing of it, for he never questioned her again. Occasionally she would run out onto the ice when the children were further out than they should be. She would scold them for their foolishness and bring them back. As the guard marched by on his patrol, he observed this and carried on his way. She was a mother looking after her children.

"One day, when the children were playing out on the ice in the middle of the river, perhaps five hundred meters from the riverbank, she shouted at them to return. They ignored her cries. The woman ran out onto the ice. Immediately her children began to run toward the southern bank, toward China. It had all been prearranged. It was the culmination of her plan. They were making their escape to China. I can only imagine how the woman must have felt, running across the ice, wondering if the guard would see her, if he would shoot at her, feeling an imaginary bullet piercing her back, at the same time hoping she or one of her kids wouldn't fall through a hole in the ice.

"Well, she caught up to her kids and they all made it across. A smuggler met her there and brought the news to her parents."

The two men were quiet for a few moments, considering the bold audacity of the mother and her children.

Abram continued. "So, my friend, I am not surprised when you tell me you want to go to Moscow. There is hope in that direction. Perhaps your route will be less dangerous than flights across the river. If the government is issuing exit visas, perhaps more of us will finally be allowed to leave as well. After hearing about what's going on in Moscow, I'm going to send a delegation to Vladivostok to see if we can get permission to emigrate that way. Perhaps the government representatives there will look upon us with kindness, though I hardly dare to think it.

"God be with you Jacob, with you and Naomi and Joseph." Abram paused. "And if anyone asks, I'll say you've gone to visit your relatives in Ukraine."

Abram took Jacob's hand in a firm clasp. He looked his friend in the eye and smiled.

"May God go with you."

Jacob Enns and his family embarked on their journey of hope on a cold morning late in November. Carrying a few possessions and a sack of dried food prepared by Naomi, the family caught a ride in the wagon of Peter Federau, a farmer going to Blagoveshchensk to pick up parts to repair a broken harvester. Federau was also their lay minister; in the villagers' homes he led prayer and teaching services. At Blagoveshchensk they would catch the train to Belogorsk. From there, the Trans-Siberian Railway would carry them all the way to Moscow.

A dusting of snow had fallen the night before. As the slanting rays of the morning sun warmed the land, the road became a patchwork of lumpy brown islands surrounded by large beige puddles and white, miniature snowscapes. Riding in the back of the horse-drawn wagon, they bumped along the rutted village street. With Joseph snuggled close on his lap, Jacob watched steaming tendrils of melting snow rise above the poorly insulated corrugated tin roofs of Alexandrovka's houses. The pickets in their front yard fences were topped with small snowy caps leaning jauntily this way and that. As the wagon jarred and shook its way from one pothole to the next, it rumbled past a few people going about their business. Jacob and Naomi waved good-bye to a few friends along the way.

It wasn't long before the snow-covered fields greeted them. Jacob looked back as Alexandrovka slowly disappeared in the distance. A copse of larch and a small hill finally hid the village from view. Above the trees he could still make out wisps of smoke from heating and cooking fires rising into the still morning air. Jacob pulled the blanket wrapped around Joseph tighter and tucked in its edges. He did not want his son to catch a chill.

He looked at Naomi and smiled. "Are you warm, my love?"

She nodded, nestling herself closer into her husband's side.

Time dragged as the wagon slowly carried them to the city. Eventually, fields gave way to houses and ramshackle businesses, and Blagoveshchensk began to surround them. They crossed a bridge over the Zeya River and looked to their left, seeing where the Zeya merged with the muddy Amur. Rattling down the cobblestone road, they watched as buildings turned from wood to stone with tops reaching ever higher into the sky. Joseph looked about with wide eyes and pointed at the wonders he was seeing.

Peter Federau turned his wagon onto Station Street and soon brought his sweating horse to a standstill in front of the Blagoveshchensk Railway Station. Jacob and his family wearily climbed down, bones and muscles numb from the jarring ride. With a friendly wave and a flick of the reins, Peter and his wagon rumbled over the cobblestones out of the square and along October Street toward the farm equipment store.

Despite measures the alarmed central government had instituted in October to keep its German colonists from traveling to Moscow, thousands had already successfully reached the capital. After two weeks of travel by rail, Jacob, Naomi, and Joseph were among those arriving in Pushkino, a suburb a few kilometers north of Moscow. Other refugees who had found no available housing in the city center had directed them there.

Two nights later, GPU and militia officers scooped Jacob and his family up in a midnight raid. A commotion outside on the street woke Naomi first, a truck coughing to a standstill, car doors being slammed. A fist pounded on the door of the dacha where they had found a bed for the night. Jacob sat up, startled out of his sleep. Fearfully, he pulled on his pants and opened the door.

"Show us your papers!" shouted an armed uniform.

Jacob shrugged helplessly and tried to stammer a reply. There were no papers. They had gone that day to register their presence in the community with the local authorities; the line in which they had stood had been long, too long for the minor bureaucrat seated at a table flanked by armed militiamen. They had been told to come back another day.

"Get dressed, immediately!" shouted the uniform.

Trembling hands had barely pulled on their coats and boots before Jacob, Naomi, and Joseph were hustled out the door. Mindful of the rifles pointed at them, the family hurried to the street where they found a flatbed truck already crowded with other detainees. Naomi clambered up. Jacob lifted Joseph up to Naomi who hugged her son close. Climbing onto the flatbed, Jacob wrapped his arm protectively around Naomi as together they shivered with cold and terror. With grinding gears and black smoke belching, the truck jarred its way over cobblestone roads and joined a convoy of similar trucks heading in the direction of the Perlovka railway station. Once there, everyone was crammed into the boxcars of a train pointed in the direction of Siberia.

The government had lost its patience. The door to freedom in the west was being barred and locked. The refugees gathered in the suburbs of Moscow were being forcibly returned to the villages from whence they had come.

December 1929

For the rest of his life, Jacob Enns would never speak of the journey back to Alexandrovka, their seemingly endless pilgrimage in the valley of the shadow of death. He would never speak of the cold, the hunger or the thirst.

Nor would he ever speak of the standing dead. Lock-kneed, those who were overcome took leave of their mortal bodies while standing silently shoulder to shoulder among those they left behind in the packed boxcar and sucked from them the meager warmth their rigid bodies managed to generate on the interminable journey from Moscow to the Far East. Jacob imagined God weeping with the living left behind in grief, anger, and despair, His holy tears becoming icy tracks on their frostbitten cheeks.

He would never speak of the sounds the dead made as they were pushed out of the open boxcar door and fell like stones to the frozen ground below. He would never speak of their frozen corpses left stacked like cordwood on railroad sidings whose names he never knew. Jacob would never speak of his shame at the gratitude he felt for the spaces left unfilled: now some of the children and elderly could lie down at last to sleep on the thin layer of straw covering the cold wooden floor; Jacob was quick to make sure Joseph had his spot. The day came when there was room enough so that all could take their turn and Jacob and Naomi could at last rest their bodies, taking their weight off swollen feet.

Jacob did not know the number of boxcars in their train. Nor could he count the number of the dead left behind. Looking out through a rough crack in the boxcar wall he could tell there are many. There was little he could do but pray. Mostly, Jacob prayed he would not become one of them. At times he prayed with less fervor, and there came a time when he prayed to join them. While the train rocked and clattered along its ceaseless track toward Siberia, he could not decide if it would be better to live or to die. He finally determined, one morning while trying to assuage his thirst by chewing a fragment of frozen breath he had clawed from the wall, since the communists were trying so hard to secure his death, perhaps it was his responsibility to deny them their wish.

"I must live, for no other reason than to foil their complete disregard for our humanity," Jacob spoke into the frigid, dispassionate darkness.

At least, that was what he told himself. The truth, Jacob would later realize, was far less politically charged and really very simple. He could do nothing other than live, because his wife, Naomi, and four-year-old Joseph, were there with him in the cruel darkness and stench of the boxcar. He could not leave them as others had left their loved ones. He came to regard the notion of his death as an act of selfish cowardice, even though he would have played no active part in it.

Yes, the Soviets made it easy for us to die, Jacob would later recall when he allowed himself to think on it. Their ally, the Russian winter played its role with its bitter, sub-zero temperatures. The guards played their part, refusing us food and water for days until they could no longer turn away from our desperate cries for mercy. Our only fortress against the Reaper who moved among us was our will to survive for the sake of those we loved.

Remembering the horror of those days, Jacob thought perhaps God had played his part as well. The God he worshipped, who promised that neither life nor death could separate His people from His love, the God who proclaimed Himself the Resurrection and the Life might have made His mysterious, incarnate appearance, for eventually, with each passing day, Jacob had found growing within himself the stubborn will to resist the cold and to ignore the hunger and the thirst, and to scorn the malevolence of the ideology that drove men to commit the unspeakably evil acts threatening to crush him. From somewhere deep in Jacob's gut had grown a deep sense of peace and the intractable desire to live.

When the train finally jolted to a stop on a railway siding at Belogorsk, the guards broke open the ice-locked boxcar doors. With great effort, the wooden panels were slid ajar. From where they lay, those imprisoned inside gaped out at the wide world. After a few minutes, having heard no shouts or commands, hesitant heads began to poke out of the iron-wheeled cells into the bright light of midday. Cautiously they looked along the length of the train, scanning from front to back, back to front, searching for the men who had tormented them so ruthlessly. The guards seemed to have disappeared. Not convinced they were safe and afraid to conclude they were free to go, it was several minutes more before some jumped out of the boxcar doorways onto the ground. Still no guards appeared, no threats were heard. Once the first brave souls had ventured out with no ill result, the rest could hardly contain their eagerness to be rid of the boxcars. Some were so weakened by their ordeal they fell to their knees on the frozen ground, the drop was too great for them. The stronger among them began assisting the weaker ones who came after. Eventually, the track along the entire length of the train was crowded with shuffling, bent figures, shielding dazzled eyes from the glare of sun on snow.

Standing on the gravel in front of their open boxcar door, Jacob reached up toward his fearful son. "Here, Joseph," Jacob encouraged. "I'll catch you." Weakened by hunger and inactivity, Joseph merely leaned forward and fell into his father's arms. He buried his face in Jacob's shoulder, so bright was the light to him after all the time spent in semi-darkness. Naomi sat on the floor of the boxcar and swung her legs out. Still holding Joseph in his left arm, Jacob caught Naomi with his right and held her while she set her feet on the gravel apron.

Looking around, Jacob saw the Belogorsk stationhouse not far off. Others had also spied it and were slowly making their way across the iron rails of tracks that blocked their way like low, metal walls over which they must lift their weary swollen feet. Strengthened by the birth new hope, Jacob carried his son and lent support to his wife as they haltingly crossed the rail yard.

Finding a bench where Naomi and Joseph could rest, Jacob looked for the nearest vendor. He spotted an old babushka with a red kerchief securely wrapping her head. Hobbling to where she sold her soup, he purchased a bowlful. It was thin, but steaming hot. A crusty loaf of black bread her neighbor sold would go well with it. Fortunately, in the mad scramble to force the refugees onto the train in Perlovka, he had not been searched. Jacob still had the money he had brought to Moscow to buy their way out of Russia.

Before he left the old granny, Jacob looked at her scarf and remarked, "Red seems to have become our nation's favorite color." He did not try to hide the sarcasm and the bitterness he felt, but afterward regretted his words, thinking perhaps he should not have spoken at all.

"Oh yes, comrade," the granny cackled in return. "We're all red now, ain't we."

As he walked away, Jacob heard the babushka's laughter broken by a ragged, roiling cough.

Naomi accepted Jacob's purchases eagerly. With tears in her eyes she gazed gratefully, greedily at the food for she was so very hungry. But it was Joseph she was more concerned about. He must eat first.

"Not too quickly," Naomi warned her son as she raised the bowl of soup to his thin cracked lips. His eyes grew large at the sight of the vegetables floating in broth. "You'll burn your mouth." Joseph sipped at the soup but there was no energy in his action. Naomi dipped a piece of the hard bread in the soup to soften it. Joseph nibbled on the dripping chunks after his mother had blown on them to cool them.

The short train ride from Belogorsk to Blagoveshchensk was uneventful. Seated on the passenger car's bench, Jacob gazed vacantly out of the window, watching the familiar, flat countryside roll past. Drained of willpower and physical strength, his thoughts refused to form into anything cohesive.

Eventually he dozed. With their bellies full and huddled tightly against him under a warm, newly purchased wool blanket, Naomi and Joseph slept the sleep of the dead.

At Blagoveshchensk, the family stood for a while in the station before venturing out into the twilit cold of early evening. They had noticed some families bedding down on the station benches and floor close to the old potbellied stove. It only provided a modicum of heat in the large, drafty building. But, staying the night seemed the sensible thing to do. Jacob, Naomi, and Joseph returned to the relative warmth of the station where they spent an uncomfortable night on the hard stone floor.

The next morning the family set out for Alexandrovka. The weather had warmed a little, dulling the cold's knife's edge. By good fortune, a farmer returning to Alexandrovka had room for them on his wagon. They rode the rest of the way to the village and before noon, the circle was complete.

They found their home empty and cold, but a blazing fire in the stove quickly remedied that. Soon, they climbed into the bed. There was no question of Joseph sleeping alone on his pallet. He needed the comfort and security of his mother's arms. They lay together under the eiderdown quilt, Joseph in the middle, his mother on one side and his father on the other. As Jacob lay with his family, luxuriating in the warm and the softness of their bed, he wondered about what had happened to them. Was it all a bad dream, a shared nightmare? The memory was too troubling to be real. He closed his eyes, grateful to be home. He listened as his family fell asleep beside him. Exhausted and at last able to relax, they breathed gently beside him. In, out, in, out, and more slowly as their sleep deepened, in, out, in, out. It is important we keep breathing, Jacob thought.

In the shadows of his exhausted mind, he entered again the darkened boxcar. He felt the cold arms of the dead leaning against him. He smelled again the reek of bodies, of clothing soaked in urine and excrement and fear. He heard the frightened moans and pitiful cries. He began to relive the indignities he and his family had endured.

Someone was banging on the door, crying out for food and water. In his sleep-fogged brain, Jacob wondered desperately, "The guards. Where are the guards?" Everything around him was still. The car was not moving. They must be parked at a station or siding, he thought. Surely the guards will finally show some mercy, some regard for their mutual humanity. Jacob briefly considered joining the person at the door. Perhaps he should add his feeble fist to the noisemaking. But he felt so tired. His legs, swollen from standing too long, felt like lead. At first they refused to move. When they finally obeyed, sharp pains shot up them.

The cramp in his calf jarred Jacob awake. He sat up groaning with pain and quickly began to massage his leg. The calf muscle was a lump of stone. Hearing his moans, Naomi woke and took over the massaging. Slowly the muscle loosened.

As the distraction of the pain eased, Jacob realized someone was knocking on their door. Naomi looked at him with large, frightened eyes.

"Who can it be?" she whispered. "Not the police, surely. Do you think they're looking for us?"

"No one ever took our names," Jacob said. "Not when we arrived in Moscow. Not when we left. First they wouldn't talk to us because they didn't want us there. Then they were in too much of a hurry to get rid of us. There's no official record of our presence in Moscow. The local GPU can't know about where we've been."

"But we had to show our documents at the train stations when we went to Moscow," gasped Naomi. "Can they find us that way?"

"I don't know. Maybe." Jacob thought a moment. "Don't worry, Naomi, they won't be looking for us. There were thousands of people in Moscow trying to leave the country. How could they ever find us? And why would they, anyway? We're just three people who don't matter to anyone." Jacob hoped he was right.

Careful not to wake his son, Jacob got out of bed and limped from the bedroom to the door. A gust of cold air rushed into the house as he opened it just far enough to look outside. Peeking through the crack between the door and its jamb, squinting at the brightness of the light, he mumbled, "Yes? Who is it?"

"Jacob, it's me, Abram."

"Abram?" Jacob exclaimed. "I didn't recognize you. One moment please." And he quickly shut the door on his friend.

With the door closed behind him, Jacob looked at Naomi still lying in bed. He was having difficulty gathering his thoughts. His brain felt addled. Finally he said, "Naomi, it's Abram. Should I let him in?" He rubbed his face. "I should let him in. Can you get up? Should I send him away?"

Naomi groaned. Her body, finally able to rest, had awakened to all the aches and pains resulting from the weeks on the train.

Gathering his wits, Jacob whispered. "It's okay. Stay in bed. Abram won't mind. He'll understand. I'll talk to him."

"No, I'll get up," said Naomi. She struggled out of bed and wrapped her frail body in a thin housecoat.

When Naomi was presentable Jacob opened the door wide. He stepped back to allow his friend space to enter. He apologized for leaving him out in the cold.

Abram waved off his apology. "I'm sorry to disturb you." It was plain for him to see he had roused them from sleep. "Ach! I woke you. I thought you'd be up. It's almost noon. But I should have known, after what you've been through."

"No, no, don't worry," Jacob said. "I had a cramp. It woke me. Come in. Sit."

Abram looked relieved for a moment, but his face became serious again. "No, I won't stay. I wanted you to know that I heard about what happened, how you got shipped back from Moscow like cattle, worse than cattle. The Dietrich Reimers are also back. They must have been on the same train as you. He's already been telling the story. We're a small community. You know how the grapevine works. Before supper the whole village will know."

Jacob was surprised. "We were on the same train? I didn't know. But then how could we. We were herded onto it like sheep to the slaughter." Then his heart sank. He said, "Everyone has heard? The teacher, too? Peter Dyck, the carpenter? They mustn't know. They'll tell the secret police!"

Abram chuckled. "I don't think you need be concerned about Yevchenko's collaborators. Everyone knows who they are. No one tells them anything."

Jacob tried to calm himself. He wasn't as convinced that such a secret as his could be kept from the sticky ears of the GPU puppets.

Abram's voice was confident. "Don't worry about it. I've come to tell you not to come to work today. When Yevchenko made his rounds after you left, I told him you'd gone to visit relatives in the Ukraine. It's the slow time of the year, I said, and it was a good time for you to get away. He seemed to buy it. On his next visit, he only asked when I expected you to return. I told him in a month or so. He didn't mention it again. He's kindly disposed to us because we're so productive and efficient. We're the model collective they point others to. I wouldn't be too concerned about him."

The icy ball in Jacob's stomach began to slowly melt.

"Yevchenko's pretty predictable in his routine," continued Abram. "He won't be back until Thursday. That gives you three days to recuperate." His voice had softened. What he left unsaid was, "You both look terrible."

Abram glanced at Naomi and back at Jacob. He was shocked by what he saw. From their protruding cheekbones and sunken eyes, he could tell they had both lost considerable weight. The skin on their faces was drawn and pale as moonlit snow. Their eyes were dull with exhaustion and something else he could only guess at. Jacob's hair had turned grey: before he left, it had been a deep black, the color of charcoal; now it was the color of coals that have cooled and are covered in a coating of ash.

"I'll arrange for some meals to be brought for a few days. You both need to rest and heal."

Abram glanced at Joseph who still slept in his parents' bed. He was oblivious to the stress and fear the new day had brought his parents. His thin, pallid face was peaceful in the restful sleep only the very young can know.

"Take good care of your family, Jacob," Abram murmured as he took his leave.

He thought of the fool's errand Jacob and his family had undertaken. He didn't know whether to be grateful they had returned or sad that they had failed in their attempt to emigrate. What is becoming of us, he wondered as he closed the door behind him and stepped into the cold of the Siberian winter's deep freeze.

"I sent a delegation to Vladivostok while you were away," Abram told Jacob the day after he'd returned to work. "I thought, if the government is issuing exit visas in Moscow, then possibly they would allow a few of us to leave through Vladivostok."

At the mention of Moscow, Jacob felt nauseous. He breathed heavily and gripped the edge of his desk firmly to hold himself steady. His mind immediately began to spin self-recriminations. "If I had known then what I know now," he thought. "How could I have been such a fool to endanger my family like that? But how was I to know? Fool! Idiot!" It was a conversation he'd had with himself numerous times since returning to Alexandrovka. He had neither answers for the questions that haunted him, nor had he forgiven himself for the decision he now regarded as having been completely reckless and foolhardy.

Jacob glanced at the portrait of the General Secretary of the Central Committee of the Communist Party of the Soviet Union. "You should have known I'd never let you out," sneered the Dictator. Jacob felt a stab of hatred for the man whose will and words determined his family's fate and the fate of millions.

Abram had not noticed Jacob's distress and was still speaking. In his moment of panicked confusion, Jacob had missed some of what he had said. When he was finally able to focus, Jacob heard Abram say, "I couldn't go to Vladivostok myself because of my responsibilities here. I sent George Reimer, Harold Ratzlaff, and Peter Penner. They're all men who've had successful dealings with the communist government in the past when we lived in Slavgorod. I thought if anyone could sway the government in our favor it would be them. I was actually quite optimistic."

Jacob didn't have to ask to know the outcome of the story.

"They talked to the American Consul, George Hanson, and got nowhere. Hanson said the United States isn't taking any immigrants. Apparently their stock market in New York crashed in October. According to Hanson, hundreds of thousands of people in the United States and in the other industrialized countries have lost their jobs. Some nations have been bankrupted. Entire industries are shutting down. There are no jobs. Unemployment is skyrocketing." He shook his head, trying to imagine the scope of the catastrophe unfolding in Europe and North America. "So naturally, they don't want to bring in any immigrants. Though I don't like it, I suppose I can understand why they don't want us."

Abram paused a moment and then mused, "We get so little news of the outside world or of what is happening in our own country. I had no idea things were so bad, even in America."

"What about Germany?" asked Jacob, curious despite the feeling of defeat that was taking hold of him. "Germany opened its doors. We were told it was welcoming thousands of refugees who'd gathered around Moscow." Despite himself, Jacob was reluctant to let go of the hint of promise that somehow Germany might assist them in their dream of emigration.

Abram was subdued. "Our representatives in Vladivostok had several meetings with the German Consul, a Dr. Stobbe. They said they pleaded our case with him and he was sympathetic. Stobbe cabled Moscow asking for instructions. In the end his instructions were clear. "We're sorry," he said. "There is nothing we can do. Our hands are tied."

Jacob wasn't willing to let it go. "What did he mean, 'Our hands are tied?'"

"I don't know. Lack of funds? Perhaps there are just too many of us. Perhaps they simply don't want to be bothered with us. Germany has its own problems. Perhaps Stalin could no longer tolerate being embarrassed in the eyes of the world and put a stop to it." Despite himself, Abram grinned. "I would imagine thousands of people camped at Stalin's front door crying to be allowed to leave his precious communist workers' paradise would light a very hot fire that boiled the acid in his stomach. Anyway, who knows why we've been rejected? The fact remains."

Jacob sighed. "Well, that's it then," he said bitterly. "We are out of alternatives." He felt the door of emigration slam shut.

Ever the one to put a positive spin on things, Abram said, "It may not be what we would choose, but, you know, we've not got it so bad here. Sure, bureaucrats who know very little about farming are dictating how we go about our business. But, so far, we've been able to raise bumper crops. The land here is fertile. The weather is ideal for growing wheat. God has blessed our efforts. We've had no problem paying their exorbitant grain taxes and special requisitions and we've been left with some for our own use. Our overseers in the local soviet are pleased with us. If we continue this way, we may be allright in the long run. We'll put our trust in God. He'll see us through."

Hearing these words, the General Secretary of the Central Committee of the Communist Party of the Soviet Union could hardly contain the smirk that threatened to spill like soured milk from his portrait hanging in its place of honor upon the office wall.

January 1930

January was tedious and cold. Winter took full advantage of its place in the cycle of seasons. The north wind drove the warmth from the land and covered the steppe in a thick coat of snow and ice that fell from the leaden Siberian sky. Gales shrieked through the villages of the Alexandrovka collective, cracking trees and whipping snow into drifts that reached the roofs of the houses.

With little to do but take care of the necessities of life, the people in the villages of the Alexandrovka collective became lethargic. When the weather permitted, the children were sent outside. When it didn't, everyone stayed close to the heat thrown by their efficient, brick Russian ovens. After the short-lived light of day, they spent the long hours of winter darkness huddled by kerosene lanterns. The men repaired tools or carved toys for their children while the women knitted or darned until fingers were sore and eyes became fatigued. Those who could, read, or taught others to read. Some simply sat and thought about those things people with little to do will think of, while others, as was their habit, discussed plans for the coming growing season. As one, they longed for the warmth the far off days of spring would bring.

There were those in the villages for whom the idea of escape from the tyranny of communism became an obsession. With no hope of a legal departure from the Soviet Union and with a growing fear of its unpredictably malevolent dictatorship, they began to consider a different route to escape. They turned their eyes to the river and its ice and to the distant snow-covered mountains of China. They prayed that perhaps their help would come from there, even as the iron clamp of the frigid cold led them to become ever more familiar with the border guards whose job it was to prevent such an expatriation.

The only people who could be counted upon to be out and about in the bitter winter weather were the border guards. They trudged the routes of their patrols with red faces framed by their ice-encrusted beards and completely inadequate budenovkas. The ties holding down the cap's earflaps were hidden behind the icy tangles, the woolen cover ineffective in warding off the cold. When their patrols occasionally brought them into the village, the people of Alexandrovka took pity upon them and welcomed the guards into their homes. They served them hot milk while the grateful guards sat beside their fires warming up and chatting about the weather, their families, and their hopes for the future. Political conversations were avoided. Most of the guards were young men. They were too young and too isolated to know anything beyond the propaganda they had been fed by their superiors. They were boys with parents and siblings living in Russian villages close by, with dreams of advancement in Moscow's Red Army. Yes, the Siberian winter created unlikely allies as all struggled to survive its glacial reign.

February arrived. Brilliant sundogs growled a warning of yet colder weather to come. South of the village, the ice covering the Amur grew thicker by the day. In places the current pushed the ice up against itself, heaving it into jags and piles so that if one had looked across the river's expanse, they would have been excused for mistaking it for a field of snow-covered stumps, branches, and other detritus left behind after clearing away trees and now waiting for the springtime bonfires.

As winter inexorably tightened its grip upon the land, the discontent felt by the some of the villagers of Alexandrovka also deepened. Naomi made it clear to Jacob that the only thing that had changed since their disastrous decision to attempt emigration through Moscow was their sleep patterns. They were unable now to find undisturbed rest, for their nights were constantly visited by visions of the hell they had lived through.

"There is still no future for our son in this country," she howled one night as they revisited their dilemma. "If anything, after Moscow, the future looks bleaker than ever."

Jacob grimaced and nodded.

Naomi's distress flowed in tears down her cheeks and fell into the mire their lives had become. "We seldom get a good night's sleep anymore. If it isn't you having a nightmare and waking me, it's me having a nightmare and waking you. Or it's Joseph crying out in his sleep. We are tied to those railway cattle wagons as surely as a heifer tied to a pole waiting for a butcher. The only way we will be free of the shackles they have clamped on us is if we somehow manage to escape from this dreadful land."

Jacob agreed without hesitation.

He looked at his son, sleeping, hopefully oblivious to his parents' anxieties. Joseph was quiet now, but Jacob's heart broke when he thought of the nightmares his son was too frequently suffering from. But then, Jacob thought, what does Joseph imagine when he is awake? Joseph had withdrawn into himself. He seldom spoke. He spent long periods at a time sitting and staring at the leafy frost designs that grew on the windowpane in the kitchen. Occasionally he licked his finger and traced the designs, slowly obliterating them. Then he hummed to himself, a toneless sound that got on his anxious parents' nerves. At those times, Jacob and Naomi would look at each other with eyes that spoke fear and concern for they didn't know how to help their son. Joseph willingly accepted their hugs, but did not return them and had no answer when they asked what it was that was bothering him.

Jacob and Naomi prayed for their son, as they did for themselves, asking God for peace of mind and heart. But it seemed the snow-covered roof prevented their prayers from being heard. This surprised them, for it did little to prevent the heat of their fire from escaping, as was evidenced by the icicles hanging from the roof outside. Massive columns had formed where the water dripping from their eaves had frozen as it fell to meet growing points of ice rising up from the ground.

"I don't know how to help him," Naomi wept, as she and Jacob lay in bed one night. "He seems to be leaving us." She sobbed into Jacob's shoulder as he held her tightly. He could give her no answer.

"Perhaps he should be seen by a doctor," Naomi tried after she had calmed a bit. "There must be a doctor in Blagoveshchensk who could help us."

"I don't know. Perhaps Abram will know," was all Jacob could think to say.

One Sunday afternoon, while Naomi was serving a lunch of cold ham, buttered buns, and pickled cucumbers, Jacob noticed she was agitated. That morning, they had met with a few like-minded villagers to worship and pray. Before the service, he recalled, Naomi had seemed content, almost cheerful for once. On the way home, Joseph had spoken to her, using more words than he had in weeks. "Do you think he may be turning a corner?" she had asked Jacob quietly so as not to draw Joseph's attention to her concern. Dare she grasp the fragment of hope his conversation presented? Regardless, Naomi always enjoyed the weekly church meeting that broke up the monotony of the slow winter days. It provided a welcome opportunity to catch up on news, to gossip, and to commiserate as the women shared their worries and cares with one another.

"Did something happen at church?" Jacob asked hesitantly.

"Not now, Jacob," Naomi snapped. "We can talk later when Joseph's asleep."

That evening as Joseph lay snuggled under the quilts on his parents' bed, his eyes closed and jaw relaxed in a moment of quiet rest, Naomi kissed his forehead and turned to her husband. Speaking softly so as not to disturb her son, Naomi announced, "This morning Anna Hostetler told me there is a group planning an escape. They're going to cross over the Amur River into China."

"Seriously?" Jacob said. He was not really surprised. Hearing about escapes across the frozen river was becoming almost routine. But the thought of a group of friends and acquaintances attempting it was another thing.

"Yes." Looking closely at her husband for his reaction, Naomi continued, "I asked if they are open to others joining them. They are."

Jacob felt a tingling in his spine. "When are they going?" he asked hesitantly.

"She didn't tell me. Soon, I think." Naomi caught her breath in a sob. "Jacob, I want us to go with them."

Jacob sat down. "Are you sure? Think of the risks involved, the cold, the border guards, the ice. It will be dangerous."

"I know," said Naomi, her voice trembling. "But we must try. We have to get out!"

Jacob thought a moment. "Are you sure?" When Naomi nodded, he said, "Alright. I'll talk to Ludwig." He pulled Naomi into his lap and held her tightly. She wrapped her arms around his neck and laid her head on his shoulder.

"We have to try," she murmured.

The next day, Jacob visited Ludwig Hostetler at his machine shop. The shop was in a large barn at the northern edge of the village. It had been transformed for its new use when its stalls had been removed. The space where once milk cows and horses had spent the winter was now a large open space interrupted only by posts at regular intervals. These supported the floor of the empty hayloft above. Pieces of machinery covered the floor in an orderly array. Some were oiled and clean, ready for spring's fieldwork. Others appeared to be broken and good only for the scavenging of parts. Against the walls, Jacob saw Ludwig had built cabinets and workbenches. These, too, were cluttered with parts from machines, buckets of bolts, and tools of all descriptions and sizes. Yet amidst the chaos of metal there was a kind of order and when needed, Ludwig was able to quickly find what he needed.

"Brother Enns," boomed the big man after Jacob had closed the door and stood in the entryway brushing a layer of snow from his coat and hat. "What brings you to my humble workshop on day like this? It's snowing as if we've had none all winter and our beloved Heavenly Father has decided today is a fine time to get us caught up on our yearly quota." Ludwig laughed. "Happily the winds aren't up, but there will be a deal of shoveling to be done when the snowfall ends. The only good that will come of a storm on a day such as this is our meddlesome Colonel Yevchenko will stick close to his fire in Konstantinovka. That GPU nose of his is small enough to fit into the affairs of anyone he decides to sniff and big enough to cause trouble the moment he smells something he doesn't like. I suspect Ivan, Gregor, and the rest of the border guards will also be warming their behinds. I doubt they'll leave their watchtower today. No sense getting lost in a snowstorm where you can't see a thing beyond your two booted feet." Ludwig finished his speech with a huge guffaw.

"Come, my friend. Sit here by the fire. I wouldn't want to have to explain to your dear wife why you developed frostbite while standing at my front door, inside, mind you." And he laughed again, loudly.

After firmly shaking Jacob's hand in greeting, Ludwig indicated a chair by a huge potbellied stove that was attempting, without much success, to heat the air in the expansive machine shed. Jacob happily accepted.

"I have some coffee brewing," said Ludwig in a voice that somehow managed to fill the void where the heater had failed. "It'll only be a moment. Would you like a cup? Mind you, it's only pripps. I charred the grains myself. Now that real coffee is only a memory, this is the best I can do." He grinned ruefully. "Can't expect much else these days can we."

As they sipped the hot liquid, Ludwig became serious. "So what brings you to my humble workplace in the middle of a snowstorm?" He grinned, shifting his mood as quickly as the pendulum of a child's swing. "I'd like to think you craved some good company, but with that wife and son of yours at home, I know you already have that."

Jacob was silent a moment, knowing the words he was about speak would alter his family's future as surely as birth or death.

"Naomi tells me you are part of a group planning an escape across the Amur into China."

"How'd she find out?"

"Anna told her. After church."

"Oh, that's allright then." Ludwig instinctively lowered his voice. "Wouldn't want the grapevine spreading our plans."

Jacob hesitated. "What gives you the courage to attempt such a dangerous venture?"

Ludwig took a long sip of pripps.

"Let me tell you a story. When we lived in Slavgorod, we had a nice home. We were comfortable. I worked hard and we saw some reward for my efforts. We were content. One night, after the civil war had ended and the Bolsheviks were tightening their clamp on our village, a group of men came to our house. We were already in bed, but they forced their way inside. They had guns. Picking and choosing our best possessions, they took what they wanted, had me load it into our wagon, and made me deliver it to their headquarters. They said if I resisted in any way, they'd scatter my ashes and the ashes of my wife and children to the four winds. Then, when we got to their place, they complimented me on how well I'd cooperated with them and told me we'd get along perfectly in the future."

As he spoke, Ludwig became restless. He stood up and began to pace. As Jacob looked up at him, Ludwig threw his mug across the room. It smashed to pieces on the iron wheel of a harvester.

Struggling to control himself, Ludwig spluttered, "Do you think our cooperation with the communists will not come with a cost? Cooperation, be damned! What is cooperation when it is given from fear of a threat? If we don't cooperate, we know what will happen." His voice was bitter. "And how long do you think it will be before they come and require our cooperation as they take from us the crumbs we are given now? The communists only have their own best interests in mind, never ours. We are their pawns and we are expendable."

Both men were silent for a time. Ludwig sat down and stared at the potbellied stove. He rubbed his hands on his pant legs. Finally, he heaved a sigh and cleared his throat.

"That is why we must leave this country by any means we can. It doesn't matter that it's dangerous. There is greater danger in staying here."

Jacob was silent a moment and then said, "We would like to join you. My family. Are you willing to have us join the group? We want to come, too."

Ludwig stroked his beard. He looked hard at Jacob. "I won't insult you by asking if you realize the commitment you are making and the risk you're are undertaking, whether we're successful," Ludwig paused, "or whether we fail."

Jacob nodded his understanding.

Ludwig smiled ruefully. "I was a little cross with my Anna when she told me of her conversation with Naomi. But I knew she and you were beyond reproach. And knowing what you've already attempted and the price you've paid, well, I'm not in the least surprised at your request."

Ludwig got up, found another mug, and poured himself more pripps. Gesturing with the pot and raised eyebrows, he offered Jacob a refill. Jacob accepted.

"There are eleven families, twelve, now, with yours. No one outside of the group has any idea of what we are planning. We are telling no one, do you understand? And that includes your boss, Abram Siemens. He's a good man, Abram is, but he still believes we can coexist with the communists. We do not. What we are going to attempt is dangerous, and some would say, absolutely foolhardy. But we are desperate, and growing more so as the months go by."

Jacob was quiet, staring into his steaming mug with the intensity of a reader of tea leaves. He was not prepared for what Ludwig said next.

"Have you heard the news? There are rumors of mass arrests, imprisonment and exile of those who had the audacity to rattle Moscow's gates in their attempt to convince the government to allow their emigration."

Jacob's heart fell to the floor. He felt dizzy. He gasped for breath and tried to take in the implications of Ludwig's words.

"All over the Soviet Union, our people who went to Moscow last fall are being rounded up. Dietrich Reimer told me. He's heard from relatives in Slavgorod. Henry Janzen also has heard from relatives, in Ukraine. They're hearing the same thing. In some cases whole families are being taken. In others it's just the men. Some are facing judges. Some are being exiled to the far north. Others are being taken out behind a barn or house and shot. It's cold-blooded murder."

Jacob felt his world beginning to unravel. Even as he grasped for the hope he and his family were still unknown to the secret police, he wondered if somehow they would discover their involvement. He had the sudden urge to flee to his home, to hide behind its locked the door, but knew the reassuring sense of safety he had once felt there was gone forever.

"Then we must leave," Jacob said resolutely. "When is the group going? What do we need to know?"

So Ludwig told him.

March 25, 1930

Ying Weimin's name literally meant a clever hero of the people. He was proud of his name and was determined to fulfill its promise. Ying had taken the name when he became an adult, a few years after his family was expelled from Blagoveshchensk. And his family had been the lucky ones.

Over the centuries, the site where the Russian city of Blagoveshchensk now stood had traditionally been a Chinese village and fort. As the Russian Tsars became more interested in expanding their empire, conflicts broke out and the majority of the Chinese residents were eventually driven out. After it was agreed upon that the Amur River should become the border between the two countries, a peaceful coexistence with those who remained began.

Ying's father found employment with a *laowai*, a foreigner who had opened a business in Blagoveshchensk. The work was difficult, but the boss was kind and tolerated no discrimination among his employees. Nevertheless, the resentment caused by their displacement continued to simmer below the surface for the Chinese living on both sides of the river.

During the Chinese Boxer Rebellion in July 1900, Blagoveshchensk was shelled for two weeks. In retaliation the local ataman ordered all Chinese who still lived in the city to be deported. However, he forbade them the use of boats with which to cross the river. Over five thousand people died by drowning or were shot by police when they refused to be driven into the river. Ying's family was among only forty Chinese who survived the massacre because their *laowai* agreed to pay a ransom of a thousand rubles for each of their lives.

Consequently, Ying had no love for Russians, whether Bolshevik or Mennonite. As a smuggler of goods across the Amur, his one aim was to further the prosperity of his honored father and mother by any means in his dealings with those he considered to be barbarian foreigners. Once a month, Ying made the five hundred kilometer trip to Harbin where he purchased the goods he took across the river to the Mennonite settlements. He loved to barter and often bragged of how he had fleeced an ignorant customer. In his trips across the Amur, it was inevitable that Ying should encounter the Russian border guards. He often gave them gifts to ensure their goodwill. In return they tolerated his illegal trade.

Knowing there was a steady stream of Mennonites and other German Russians attempting to escape across the Amur into China, Ying saw an opportunity to profit from their desperation. He whispered in the ears of a few residents of the Alexandrovka collective his willingness to act as a guide should they decide to attempt a crossing, for a fee, of course.

So it was that Ying Weimin agreed to guide twelve Mennonite families in their attempt to flee across the Amur River. It was a Tuesday night. The waning moon sent a sliver of light across the white barrens and cast dark shadows among the ten sleighs closely parked together. The long trek from Alexandrovka had been nerve-racking but uneventful. The group had skirted unseen around the Russian villages of Voykovo and Orlovka that stood between them and the river. Above them, the uncounted multitude of stars in the Siberian sky flickered in the dispassionate darkness of the heavens. An occasional shadow of passing cloud blocked their view of the anxious, hopeful band gathered at the appointed meeting place. The clearing had been carefully chosen far enough away from the riverbank to hide their presence from the patrolling guards, yet close enough that when the moment came, they'd be able to make a quick descent onto the ice.

Jacob, Naomi, and Joseph were among them as the tense group waited for their guide to appear. The women and children sat bundled under blankets on sleighs packed to the gunnels with the few precious household goods there was room for, and enough food for a week on the run. Naomi and Joseph shared a sleigh with Anna Hostetler and her children. Jacob stood with the rest of the men who held their horses' bridles and soft noses, or stroked their heads to quiet them. The horses stamped their hooves and ground their teeth in impatience, wanting to get on with the chore they had been trained to do. Fortunately, the gathered snow on the ground and in the bushes helped to muffle their commotion.

As the hours of waiting passed, the nervous impatience of the group grew. Where was Ling Weimin? Why was he taking so long? What had become of him? Finally, it became clear that Ling was not coming. Who could know what had happened? It seemed he had taken their money and run.

Ludwig Hostetler gathered the men of the group together. He led a quick, muffled conversation. Agreement was easily reached. All knew they had no choice; the decision was made. Without a guide, there would be no thought of escape that night. They needed to begin the long journey back to Alexandrovka before the coming daylight betrayed them.

With heavy hearts, yet with some relief as well, the small band dispersed. The hissing whispers of the sleighs' runners dissolved into the night along with the vapor of the abandoned dream of freedom.

A Siberian wolf observed the strange gathering in the forest clearing. From its resting place some distance away in a thatch of low snow-covered bushes, it watched with regret, and also some relief, as the horses and their human masters disappeared into the night. Though the scents had been appealing, it knew there was no dinner to be had from that dangerous prey this night.

The brilliant stars continued their indifferent vigil while the grey shadows of the night moved like the hands of a clock in their ordered paths.

The next morning, Jacob and Naomi could hardly contain their disappointment. They had failed again in their attempt to escape from the oppression of the Soviet Union. Exhausted by a tense and sleepless night, they shared a quiet breakfast before Jacob stumbled out the door and walked the quiet dirt pathway to work in the business office of the Alexandrovka collective.

Jacob had not been at his desk for more than a few minutes when Colonel Yevchenko of the GPU threw open the door. Colonel Yuri Yevchenko was a veteran of the bitter Russian civil war. As a Red Army Major, he had pursued the fleeing White Army all the way from Perm in west Siberia to the port city of Vladivostok on the Sea of Japan. He became known for his daring and ruthless tactics. After the war ended, he found his way into the ranks of the secret police where he was quickly promoted. He considered his posting to Konstantinovka a steppingstone to greater responsibilities in larger centers like Irkutsk or Omsk. Perhaps even Moscow.

Abram Siemens and Jacob had just begun to go over an inventory of stored seed grains reserved for the spring planting when the colonel stomped into the office.

"Comrades!" Yevchenko boomed. His face was red and puffy. The bags under his eyes bulged like two rounded halves of boiled egg white pasted under his blood-shot eyes. He looked like he'd been on an all-night bender.

Jacob cringed and thought, "I'm not your comrade," even as he noticed a hint of threat in the inflection of the Colonel's voice. Yevchenko's "Comrades" had begun cheerily enough but had ended sourly, like the tart aftertaste of curdled milk.

"Good morning, Colonel," Abram said. Unlike Jacob, he had noticed nothing amiss, other than the timing of Yevchenko's visit. "You're early this week. We weren't expecting you until tomorrow."

Yevchenko unbuttoned his greatcoat. "There is a matter of grave concern we need to discuss." His pupils were dark, his eyes heavy lidded behind his fleshy cheeks. His lips were compressed in a straight thin, pale line.

"Oh?" Abram's voice was light, though his confusion was becoming evident. His brain raced to find the "matter of grave concern" Yevchenko spoke of. In the moment, he could think of nothing.

Yevchenko lifted his meaty finger and pointed at Abram. His brow furrowed. "There are reports of an attempted escape last night," he spat.

Jacob reeled from the current of shock that threatened to toss his body off his chair. Struggling to steady his nerves, he thought, "Ling Weimin must have played both sides of the fence. The bloody scoundrel!" Jacob lowered his face and stared at the page, barely seeing the figures written upon it. "Don't look at me." He threw the thought at Yevchenko whose attention at the moment was focused on Abram. Jacob concentrated on controlling his breathing.

Abram was talking. "That can't be," he flustered while Jacob frantically wished an impenetrable wall into existence around his desk. "We are all happy here. We have a good life. Why would anyone risk a crossing on the ice?"

"Apparently you are mistaken," growled Yevchenko. "Nevertheless, it's true."

Abram was deeply shaken by Yevchenko's accusation. He was confused and filled with turmoil. "Could it be true?" he thought. "Might someone have tried a crossing without telling me?" As he thought the question, he knew the answer. "It can't be!" he bleated.

Colonel Yevchenko ignored Abram's protestation. His voice became menacing. "I want everybody in this village assembled on the street in front of this office in one hour. No exceptions. Men, women, and children. Everyone, do you understand? If there is one person missing, I will hold you personally responsible."

Abram knew desperate people were regularly risking their lives by attempting to cross the river into China. But with the life they had managed to build in Alexandrovka, he thought people had become resigned to their situation. Sure, the government dictated much of what they did. But life here wasn't that bad, surely. Could such desperation flourish in his village? What had he missed? If Yevchenko's accusation was true, who could it have been?

Abram pushed the rush of thoughts aside for the moment. "Jacob, will you go and gather the people?" he said in a subdued voice. "It shouldn't be difficult. No one will be out in the fields yet. It's too early; the ground is still thawing. As far as I know, no one has gone to Blagoveshchensk today."

Jacob quickly rose from his chair. "Yes, right away," was all he said. He was grateful for any excuse to escape the anger and the notice of the Colonel. As he stepped outside, Jacob saw two secret policemen were standing there, one on either side of the door. Both had a Mosin-Nagant rifle slung over their shoulder. Three horses stood close by. Their reins were tied to the hitching post. The horses shook their heads and flicked their ears as a few hardy flies, early for the season, sought a warm spot to land.

An hour later, all of the residents of Alexandrovka had gathered in front of their collective's office. The dirt road was beginning to thaw and everyone's boots were sinking into the sticky mud. A few children, oblivious to the gravity of the situation, took the opportunity lift their legs up and down, watching as the muck rose and fell and sucked and squished in time with the pressure they exerted or released.

Fortunately it was not cold or raining. A light breeze ruffled uncovered hair. Though cloudy, here and there bright spots showed where the sun's rays broke through the veil to bring color to the land: deep browns, dirty and dazzling whites, and here and there, a small flash of green. But for the mud and in different circumstances, it would have been a pleasant time to stand outdoors and chat with one's neighbors as the promise of spring suffused the air.

A few last stragglers were joining the crowd as Colonel Yevchenko stepped out of the office. He stood on the small landing at the top of the short stairway leading into the building. It put him above the people who looked up at him with wary eyes. Abram Siemens had preceded him and now stood on the ground by the first step, looking pale and shaken, not knowing if he should stand facing his fellow villagers or the colonel.

A murder of black crows flew overhead. Their raucous cries rang out in sharp contrast to the muttering villagers standing nervously below. Some children looked up. They wished for their slingshots even as they remembered crows were very clever. They knew after a crow had been shot at once it would seldom sit still to allow for another chance.

Yevchenko raised his hands and his voice. "Is everyone who lives in the village of Alexandrovka here?" The tone of his voice scythed the crowd into silence. Some looked around to see if there were any faces missing. Most looked stolidly at the colonel. He waited while his audience grew uncomfortable in the stillness. Finally he said, "I am told there has been an attempt by people of this village to escape across the river last night. Does anyone know anything about this?"

Silence.

Standing close to the front of the crowd, Jacob's heart began to thud heavily against the walls of his chest. He wondered how Yevchenko could not hear its beating. He glanced over to where Ludwig Hostetler stood. Ludwig was staring at the colonel, shaking his head like many others in the crowd. No, we know nothing about an escape, they were saying. Jacob did the same. Naomi was standing holding Joseph's hand. She pulled him closer to her. Her son looked up at her with wide, frightened eyes, but, hidden as he was behind the taller persons standing in front of him, she was sure the GPU officers could not see the guilt written on his face.

The crowd was silent. Some were shocked at the allegation. Others were shocked their attempt had so quickly become known. Some assumed puzzled expressions and looked at the faces of those around them, pretending to search for guilt, or attempting to hide it. Others, amazed that such an accusation could be made in the village of Alexandrovka, wondered at the temerity of those whose selfish ambition had the potential to bring the wrath of the GPU down upon all of them. After the ripple of emotions had made its way through the crowd, all stilled their faces and their breathing. They looked at the colonel and his officers as calmly, as matter-of-factly as they could.

No, we know nothing about an escape.

Nervously, they waited for what would come next.

Getting no satisfactory reaction from the people, Yevchenko commanded, "Organize yourselves in rows. Then stand at attention while we do a head count. We'll soon know if anyone is missing."

The crowd shuffled about until a number of rows began to take shape. The two GPU officers walked down the rows, pushing a person into place here and there, counting as they went. Yevchenko looked on threateningly. In his hands he held the book containing the tally of all who lived in Alexandrovka, their names and dates of birth.

When they were finished counting, one officer approached the colonel. "One hundred and ninety-eight," he said.

Yevchenko looked in the book. The number neatly printed there was the same. Watching him, Jacob thought he detected a hint of disappointment on his face. Then his face changed as, with a dawning realization he shouted, "I'm going to call the roll. When you hear your family name called, come to me to be recognized." And Yevchenko thought, "Perhaps they have stacked the deck to hide the fact some are gone. Maybe some of these people don't actually live here. We'll soon see."

The roll call began. Families shuffled forward and retreated again like floating branches in the ocean tide. They were all captive to the power of the red star on the colonel's military cap.

When Jacob's family was called forward, he repeated each of their names firmly, despite the thickness in his throat and the acidic reflux that threatened to choke and expose him. "Jacob Enns. Naomi Enns. Joseph Enns, our son."

The colonel held Jacob's eyes for a moment, looking for the lie, digging for the truth. Finding only wariness, he turned his attention to Naomi. He was pleased to see she was a pretty woman. He stared greedily at her. Seeing the beauty of defiance in her clear eyes, he was momentarily aroused. Her contempt surprised him. "I could break you," he thought. He had a fleeting memory of another time and place; distracting thoughts of bare skin, screams, and begging for mercy.

It was Yevchenko who broke eye content. Realizing there were many more people to account for, he reminded himself he could not dally with lustful fantasies. Furthermore, he was growing bored. This woman had been an engaging diversion, but the process was tedious. He was losing his enthusiasm for the hunt. But then a thought struck him. He stared first at Jacob, then at Naomi. He shifted his gaze back to Jacob.

"Tell me. How are your relatives in Ukraine? Did you have a pleasant visit?"

The questions were so unexpected Jacob could manage no reply, caught as he was in the vice of Yevchenko's red stare.

Naomi, who had relatives in Ukraine, answered calmly. "They are well, sir. Thank you for asking." She had even managed to frame the words with a veneer of sincerity.

Glancing at Naomi, Yevchenko was vexed. Tired of the game, he replied sarcastically, "I'm glad to hear it."

The colonel looked at the names in the book. "Next!" he shouted.

At the end of the roll call, the colonel was frustrated. His source had assured him there was a group of villagers who were going to attempt a crossing. Yet, all names called matched those standing in the crowd in the street before him. He was forced to acknowledge the entire population of the village of Alexandrovka was present and accounted for. It was clear no one was missing. He decided to try another angle. His voice took on a conciliatory tone. "Does anyone know of an attempted escape? You know of someone who was out last night hoping to cross the river, but for some reason, changed his mind? There's no need to be afraid, you can tell me."

Numerous heads were shaking, lips pursed, brows furrowed in feigned concentration as the colonel scanned the crowd. A few parents gripped their children more tightly, hoping their lessons in truth telling would not bear fruit on this day. One or two looked down at their children and silenced them with their eyes or with a firm squeeze on their arm.

"No one?" Yevchenko was not surprised. It was as he expected. Nevertheless, the attempt needed to be made. The signal needed to be sent. These farmers needed to know they were being watched.

As he paused, the colonel made a mental note to question his collaborators in the village. The carpenter, Peter Dyck, and the teacher, Gerhard Wieler. Perhaps they'd know something. Otherwise, what good were they if they knew nothing about what was going on in the village? However, there, too, the colonel would be disappointed. He would find that Wieler and Dyck were completely in the dark.

"Well," Colonel Yevchenko finally conceded. "Perhaps I was misled. I apologize for the interruption to your day. You are free to go about your business."

Jacob breathed deeply, slowly. He hoped his relief wasn't evident on his face. He pressed Naomi's hand as she turned to go. They made eye contact briefly. "I'll see you later, after work," was all he said.

As the crowd dispersed, Colonel Yevchenko thought, "I shouldn't have trusted that chinaman. Why would he lie to me?" So no one could hear but the officer to whom he spoke, he muttered, "The next time you see Ying Weimin, arrest him."

Yevchenko took the reins of his horse from the officer who held them. Walking to the horse's side, he straightened the stirrup and lifted his booted foot into it. As he hoisted himself into the saddle, his conversation with the Ennses came to mind. Turning his head, he saw Naomi Enns and her son walking away. He made a mental note to remember the family. Perhaps they warranted another visit. Yes, he would look forward to it.

Jacob watched as Yevchenko and his men got on their horses and trotted briskly out of the village in the direction of Konstantinovka. The mud of the road clung to the horses' hooves before being flicked off as the secret policemen rode away. Seeing the flying clumps of earth, Jacob was reminded of Jesus' admonition to his disciples to wipe the dust off their feet as they left any village that did not welcome them.

The colonel's visit had frightened him badly. "We need to wipe the dust of this village off of our feet," he thought. "Otherwise…"

He didn't want to finish the thought.

Did You Consider the Consequences?

Returning to the office after Colonel Yevchenko and his GPU secret policemen had gone Abram was quiet. In shock at what had just occurred, he took some time to collect himself and to ponder. He remembered Jacob's discomfiture when Yevchenko had appeared and begun his accusations. He was surprised the colonel had missed the obvious signals. Abram decided it was time to ask his own questions and, perhaps, to make his own accusations.

While Jacob busied himself on the other side of the room, Abram stared absentmindedly at the grains in the wood of his desktop. Once or twice he glanced at Jacob. As his thoughts started to take shape he began.

"You knew, didn't you," Abram said softly, a hint of bitterness in his voice.

Jacob looked at Abram. Worn out and unsettled by the colonel's inquisition, he could no longer deny the truth. He collapsed into his chair.

"Yes."

A pause.

"Were you part of it?"

"Yes."

Another pause.

Abram's voice took a harder tone. "What happened?"

"The guide didn't show up. We couldn't go without him."

Abram was silent a moment as he digested Jacob's words. "How many?"

"Twelve families; forty-one people, I think, including children."

Abram convulsed as if he had been struck across the face.

"Twelve families? Forty-one people?" he repeated slowly, his voice rising in anger. "How could you? How could you put this entire village in jeopardy? Do you realize the consequences your escape might have had for us all? Forty-one people suddenly gone?" Abram was aghast. "We are friends! We are brothers! Do you realize the consequences your escape might have had for those of us you left behind?" He stopped before sputtering, "Do you realize what it would have meant for me?"

Abram pointed at the portrait of the General Secretary of the Central Committee of the Communist Party of the Soviet Union hanging on the wall between them. It's monochrome brow seemed especially furrowed, the black eyes piercing, the mouth twisted in a frown.

"Do you realize what he might have done to us? You know how hard life is becoming for those who do not cooperate with his atheistic communist utopian vision. My God, forty-one people disappearing from our village!" Abram was livid, incredulous. "They'd have sent the rest of us to the Gulag, the work camps! If we were lucky!" he barked.

"We didn't think about any of that." Jacob was embarrassed. "I'm…I'm sorry. Naomi and I were thinking only of us and of our need to get our child out of this god-forsaken country. We must give him the hope of a better future."

Abram snorted mirthlessly. "Yes, well think about the children you'd have left behind, and the kind of future you were giving them." He became silent as he considered what to say next, whether he should ask who else was involved. Even as he thought it, he was sure he didn't want to know. Not now. Not yet.

Instead, Abram asked, "Why didn't you tell me? Ahead of time, I mean." Though still hard, Abram's voice had begun to soften.

"It was agreed. No one was to know. I could not tell you."
Abram sighed.

"Yes, I suppose I see that. If I had known, it would have made it awkward for me with Yevchenko. But, I wish you would have trusted me. As I said, we're friends, and brothers in Christ." His voice trailed off. Despite himself, he felt hurt at Jacob's lack of trust in him.

Jacob said nothing. He didn't want to remind Abram that it was not uncommon in the Mennonite colonies for "brothers in Christ" to take advantage of others if it was to their benefit. And when it came to obeying their communist lords, such behavior was being actively encouraged and rewarded by the secret police. Why else were there those willing to act as collaborators in their village?

Abram was silent. The conversation was over. He shuffled through some papers on his desk, but could not concentrate. He turned to Jacob. "I couldn't help but hear Yevchenko questions to you and Naomi. He is a dangerous man. Be careful." He paused briefly. "And, don't worry. Your secret is safe with me."

Jacob nodded weakly.

Abram stood up.

"I'm done for the day. I'm going home. You should, too. Go home and be with your family. I'm sure Naomi needs your support right now after all she's been through. And take care of that boy of yours. He doesn't look well."

As he rose to leave, Jacob was grateful Abram hadn't ask him for a promise to not make another escape attempt. He knew that would have been a promise he could not keep.

When Jacob arrived home, Naomi was standing at the table furiously kneading dough. He thought it odd, for on the shelf were two large bags full of twice-baked buns. She had made these in preparation for their failed escape attempt the night before. Naomi looked up briefly as he closed the door. While he removed his coat and boots, she redoubled her efforts, lifting the ball of dough she had created and slamming it down, pounding it, hammering into it her anger, frustration, and fear. She stopped, breathing hard and stare at the dough with a look of disgust on her face.

"How did they find out so quickly?"

"The guide must have told him," Jacob offered.

"After all the money we paid him, he had the gall to betray us?"

Jacob didn't respond. The truth ended all speculation. He watched as Naomi worked the dough.

She stopped for a moment and looked at Jacob. Her eyes were shiny, wet with tears that spilled down her cheeks.

"Did you see the way he looked at me?" she fumed.

Naomi took a handful of flour from the sack on the table and threw it onto the mound of dough beside it.

"Who?" he asked tentatively, not following her thinking.

Naomi had resumed her pummeling.

"Who?" she echoed. "The secret policeman. Yevchenko." She spat out his name. "Did you see how he looked at me?"

"No," Jacob admitted. He remembered standing before Yevchenko and nervously fixating on his belt buckle once the colonel was through with him. He'd noticed the hammer and sickle embossed on the golden star at its center.

"Well, you wouldn't, would you," Naomi snarled. "You never see what goes on. Your head is always either in the clouds or in your books. Anyway, you're a typical man with the observational skills of a gnat. What do you know about how men treat women? No one looks at men the way the colonel looked at me. It is only men who look at women as he did and imagine the things he was imagining."

Jacob was shocked by Naomi's words. What had he missed? He felt ashamed at his inattentiveness, his lack of awareness of what Naomi had felt. He wanted to protect her; he had much to learn.

"I'm sorry, Naomi, I really am. For my failure, for what you felt." Jacob pulled Naomi into his arms and embraced her. Weeping softly, she pulled away from him and plunged her hands into the lump of dough on the table.

Looking toward where Joseph was playing, Jacob saw he was lying on the floor in the corner of the room. He had put down the carved, wooden miniature horse he'd been playing with and covered his ears with his hands. "Joseph," Jacob said quietly, a note of concern creeping into his voice. He watched as Joseph lay down and curled into a fetal position, tucked tightly against the wall. He had closed his eyes.

Jacob reached out to touch Naomi's arm. "What's Joseph doing?" he asked quietly.

Naomi stopped kneading. She looked over to where Joseph lay motionless on the floor.

"I don't know," she said through tears that had yet to stop. "He's having a rest. Are you listening to me? Have you heard anything I've been saying?"

While she spoke, Joseph sat up. He began to bang his head against the wall, slowly, rhythmically: bang, bang, bang, bang, bang, bang, bang. The dull thuds reverberated around the room, their echo far exceeding the volume of their point of origin.

"Joseph, what are you doing? Stop that," Naomi said sternly.

Joseph did not stop.

Frantically, Naomi started pulling shreds of dough from her fingers, stabbing them into the mound of dough on the table. With quick steps, Jacob reached the corner. Wiping her doughy fingers on her apron, Naomi was close behind him. Jacob picked up his son, but Joseph immediately began kicking him and hitting him with his little fists. Jacob held him tighter, struggling to hold his legs still while grasping at his arms. Naomi tried to calm her son. She stroked his hair and his back, and spoke words of love into his ear.

As quickly as Joseph's anger had erupted, it ended. He collapsed into his father's shoulder. As she watched her son surrender to his father's firm grip, Naomi realized that throughout his tantrum, Joseph had uttered no sound. Utterly alarmed, she hugged her son and her husband to her, pulling her family together with all her strength.

She looked up at Jacob. "We must leave this country," she whimpered. "If we stay, it will be the death of us all."

Still holding his son, Jacob moved over to their bed and sat down. Naomi sat beside him. Taking Joseph into her arms, she buried her face in his hair and wet it with her tears. Drawing back, she kissed the bright red lump forming on the center of his forehead.

For a fleeting second, Jacob thought of his conversation with Abram. He thought of Abram's warning and his plea. Consequences; perhaps they would be less severe if it were only one family that crossed the river.

"Yes," Jacob agreed cautiously. "We must leave. But they will be watching the river more closely for a while now. When the ice breaks, we will go on our own. We won't tell anyone. We'll go by boat. I'll arrange it."

Naomi nodded.

Joseph lay in her arms sucking his thumb, silently staring at his mother's face.

This May Be Our Last Chance

April 1930

On the banks of the Amur River lived an old fisherman. Both he and his wife were bent and gnarled by years of hard labor. Their home was a small hut made of logs so weathered they had assumed the color of roasted coffee beans, a beverage he and his wife had never had the pleasure of sipping. On its sod roof grew a splendid display of the local grasses and colorful weeds.

While her husband fished, his wife spent her days tending the large vegetable garden planted beside their shack. Thus they eked out their living for decades before the outsiders had arrived to set up their villages and their farms. They raised their children as best they could and waved good-bye as they were taken away by promises of love, adventure, and for one, a Red Army uniform that guaranteed three meals most days. The years had not been kind to the old fisherman. Arthritis was in his shoulders and wrists now. It made it impossible for him to work the oars of his rowboat against the strong currents of the river.

When Jacob Enns thought about where he might obtain a boat for his family's escape, he remembered the old fisherman. Once, when he traveled along the river's dyke, he had caught a glimpse of him through the trees. The man was well known in the region for the fish he sold to customers in the villages. Now, Jacob knew, the crippling effects of age kept the old man seated on the bank of the Amur where, when the river ran free, rain or shine, he fished with a pole and line. Jacob hoped the old fisherman still had his boat. Perhaps, since he no longer could use it he would be willing to sell it.

In mid-April, after the snow on the steppe had melted and fled to the Amur, and the river itself had heaved and shrugged off its thick, five-month old coat of ice, Jacob went to visit the old fisherman in his hovel. The day was cloudy with rain spitting intermittently.

When he arrived at the fisherman's door, Jacob was invited in with the grudging hospitality reserved for the stranger. After some small talk he made his request. Jacob missed the look of resentment that flitted across the fisherman's face before his visage settled into the stony look of a seasoned haggler. The man resented the newcomers he regarded as foreigners, German colonists who had no business living in Mother Russia. He resented the wealth they had so quickly wrested from the Siberian soil while he and his wife continued to subsist in poverty. However, when Jacob showed the man and his wife a handful of rubles, the old fisherman saw that here was a chance to reap some profit and he was determined to take it.

Since neither man wanted to appear eager, the bargaining was slow and filled with pauses of feigned indifference. Knowing the absolute necessity of the deal, Jacob watched with fluttering heart as the cagey fisherman often stopped to make a show of stroking his long grey beard thoughtfully. The fisherman's wife sat on a stool in the corner, eyeing the men disapprovingly. After much hemming and hawing, a price was finally agreed upon. Jacob politely accepted the proffered glass of celebratory vodka that would seal the deal, though he would rather have declined. Knowing the importance of the custom, he threw the clear liquid back and coughed as it hit the back of his throat.

The fisherman agreed to hide the boat at a place chosen by Jacob. He would moor it at a certain spot in a bend along the bank of the Amur River where the thick willow bushes growing there would hide it from the eyes of the border guards patrolling along river.

Knowing the moon would be full in a week or so, Jacob and Naomi decided to make their crossing the next night. No sense in risking a crossing when the land might be lit with a glow that would multiply a watchful border guard's vision. And if today's overcast held, the clouds promised to hide the moon and stars' ambient light. They would provide a cloak under which Jacob and his family could attempt their escape.

That evening Jacob and Naomi lay in bed, their nerves stretched tight by the uncertainty of the morrow's daring plan.

Naomi listened for the sounds that would tell her Joseph was asleep on his pallet on the other side of the room. When his breathing slowed into the telltale steady rhythm, broken occasionally by a childish snore, she whispered to Jacob, "Make love to me."

Jacob turned onto his side to face her. With his help, Naomi's nightdress was soon above her hips and over her head. Facing each other, Jacob felt Naomi's hand reach over him onto his back. Her fingers began to play a slow four-note scale rising and falling, each note in turn pulling him fractionally closer to her. Through his nightshirt, Jacob felt the insistent prick of her nails. Naomi began to undo the buttons of his shirt and soon they were both fumbling with them. When Jacob's clothing was gone, Naomi kissed him hard, impatiently, her soft breasts pressed into his chest. Holding him tightly, she murmured, her hot breath in his ear signaling her deep desire, "This may be our last chance for who knows how long."

While their son slept, Naomi and Jacob nervously watched the minutes tick by. Their only time piece was an old windup clock. It glowed on their sideboard in the reflected light of the kerosene lamp. Try as they might, staring at the clock would not hasten the night along. It seemed the progress the hours made was as slow as that of a beetle crawling through a puddle of molasses. There was no question of their catching some sleep. On this night they intended to make their escape.

Finally, when the clock's hands showed eleven, Jacob and Naomi embraced tightly. With no words needing to be spoken, Jacob lifted Joseph up out of his sleep. Naomi took hold of the sack of food she had prepared for the journey.

As they stepped out of their cabin, Jacob looked gratefully at the blackened Siberian sky. A thick cover of low-hanging clouds hid the waxing moon. He breathed in the night air, fresh with the scent of the soil from the rain that had fallen during the day. The wind that had accompanied the rain had died a little so it looked as if the clouds might be left stranded, a shadow blanket covering the land. "Good," he thought. "The darker the night, the better." The breeze ruffled his hair; he didn't allow himself to consider what effect any wind might have on their boat as he rowed it across the river. Quietly he latched the door behind him and went to the stable to get their horse.

In order to keep the boatload as light as possible, Jacob and Naomi had decided they would take no unnecessary belongings along. With only the clothes they were wearing and their sack of buns and cured meat, the small family climbed onto the horse, Jacob in the middle holding the reins, Naomi holding on tightly from behind, Joseph sitting in front of him. Hoping the clip clop of the horse's hooves would not betray them, they trotted along the dirt road out of the village and onto the open steppe. The darkness was thick, but the horse knew the track and when they needed to leave it to ride across fields, Jacob's sense of direction didn't fail him. Eventually they found the road that wound its way along the riverbank. This they would follow to the place where Jacob expected they'd find their boat.

As Jacob rode along, he thought about the craft he had purchased. He had examined it briefly under the watchful eye of the fisherman. Now he wondered if it was strong enough to make the journey across the river. Were its seams tight? Would it leak? He hadn't thought to bring a bailing bucket. Going back for one was out of the question; he was unwilling to risk the delay. His family would take its chance on the strong currents of the river.

Their progress was slow for the night was black and they had to stop often to gain their bearings. Knowing the border guards would be patrolling the riverbank, they were alert for any sound of leather boots or horses' hooves on the muddy track, or the snapping of trodden sticks that lay upon it. Should they be discovered, there would be no satisfactory explanation for their presence on the dyke at that time of night. They stopped often to listen, but the whispering leaves hid any sound that might betray the approach of a patrol.

It was only his familiarity with the area that allowed Jacob to finally lead his family to where their boat was tied. Naomi slid off of the horse before Jacob dismounted. Jacob lifted his son from the horse and set him on the ground. Reluctantly he patted the horse on the rear, giving it its freedom.

Jacob carefully climbed down the steep bank of the river. Weaving his way through the willow bushes using some as handholds and pushing others aside, he stared into the darkness for the outline he expected to find. When Jacob's hand fell on a rope tied to a branch, he knew he had found the boat. He breathed a sigh of relief, for he had wondered if the old codger would follow through on his part of the deal. There would have been little he could have done, should the fisherman have decided to keep his money and his boat.

Clambering back up the slope, Jacob returned to Naomi and Joseph. Using hand gestures, he told them he had found the boat. Holding each others hands tightly, the family crept down the bank to the boat. Naomi's coat caught on some branches. It took a moment to free it—they held their breath at the racket the cracking branch made. Frozen in place, they listened for any sign they had been heard. They heard only the sloughing and gurgling of water against the weeds that grew in the marshy shallows, the timpani of crickets and the croaking of distant frogs. Jacob gingerly helped Naomi into the boat. When she was seated at the back of the boat, he lifted Joseph into her waiting arms.

With Naomi and Joseph in place, Jacob untied the painter. He pushed the boat into deeper water and hoisted himself in, cringing at the sloshing sounds he made. Whispering a prayer for safety and guidance, Jacob settled himself on his seat and took hold of the oars. The shaped, worn wood felt strange in his soft hands. He pushed aside a fleeting thought of the fisherman whose gnarled hands had worked these oars for decades. He could feel the boat begin to drift into the current.

For a moment Jacob hesitated, wondering if what his family was attempting was complete folly. But no, for years now, people just like his family had successfully made the crossing into China. He would not allow himself to think of those who had tried and failed, caught by border guards or overcome by the power of the river. In the darkness he could make out the dim forms of Naomi and Joseph. She had wrapped her arms around her son in a motherly attempt to protect him and keep him warm.

Jacob looked into the darkness at Naomi's face. She nodded silently. Jacob nodded in reply. It was time.

Jacob took a deep breath. He dug the oars deeply into the water, working them in opposite directions in order to turn the boat. He needed the bow to be pointed at China. The boat turned slowly, the current now helping his efforts. Jacob felt the strong pull of the river. He quickly realized that this night he would need to work harder than he had at any other time in his life if they held any hope of success. He hoped his body would be up to the task.

Jacob put his back into it and pulled on the oars. Slowly he worked his way into a comfortable rhythm.

They had not been on the water more than a couple of minutes, when Naomi hissed, "Listen!" Jacob stopped rowing. He listened; he heard it. It was the faint putt-putt putt-putt sound of a motorboat. It was coming closer, though slowly. He sat still a moment longer, feeling his rowboat beginning to drift with the current, anxious because of it, anxious because of the motor chugging toward them. Yes, he decided, it was definitely coming closer. The boat was downstream coming in their direction. The sound of its motor was growing louder. Jacob knew it would clear the bend in the river soon.

Who could be out on the river at this hour? In a motorboat? Even as he thought it, Jacob knew the answer. He felt panic rising within. His limbs suddenly felt limp, his hands weak, his head dizzy.

"Row!" hissed Naomi. "The current is carrying us toward them! Row!"

Jacob pulled fiercely on the oars. The boat began to straighten. But then the thought occurred to him, "In which direction should we go? Back toward the riverbank or out onto the river?"

Ludwig Hostetler could not sleep. He lay in bed tossing and turning. He tried to calm his thoughts, but his mind refused to be still.

Earlier that evening, Jacob Enns had knocked on his door. "May I have a word?" he had said, ignoring Ludwig's invitation to enter.

As they had stood in Ludwig's front yard a sudden breeze had carried to them the smell of rain falling somewhere nearby on the steppe. Jacob told Ludwig that he and his family had decided to cross the Amur River to China in a rowboat he had purchased from an old fisherman. Ludwig hid his surprise and nodded. He knew there was no sense in trying to dissuade Jacob.

"Do you trust the fisherman?" Ludwig had asked.

Jacob had paused.

"I have to. God knows I paid dearly for his boat. He should be satisfied."

Ludwig had been silent.

"We're going tonight." Jacob's voice was matter-of-fact. It betrayed none of the fear or apprehension he was feeling.

"Have you said anything to Abram Siemens?"

"Yes."

"How did he take it?" Ludwig had wanted to know.

Jacob had shrugged. "He appreciated me being straight with him. He tried to talk me out of it; talked about the danger I was placing my family in. But he's beginning to understand the desperation we and others like us feel."

For a time the two men stood in silence, feeling the moving air on their faces.

"It's going to rain."

The observation had seemed banal, given the danger that would be faced that night, and Ludwig had regretted his words.

They had embraced.

"God be with you," Ludwig had whispered.

And then Jacob had gone.

Ludwig shifted his body on the feather mattress. He opened his eyes. Anna was lying on her side facing him, her mouth hanging open in deep sleep. Ludwig smiled; he loved his wife, no matter how unflattering her posture. Baby Peter slept in the cradle next to her side of the bed.

Thoughts of Jacob, Naomi and Joseph crowded in: a premonition of great danger. "I can't sleep," he mused, "should I be going down to the river to see how the Ennses are doing? That's twenty kilometers in the dark." But the feeling that this night evil would be done would not be shaken. Wide-awake now, Ludwig sat up. Whispering a prayer for Jacob and his family, he swung his legs out of bed. He picked up the clock that ticked by his bedside and squinted at the numbers. Eleven-thirty. There was still time.

Ludwig pulled his pants and shirt on over his nightclothes. He padded by where Margaret and Judith slept on his way to the door. Taking his jacket from the peg where it hung, he looked back and noted that his wife and children still slept. Slipping into his shoes, Ludwig went out into the night.

Rousing his horse from its slumber, Ludwig mounted and urged it into a quick trot, hoping there were no hidden obstacles that might trip it up, hoping the noise it made would not be heard by unwanted ears. Following the darkened paths, he finally came to the dyke that formed the bank of the Amur. Ludwig halted his horse and patted it quiet, standing still awhile listening. Between gusts of wind that sent the larch leaves into rustling tremors, he strained his ears for any sounds of border guards who might be nearby on their nightly patrol. He doubted they would be. The guards were not as diligent as their commander wished. He knew they loved a warm fire and a glass of vodka to chase the chill from the night air. With any luck, on a dark night such as this, he hoped their patrol might be haphazard at best.

Hearing nothing, Ludwig urged the horse out onto the dyke and trotted along the track. Out in the darkness he heard the nickering of a horse. Ignoring the fear that it might be a border guard, he rode in the direction from which the sound had come. Coming close, he recognized Jacob's horse. "I must be close," he thought. Jacob had told him the approximate location from which his family would leave. Ludwig dismounted and tied the reins of the two horses to a stout tree branch.

Walking along the dyke, Ludwig heard a sound coming from the river. "A motorboat," he thought. He had just enough time to ask himself why a motorboat would be on the river at this time of night when he heard another sound. Was it a shout?

Crack!

Ludwig stopped. He was a hunter. He knew that sound.

Crack!

A pause just long enough, he imagined, for a bolt to be drawn back, a spent shell to be ejected and another cartridge to be rammed into the barrel of a rifle.

Crack!

Pause.

Shouts.

Crack!

Ludwig stopped at a place where he had a clear view of the river. In the dark he saw a light sweeping the water.

Crack!

More shouting.

Despite his sudden fear, Ludwig found himself running along the dyke in the direction from which the shots were coming.

The motorboat was coming closer. The sound of its engine was slowly growing louder.

Jacob pulled on the oars with all his strength. In his panic he lost control of one. Its tip skidded across the surface of the water, splashing Naomi and Joseph.

"Hurry! Jacob, hurry!" said Naomi, her voice rising.

As she looked frantically toward the bend in the river from which she expected the motorboat to appear at any second, she saw a light weaving this way and that over the water. After a few moments it was lost to her sight. Then it flashed back onto the water.

"Jacob, they have a search light!" she cried in alarm.

Jacob knew what he must do. They had only one chance of survival. He managed to turn the rowboat around. He pulled hard for the bank they had just left. He knew their only protection would be amongst the thick willow bushes growing there. Their branches hung low over the water. Perhaps the border guards wouldn't see them hiding amongst the underbrush. Perhaps the light wouldn't catch them out. Perhaps the guards wouldn't find their boat. Perhaps time would reverse itself and the boat with its searchlight would slowly disappear downriver from where it had come.

Jacob pulled on the oars, once, twice, three times, four times, five.

The motorboat was still hidden by the bend. The light coming from it clawed at the water this way and that, in front of it, beside it, scanning the water, scanning the riverbank.

Jacob pulled on the oars.

The motorboat was certainly coming nearer.

Jacob heaved on the oars.

The rowboat dragged bottom as it struck the shallow. Heedless of the noise it would make, Jacob jumped out of the boat. Naomi stood, pushing Joseph into her husband's outstretched arms.

The motorboat was closer now.

With his son in his arms, Jacob turned and splashed through the shallow water. He came to the bank and climbed amongst the willows, oblivious of the branches whipping him as he went past. Terrified, Naomi jumped into the water. She turned toward the willows. For a brief moment they were bright as day around her as the light swept past. She marveled at the sudden clarity, the sudden contrast of light against darkness. And then it was gone. She splashed toward the willows. As she leaned forward to push aside the branches the light returned.

A shout, "There!"

Naomi scrambled into the bushes.

CRACK! The night air shattered.

Jacob jumped at the sudden explosion. His ears did not catch the snick of the bullet as it sped past and struck the riverbank.

"Can he see us?" His thought was half-formed and fled.

Jacob heard the metallic snap-click of a bolt-action rifle.

Naomi dove into the thicket. She clawed at the riverbank as she climbed higher, to where she thought Jacob and Joseph had fled.

CRACK!

Someone on the river was cursing as he pulled the bolt of his rifle to reload. The staccato beat of the launch's two-stroke motor set the tempo and Jacob's racing heart kept time.

In the dark shadows behind the brightly lit bushes, Naomi found Jacob and Joseph. They were huddled together in the cover of the thick willows.

"Thank God!"

Jacob grabbed her. She sank down beside him. He pulled her close.

CRACK!

The light from the boat started to move again. It swept back and forth, up and down, searching the riverbank, searching among the willows. But the boat came no nearer. Its hull was too deep; the shallows prevented its approach and evidently the border guards had no wish to wet their boots and trousers.

A voice shouted angrily, "Hold the goddamn boat steady, you bloody fool! I saw someone! I'm sure of it! They're there! I know it!"

He pulled the trigger.

CRACK!

A high-pitched, plaintive voice, apologetic, "The current's too strong, sir. And the wind's come up. I can't hold her."

CRACK!

Jacob crouched over his son, pulling him close with his left hand. His right arm held Naomi tightly to him.

"Ah, you bleedin' idiot," shouted the voice. "You son of a poxed whore. How am I to aim if you can't keep the goddamned boat steady? If I've missed, I'll skin you for this. Bastard! Get me to a place where I can land. I want to see if I've caught the traitors."

"I know that voice," thought Jacob absentmindedly in his terror.

Jacob heard the motor speed up as the boat veered away. The sound grew quieter as the launch disappeared around the bend from which it had come.

Shocked by what they had just endured, it took Jacob a few breaths to calm himself. "We're safe for the moment," he whispered. "Let's go. Quickly now. It will be a while before they are able to get here, but we want to be long gone. We must find our horse."

Joseph uncurled himself from beneath his father and stood, grasping a branch to steady himself. He was trembling violently. Naomi did not respond. She leaned heavily against her husband. She seemed to have suddenly become very small, as if she had shrunk into herself.

"Naomi?" Jacob said softly.

She began to slip from his grasp. Jacob shifted his arm on Naomi's back, trying to keep her from falling over. His hand touched something warm and sticky. Frantic, Jacob reached for his wife's face. Her jaw was slack.

"No breath," he realized. "Oh God, no breath! Naomi! My love!"

Jacob's breath was coming in great gulps, as if somehow he might have enough air for both of them. He clenched his teeth to keep back the cry of anguish that was rising up from deep within.

The sluice gates of the heavens split apart. Cold rain fell in great gouts and squalls driven by a sudden wind howled through the weeping willows on the riverbank. The sound of leather boots pounding upon the dyke road was lost in the tumult.

Huddled with his wife and child, Jacob was unaware of the storm and the approaching steps. His entire world had collapsed into a tiny oasis of grief. Jacob held Naomi's limp body tightly enveloped in his arms and rocked her in mute disbelief. Again and again he kissed her wet cheeks, her dripping hair, her dull eyes. He pleaded with her to take a breath, one small breath that could lead to larger ones.

Watching his father, Joseph began to wail in shocked, helpless bewilderment. Seeing but not understanding what had happened, he wrapped his arms around Jacob's neck. He mindlessly pulled and tugged at his father with all his small might. When this elicited no response, he began to hit his father with his small fists.

And so it was that Ludwig Hostetler found them there, a family of mourners locked in a confused combat grief and terror. A horror that could not be contained betrayed them in their hiding place. Scrambling down the embankment, Ludwig approached with disbelief. The rain-soaked skin of their hands and faces shone like marble in a sudden flash of lightning. The thunder crashed, and for a moment he halted, instinctively recognizing the sacrilege of his intrusion into their anguished tableau.

Yet, there was no question of delay. Ludwig stepped forward. Angling around a clump of underbrush, he made his way so he was on the lower side of the family upon the slope of the riverbank. He knelt down. Ludwig put one hand on Jacob's shoulder even as he gathered Jacob's son to him with the other.

"We must go from here, Jacob," he breathed. "Quickly." And to Joseph, gently, "Shhh, little one. Shush." As he sought to calm Joseph, Ludwig made no promises of a better life, or of an end to his suffering. He knew there would be no comfort in words. He offered only a caring embrace. "Shhh, Joseph. Shhh."

Joseph buried his face in the shoulder of the man he knew to be his father's friend. He shuddered repeatedly as he sobbed. It seemed all strength had left him and he gave in to the comfort of Ludwig's shoulder, weeping inconsolably.

It seemed a lifetime before Jacob turned his head to peer at Ludwig. Ludwig saw his distracted eyes and knew Jacob looked without seeing. Jacob's hold on his wife was strong; their slow rocking dance continued.

Ludwig tightened his grip on Jacob's shoulder. Lightly, he shook him. "Jacob, we are in great danger here. The guards will be searching. They will have landed by now. They will find us."

Slowly recognition dawned in Jacob's face. His eyes began to show understanding.

"Jacob, take Joseph." Ludwig pushed Joseph toward his father's chest. "Here, take your son. He needs you. I will bring Naomi." Though he spoke softly, there was the urgency of command in Ludwig's voice.

For the first time Jacob heard his son's pitiful cries. Unwilling to release his wife, with one arm he wrapped Joseph in a tight embrace. Hampered by the thicket of willows, Ludwig reached around Jacob to steady Naomi's head. Jacob relinquished his grip and stood so Ludwig could reach her fully. Ludwig took Naomi into his powerful arms and as he did his heart cried out for he saw there was no life in her.

Thus did they begin the arduous climb to the top of the embankment. Somehow, their sight blinded by tears and rain, their breath ragged with the effort, they reached the top and stepped onto the roadway.

After a brief rest Ludwig urged them to move forward. "The horses are close by. We must get off of the road as quickly as possible. The border guards will be coming. Our best hope lies on the narrow path up ahead that leads into the forest. Come."

As a patient father leads his child, so Ludwig urged and cajoled Jacob until his feet began to move. Jacob stumbled along until they found the horses. He struggled into the saddle and rode as if in a dream, at first slowly, but then, gradually with greater urgency, as Ludwig urged them to hurry. They soon left the road and moved silently along the trails among the wind-whipped evergreens and dripping bracken where there was less danger of being found. They moved unseen, for the dark of the night and the relentless power of the storm had taken the village of Alexandrovka into its firm, unyielding grip so that those who hunted were blinded and forced to seek refuge.

When they arrived finally at Ludwig's home, they found a dim light in the window. Having awoken to find her husband gone, Anna had gotten up. She had lit the lamp and stoked the fire in the stove. Great was her shock and sorrow when they entered and Ludwig laid Naomi's body on the kitchen table.

But this was not a time for tears. Danger surrounded them like a death shroud. Anna asked no questions for there was not time for them, and she guessed their answers anyway.

Knowing the dead for the moment could wait Ludwig and Anna busied themselves caring for the living. Jacob and Joseph were both numb with shock and cold. They were shaking uncontrollably. Anna found suitable, dry clothes from amongst her husband's and children's things. Ludwig put a kettle on the stove to boil.

Later, warmed and dry, Jacob and his son were put to bed. Jacob made no protest, though he and Joseph were made to lie in Ludwig and Anna's bed. He had no words to express his sorrow or his gratitude for his friends' kindness.

As Anna pulled the coverlet snug against Jacob's cheek, she whispered, "Rest now, Jacob. Ludwig and I will think of what must be done. For now you must rest."

Jacob lay with his eyes wide open, while his son fell into a deep sleep tucked up close in the safety of his father's arms. Sitting at the table, Ludwig and Anna faced the questions that now demanded answers, questions not about what had happened but of what must happen now.

Rays of light danced through the window and, splintered by a glass cup on the table, flashed rainbows upon the wall. The storm had blown itself out; the clouds had fled and the sky was painted with the pale blue hues of springtime. When Jacob woke from his sleep, his eyes caught the splash of color. Its beauty seemed to mock him as in an instant he recalled the horror of the night before. He closed his eyes and for a moment wished them never to open again. Then, feeling his son stir, he knew he must gather the strength he would need to face what lay ahead.

Snuggled beside him, Joseph slept on. Jacob slowly removed his cramped arm from under his son's shoulders. Worried the creaking mattress would awaken him he arose slowly from the bed. Tiptoeing from the bedroom, he found Ludwig and Anna seated at the table where last he had left them. His wife's body was no longer there.

"Naomi?" he choked. "Where is she? What have you done with her?"

Understanding his friend's alarm, Ludwig said, "She is safely resting, Jacob. I have laid her in our shed. I am sorry, but it is the best place for her." His voice was subdued. It was edged with fatigue and grief.

"We could not have the children waking to find her here," murmured Anna. A tear slipped from the corner of her eye. "While you slept I have washed her body and dressed her in fresh clothing."

"I must see her," pleaded Jacob, grateful for Anna's ministrations but unable yet to thank her.

"You two go while I fix some breakfast," Anna urged Ludwig.

Ludwig and Jacob stepped outside. The door was at the back of the house so they could not be seen from the road. Even so, Ludwig paused to scan the road from behind the corner of the house. Seeing no one, they walked quickly to the shed. Ludwig unlatched the door and held it open. Jacob breathed deeply before stepping inside. He found his wife lying upon a workbench that had been cleared and wiped clean. A quilt was wrapped around her and Jacob was briefly grateful for the blanket that had somehow kept her warm. Ludwig held back while his friend bowed over his wife's body and wept slow tears of mourning.

After a time, Jacob turned. "We must build a coffin."

"Yes," said Ludwig. "I have thought of that. I have some boards laid aside in the shop. Let us build it now while it is early and not too many folks are about. Before prying ears and eyes think to ask questions, though it is not unusual for me to practice my carpentry here." He hesitated. "Naomi's death must go unnoted."

It was while they sawed and hammered that Ludwig and Jacob faced the difficult question of burial. Naomi could not be laid to rest in the church cemetery. For obvious reasons, it would invite scrutiny and inevitable discovery.

"I know of a glade in the forest not too far from here," offered Ludwig. Pine and larch trees surround it. I sometimes go there when I need to think. It is a quiet place and unlikely to be discovered by the secret police who like to stick to the roadways and river."

"Yes, that would be good," agreed Jacob readily. He attempted a smile. "Naomi loved the pinewoods. In the springtime, she often remarked about the scent of the sap in the air when it began to flow beneath the trees' bark. On summer evenings, she often walked among the trees and looked for wildflowers to pick. She'd put them in a jar on the table. Yes, she would welcome such a place to rest as she waits for the Day of Judgment. And it doesn't matter if she is buried in a churchyard or a forest glade. On that day, God will find us wherever we may be."

The coffin was soon made. It was a crude resting place for one so loved, but it was made with love.

After they had breakfasted, Anna lined the box with a fine quilt. Though Jacob objected to her sacrifice, she would not entertain his disagreements. "I have other quilts. This is the least Naomi deserves," was Anna's unmoving response.

That night, while the village slept, Ludwig, Jacob, and two trusted neighbors bore Naomi's coffin to the clearing in the woods. Anna had said her good-bye to Naomi and remained with the sleeping children. It had been agreed that they should not know of the night's events or the grave's location. They could not reveal to playmates or strangers what they did not know.

All that day, Joseph had been easily irritated and often angry. By evening, none of Ludwig and Anna's children would allow themselves to be left alone with him. He had refused to speak to anyone, even his father. For better or worse, it was judged he should not be exposed to more traumas in the night burial of his mother.

The skies were clear and the moon offered a bathing glow to help the men when they began their trek through the forest. The task was difficult and tiring. Moving among the trees carrying their load was slow going. When they finally reached the glade, the men put the coffin down and rested a few moments. It was Jacob who roused the men. He began to furiously hack at the sod with his shovel until Ludwig laid a hand on his shoulder to stop him. Ludwig then showed them all what must be done.

Being careful to first remove and lay aside the layer of grass, weeds, and wildflowers that grew there, they began the task for which they had come. Taking turns, the men dug deep into the ground. The loamy soil made it easy for them, though there was the occasional tree root needing to be cut. Once they were satisfied with the depth, they lowered the coffin into the hole. The dirt was replaced and the sods were fitted on top so that anyone walking there would soon see no evidence of the grave in the center of the clearing. Finding they had a mound of dirt left over, the men carried it a little way away and scattered it among the bracken and trees.

When the work was done, the four men stood around Naomi's grave. It was suffused in the soft light of night and Jacob considered it beautiful. He had the fleeting thought there was divine approval in their choice of his wife's resting place. In the absence of a minister, the men recited meaningful passages of Scripture from memory. While Jacob wept, his comrades prayed for him and for his son. They beseeched God for help in their time of grief and thanked Him for the promise of resurrection and new life to come.

Lord have mercy.

When Jacob Enns stepped into the office of the manager of the Alexandrovka collective the next morning, Abram Siemens did not notice his red-rimmed eyes and haggard face. He was preoccupied with his accounts and seemed to have forgotten that Jacob wasn't supposed to be there at all.

It had taken Jacob most of the night to find the resolve to carry on the charade Ludwig had urged upon him. "You and your son must either leave Alexandrovka or you must pretend your wife has gone away. You must explain her absence; tell people there was a family emergency that required her to travel to Ukraine. You must carry on with your life as if nothing were amiss," he had said. Not knowing where he would go, Jacob had elected to stay.

"Jacob," Abram finally said, his voice full of surprise, "You didn't go. What happened? Did you change your mind?"

After hanging his sodden jacket on the coat stand in the corner—it was raining again—Jacob sank into his chair. He busied himself sharpening a pencil with his pocketknife. The little shavings cascaded into the wastebasket like the fragments of broken tears.

Jacob took a breath. He didn't know where to begin. Collecting his thoughts, he was about to speak when the office door banged open and Colonel Yevchenko stepped inside. The colonel took great swipes at his shoulders and arms as he wiped the droplets of water from them. Small puddles began to form around his boots. It was the day of his weekly visit.

"The cursed rain!" griped the colonel. "When will it stop?"

"We'll appreciate it when the spring seeding is done, sir," offered Abram Siemens. "The soil needs all the moisture it can get to grow our crops."

"Bah! By the holy Mother-of-God, the timing could not have been worse!"

Siemens look puzzled.

"You haven't heard?" growled Yevchenko. "We had a little action on the river Monday night. Someone tried to escape."

Jacob blanched. His gut wrenched and he felt again his terror on the riverbank. He heard again the shouts from the motorboat and to his horror realized this was the voice he had heard that night.

Yevchenko was bellicose. He angrily exclaimed, "These people from the west. They keep coming here thinking they can get over the river to China. What misguided, treasonous fools! I don't know why the police in Blagoveshchensk don't put a stop to them. Round 'em up and send 'em to the work camps where they'll do some good for the nation. Or line 'em up against a wall and shoot 'em."

Jacob felt the gorge rising in his stomach.

The pool of water around the colonel's feet was growing. When he spoke again his words were threatening. "I have many eyes and ears in the villages and countryside. They see; they hear. They talk to me. I know when things are going to happen. People are such bloody dimwits."

Jacob felt dizzy. He thought he might faint. He gripped the edge of his desk to steady himself.

Yevchenko bullied on. "I knew they were going to try the crossing. I knew they had a boat. I knew where they got it and I even knew how much they paid for it. But I just didn't know who they were or where they hid the thing. The border guards are useless, so I decided to go out myself. I thought I'd do a little hunting. But wouldn't you know it? The buggers heard me coming. The motor on that boat is loud enough to wake the dead. Hah! They paddled back to the bank and fled into the bushes like scared rabbits. I'm not sure, but I think there were three of 'em. Two big ones and a little one. I took a couple of shots, but it was too dark to see 'em once they got in amongst the trees. We beached our boat and went and had a look. But with the rain, there wasn't even any blood sign. Probably washed away. So who knows. Maybe I got one; maybe I didn't. We found their boat downriver this morning. Nothin' in it but a bag of soaked bread."

Jacob grabbed his wastebasket and vomited. He heaved and heaved and all the while he was thinking wildly of how he wanted to stand and smash the pail down on the colonel's head.

Yevchenko looked distastefully at Jacob. "What's the matter with him? Too much vodka last night?" He laughed uproariously. "Nah, you people don't drink the stuff, do you." He became serious. His nose turned up at the sour smell that was beginning to pervade the room. "Do you have the influenza?" He looked at Abram. "This man should not be here. He's going to sicken us all. Send him home."

Abram stood. "Yes, sir. I will."

Yevchenko buttoned his coat. He was in a hurry to leave.

"There's nothin' goin' on here that I need to attend to anyway. I'll see you next week."

When Colonel Yevchenko had gone, Jacob broke down completely. He wept in great gasping sobs while Abram Siemens looked on with consternation.

"Jacob, what is it? What's happened?"

When Jacob could finally speak he told his friend the whole bitter story: the escape attempt, the motorboat, the shots in the dark, Ludwig's rescue.

Abram was shocked. He struggled to understand what Jacob had told him even as he felt a mixture of grief and horror. "Oh, Jacob! Naomi is dead? And the colonel? Yevchenko? You think he shot her? He killed Naomi?" He sat for a moment in stunned disbelief. "And now he laughs about it? It is a lark for him to hunt and kill desperate people?"

Abram could not fathom the insanity, the inhumanity of it. "You're sure it was him? Colonel Yevchenko? You're positive?"

Jacob could only nod his head.

"And Naomi? Where is she now?"

Jacob described the night burial.

Abram listened, his head shaking slowly back and forth, as if somehow he could defend himself from the truth of what Jacob was saying, as if he could shake off the brutal reality of their lives in the workers' paradise that was the Soviet Union of Socialist Republics.

Jacob glanced at the stern portrait of the General Secretary of the Central Committee of the Communist Party hanging on the wall. He knew the madness rampant in his country was a result of the madness in that man's heart. It was a contagious lunacy that corrupted all who were susceptible to it. Stalin's piercing eyes seemed to mock Jacob. He was filled with hatred for this tyrant and for the man who had killed his wife.

Jacob Enns' dream of a new life was shattered. His beloved Naomi was dead. There would be no new life in a country where people lived in freedom. In the days that followed, Jacob's sorrow consumed him. He felt no joy when he looked at his son. Indeed, he was hardly aware of him at all. It was only Joseph's temper tantrums that broke through his desolation. Then he would look at his son with surprise and amazement that he should still live. Jacob stumbled through the daylight hours, knowing only that he breathed and resenting the need to place one foot continually ahead of the other.

Jacob was aware that for him the future had ceased to exist. It lay buried in the forest grave encased with Naomi's body in a pinewood box. He imagined his future washed into the rain-soaked soil of the riverbank together with Naomi's precious red blood. And he put all the blame for what had happened upon himself.

Jacob's nights were filled with the exhaustion of anguish and self-recrimination. Lying on his bed in the darkness, listening to his son cry out in his sleep, Jacob's mind grew darker still. He twisted and tumbled ever deeper into his thoughts, wrestling with them like his biblical namesake wrestled with the angel in the wilderness. But unlike the Jacob of old, the morning did not bring clarity. There was no revelation, no epiphany. He did not see God when he woke. There was no angel, no mysterious being to explain for him the events of his life, to give him a new name and a new hope.

But as much as he resented it, his life did go on. In the days following Colonel Yevchenko's precipitous visit to the office of the Alexandrovka collective, Jacob took Joseph to the Hostetler's home each morning before he went to work. Anna had offered to care for the boy who, after the events at the river and his mother's death, was no less traumatized than his father. At the end of the workday, Jacob and Joseph would join the Hostetlers for their evening meal. "The last thing you need is to go home to

114

an empty house and have to prepare a meal for yourself and Joseph, what with everything that's happened," she blustered sympathetically. Her words were a kindness, for she knew, with Jacob's paternalistic upbringing, it was unlikely he would know how to boil an egg. Even so, she watched with concern as both Jacob and his son picked at their food with little interest.

One evening, Jacob and Ludwig lingered at the dinner table. They sipped their tea and the silence grew long between them. Anna was rummaging about nearby, cleaning up what was left of the meal. It was raining, so the children had been sent to their bedroom to play. The calm of the household acted as a balm on Jacob's frayed nerves. He found himself enwrapped by the love that so obviously permeated Ludwig and Anna's home. And somehow this love gave him the courage to finally verbalize his thoughts and feelings. For Jacob, steeped in the faith of his fathers, life needed always to be explained in relation to the God he worshipped.

"I feel lost, Ludwig," Jacob began. "I do not believe that God is responsible for what happened at the river. I do not believe that God orders the events of our lives." Jacob paused. "If God did arrange the things that happen to us, it would be like Good walking hand in hand with Evil, right? I mean, if the good we experience is from God's hand and if His hand also directs the evil we experience, well then what kind of God is it that we worship? That is certainly not what Jesus modeled. And he was God incarnate." He paused. "And I don't believe God sits back and allows things to happen to us because of some greater plan He has in mind. Like the absurd notion that Naomi had to die so that through experiencing her death I or—God forbid—Joseph should become better persons, better Christians, or somehow more spiritual. If that were the case, God might as well have pulled the trigger Himself."

Jacob paused, a grimace on his face. He was slowly shaking his head. "Yet, if, as I have said, I don't believe God interferes in the events of our lives, why do I so wish that He had shifted Yevchenko's aim? Tell me. Why could He not have done that? One more gust of wind. A large wave at the right time. A trick of the river's current. A speck of dust in his eye to distract him.

Something, anything to change the direction of the bullet at the last second." Jacob's voice was rising. "What bit of difference would it have made to Him who created this miserable world— and as we are told holds everything in it together in His all-powerful hands—what difference would it have made to Him to have done such a thing?"

Ludwig looked bleakly at his friend. From the corner of his eye he could see the children peaking out of the bedroom door with frightened eyes. They had heard Jacob's cries. He looked at Anna and gestured with a nod of his head toward where the children stared. She took his hint and hurried to the doorway, wiping her dish-water-wet hands on her apron as she went. She shooed the children into the bedroom and, following them, closed the door behind her.

The words began to spill from Jacob's mouth. "Why did Naomi have to die? If anyone had to die why couldn't it have been me?" His voice cracked. His tears began to flow. "I should have died. Not her. It was I who planned our escape. It was I who bought the fisherman's boat. It was I who chose the night we left. It was I who told the fisherman when and where he should leave the boat. It was I who took my family to the river. It was I who was unable to row the boat to safety before we were seen. It was I who crouched in terror on the riverbank. It was I who failed to protect Naomi. It was all my doing!"

Jacob was sobbing uncontrollably. He gritted his teeth and found himself shouting between sobs, the words coming from he knew not where, "I. Am. So. Angry!"

Tears filling his eyes, Ludwig laid his hand on his friend's heaving shoulder. He had no answers for Jacob's questions. All he could do was weep with him.

The next Thursday Jacob woke with the taste of blood in his mouth. His dreams had been violent and persistent. During the night he had frequently crawled out of his dreams toward consciousness, sweating and shaken by the paths his subconscious mind had taken. He had tried to rearrange his thoughts. But each time he fell asleep again he found himself pulled into the same ordeal. Swallowing his bloody saliva, he thought sometime in the night he must have bitten his tongue. He shrugged it off. This night had been no different from many nights since the horror at the river.

Jacob splashed his face with cold water from the bowl on the table. He wiped his face with the shirt he then pulled over his head. "I must go to work today," he muttered under his breath. "For everyone's sake, I must stick to my routine."

As he picked up his pants, he looked over to where Joseph lay on his sleeping bench. Joseph's eyes were open. He was watching his father impassively. "Come, Joseph. It's time to get up."

Joseph sat up. After a moment, he pattered out the door and peed on a bush growing there. Jacob thought to reprimand him—their outhouse was only a few steps further along the path. And the boy needed to learn to use it. However, he decided, he didn't have the energy for it this morning. "What difference does it make?" he thought. "The boy will learn when he's ready."

As Jacob pulled on his pants he felt an oppressive sense of dread settling over him. He remembered that today was Thursday. He knew he would again be confronted with the need to endure the loathsome presence of his wife's killer. On this day, Colonel Yevchenko of the GPU would be paying his weekly visit to the collective's office. Jacob shuddered at the thought.

After breakfasting on a slice of buttered bread and tea, Jacob took Joseph's hand and walked him to the Hostetler's. It was a fine April morning. Birds chirped merrily in the budding trees. Others busily pecked at the ground looking for food or bits of dried grass for their nests. The sun on Jacob and Joseph's backs warmed them, and if it hadn't been for the constrictions of memory, Jacob would have thought it a fine time to skip along the path in the joy of spring's renewal. As it was, they walked hand in hand, without speaking; the rutted ground and the new tufts of grass before their feet the only thing they saw.

After leaving Joseph with Anna Hostetler, it was all Jacob could to do force himself to walk the steps it took to reach his workplace. He dreaded what the day would bring. He had no idea how he could face it.

Abram was already at his desk when Jacob entered the office. He nodded a greeting to Abram as he hung up his cap and jacket. Jacob sat down at his desk and immediately began to tremble. His whole body began to vibrate in spasms, alternately softer, then slowly growing more violent. Jacob hugged himself and wondered that his chair and desk could remain in place. He was amazed that his tremors did not knock the hated picture hanging on the wall behind him out of kilter, that Abram sitting across the room did not feel his vibrations through the floorboards.

Abram may not have felt Jacob's trembling, but he noticed his distress. "What is it, Jacob?" he asked, a look of deep concern on his face.

Jacob gritted his teeth and looked down at the papers on his desk.

It took a moment for Abram to realize the obvious. "Of course. The colonel's visit today. Such a dummkopf I am."

"I cannot be in the same room as that man," said Jacob, his fierce whisper uttered from beneath the inconceivable weight of fear and suppressed rage. "I don't know what to do."

Abram was silent a few moments. He looked at his friend and co-worker. He could not imagine the pain Jacob must be feeling. Then, "Yes, of course," he said. "I should have known. I'm sorry. A man can only bear so much." He paused again. "Let me think."

Jacob's teeth were beginning to chatter. He clamped his jaws together and hugged himself tighter, willing his body to relax.

"Go home, Jacob." Abram had the beginning of an idea. "Go home. I'll make up an excuse for you if the colonel asks. You're still ill. Remember last Thursday. You were sick. You have the flu. It won't be a problem, you not being here. Go home."

Through his gritted teeth Jacob muttered, "I don't have a home anymore." But he got out of his chair anyway. He grabbed his jacket and hat and almost ran for the door, released from the prison of apprehension that had gripped him, the fear of what he might do, his hatred of the man who had killed his wife. He managed a grateful grimace as he opened the door to leave.

Abram said, "Leave it with me. I have an idea. You won't need to be in the office on Thursdays for a month or so. Probably longer. I'll talk to you about it tomorrow. Now go."

Jacob fled out the door.

In the end, the solution was rather simple. As it happened, Abram needed to coordinate a series of meetings with the farmers of the villages in the Alexandrovka collective. A new set of directives had been delivered from Moscow: schedules for planting, instructions on crop rotations, dates to begin harvesting, deadlines for grain deliveries and meat requisitions. He had shaken his head in disbelief when he first read the directives—bureaucrats telling farmers how to do their farming, disregarding their skills, the weather and local conditions. How absurd! Yet the government's edicts still needed to be, if not obeyed, then at least conveyed to those for whom they were intended. He would send Jacob to explain the directives. Jacob was educated, a fast learner. He could discuss what needed to be done, say what needed to be said. And, Abram decided, he would schedule the meetings on Thursdays. That would keep Jacob out of the office during Colonel Yevchenko's visits for weeks to come.

He only hoped the stress of the meetings with what would surely be unhappy farmers would not be too great for Jacob. More stress was not what Jacob needed.

It was the end of May. Jacob had spent his Thursday meeting with farmers in Halbstadt, one of the villages in the Alexandrovka collective. Now, as the light of early evening peaked through high wispy clouds and played magic with the land around him shining spotlights of color here and there, he let his horse have its rein as he rode the ten kilometers back to Alexandrovka. Jacob was in no hurry. There were too many things to mull over. The horse plodded along, occasionally dipping its head to grab a mouthful of grass, never stopping, just moseying along. The mare was a dawdler, Jacob thought, but on this day he didn't mind.

May was Jacob's favorite time of the year. It was the month when spring's new growth was coming into its own, the time before the heat and drought of summer caused it to dry up and wither. Jacob marveled at the seemingly infinite variety of lush green hues splashing in every direction he looked. On both sides of the narrow road, long rows of feathery yellow-green stalks of wheat sprouted in the fields. In the distance, towering above the fields along their edges and mixed among the dark pines that hovered there, the larch and birch trees were bursting with new leaves glistening silver-green, their mottled feet hidden in a thick carpet of tall asparagus-green weeds standing proud and arrow-straight. The columbine and daisies struggled to be seen among their larger cousins and added a hint of purple, yellow and white to the palette.

His eyes taking in the mottled delights of spring, Jacob's thoughts turned to his latest meeting. The farmers in Halbstadt had been as incredulous and unhappy at the new directives as were the farmers at Friedensdorf and New York when he had met with them earlier in the month. Many farmers had been outraged. These were men who had learned the secrets of their vocation through years and generations of experience. "We don't tell the government how to go about its business. Why must ignorant bureaucrats dictate to us how we are to farm?" asked one. "Why must they continually meddle in our affairs? They have no idea how this works," said another. Someone else had chimed in, "Imagine! Telling us the dates on which we must harvest our crops; the dates! It beggars belief!" Another farmer had added, "Do they have a crystal ball that can foretell the weather, how much rain we're going to get, the amount of sun, the temperatures, the condition of the soil, when the grain will mature?" The others had laughed rancorously. As in the other village meetings, Jacob had tried to mollify the agitated farmers. He'd said, "I know you're the experts. Don't worry. Moscow loves its formulas, but you know how to get the best from the land. We'll humor them by listening to what they have to say; and then we'll do things our way. In the end, they'll get the quotas they require of us." All things considered, the meeting had gone well.

Jacob's reverie was broken as his horse shied. "Whoa, girl," he muttered pulling on the reins as a ground squirrel ran by. Looking at the pines in the distance Jacob was reminded of the glade in which Naomi lay. He missed Naomi dearly. He still felt physical pain at the thought of her horrible death. He sighed deeply as he thought of her.

Everyone in Alexandrovka was now aware that Naomi was dead, though the details they had been told were far from the truth. It was now a little over a week since Jacob let it be known he had received word of the tragedy via a letter from his mother-in-law in Ukraine whom she had been visiting. Naomi had suffered a sudden and fatal illness. In answer to their questions he had said, no, he would not be traveling to the funeral. The letter had taken far too long to arrive. Naomi had long since been laid to rest. He would go in fall when the fieldwork was done.

As fate would have it, three weeks after Naomi's death, Jacob had received a letter. But, while giving him the pretense he needed to explain his wife's prolonged absence, the letter contained only the news of the happy birth of a nephew. And when the teacher, Gerhard Wieler, casually inquired of the man who delivered the few articles of mail that arrived from Blagoveshchensk each week about a possible letter from the Ukraine addressed to Jacob Enns, the mailman was able to say, "Yes, there was such a letter."

Hearing of the inquiry, Jacob was alarmed that the collaborator should take an interest in his family. He wondered, did the GPU have a file in their cabinets entitled, Jacob Enns? Were they suspicious of him in particular or did they watch anyone who had made the disastrous trip to Moscow in the fall of the previous year? Surely they had no clue of his family's attempts to cross the Amur in March and April. No, he decided, they couldn't know. Otherwise, he'd have been arrested long ago. Despite his rationalizations, Jacob felt a chill creep down the back of his neck.

For a while Jacob's thoughts turned dark as he considered the man who had caused his family so much pain. He felt the low burn of anger and hatred in his gut. What would it be like to pull the trigger, he wondered. Would it be the same as killing a pig or a cow to be butchered? Did Colonel Yevchenko have any right to continue his evil existence? God said that vengeance was His; could Jacob not act as the hand of God and speed up that judgment?

Coming to a crossroad, Jacob nudged his horse so it chose the path leading to Ludwig and Anna Hostetler's house. Joseph was waiting for him there.

Joseph. Thoughts of his son brought warm feelings of love and concern. Anna took care of Joseph each day while Jacob was at work. But since his mother's death, the boy had become harder to manage. Anna was worried about him. Jacob recalled a conversation they had recently had.

"I don't know what to do with him anymore," Anna had said. "Joseph refuses to play with the other children. He cries when you leave and clings to me all day long. That's not normal; he's five years old. And then, out of nowhere he throws a fit of temper. I've never seen such anger in a child. Next minute, he is nervous and jumps at any sudden noises. I can't expect the other children to tiptoe around him all day. I'm sorry, Jacob, but I'm at my wits end. I don't know how much longer I can do this."

Jacob had to agree with Anna. His son had become a handful. He was as much at a loss as to how to handle Joseph as she was. He was leery, though, of Anna's solution to the problem.

"You know what Joseph needs, Jacob?" she had said, a stern look on her face. "He needs a mother. I know you're trying to be a good father to him—and you are—but you're hardly ever around. I'm doing everything I can for him, but I have my own children to think of. What your boy needs is his own mother. Someone who'll hug him when she puts him to bed at night and who hugs him when he gets up in the morning—I know you do that, but it's just not the same. Joseph needs a mother who'll care for him in his own home when you are at work, someone he can count on to be there every minute of every day that he needs her. I know you love your boy, but it's not enough. He also needs the love that only a mother can give. Naomi is gone, God rest her poor soul. And now you need to find Joseph a new mother."

Jacob had been put off by Anna's candor and by her audacious suggestion. Him, remarry? Naomi had barely grown cold in the ground. At the same time, he had realized there was something to what she'd said. Joseph did need a mother's love. But would it be fair to marry another woman? Jacob didn't know if he could love another as he had loved Naomi. And if he couldn't give her that kind of love, would it be right to ask that of her, to be his wife, to be a mother to his son? And anyway, he had decided, it was a moot point. He wasn't aware of any women who were even available. Aside from a couple of grannies and teenaged girls, there certainly were no single women in Alexandrovka.

But, that didn't change the fact he needed help with Joseph, Jacob realized. And no one would be better for the boy, he thought, than a loving mother.

Leaving his reverie, Jacob looked along the track. The light was beginning to fade and he had still some distance to go. He dug his heels into his horse's ribs. "Come on old girl. Any slower and we'll be spending the night out here."

The horse responded with a snort and a shake of its head. Jacob flicked the reins, gave her another kick, and soon they were trotting down the darkening path.

Rachel Hiebert lived with her mother, Ruth Hildebrandt, in the neighboring village of New York. Rachel and her husband, Henry, together with her mother had come from the village of Rosenfeld in west Siberia the previous summer, after her father's arrest and execution. He had been jailed on a charge of supplying grain to the White Army during the Civil War. The fact no evidence was offered at his trial to support the charge made no difference to the judge. A guilty verdict was swiftly pronounced. The sentence was carried out without delay. Promises to return the body for burial by the family were left unfulfilled.

Soon after arriving in New York, Henry began complaining about an ache in his belly. The pain grew severe, settling in his right side. He had little appetite and began to throw up what little food he managed to swallow. His abdomen became swollen and hard. He developed a high fever. Despite the homeopathic remedies Rachel and her mother administered, within days he was dead.

After her husband's death, Rachel and Ruth were forced to go to work in the collective's fields. To survive, they gleaned what they could after the harvest had been gathered. And, thanks to the kindness of the collective's manager and the generosity of their neighbors, they were never in want. They lived hand to mouth and were grateful for the blessings each day brought.

One day as he idly considered Jacob Enns' situation, Abram Siemens thought of Rachel Hiebert. He looked at Jacob seated at his desk on the other side of the office, his head bent over a stack of papers, pencil poised like an acupuncturist's needle. Abram cleared his throat. "Jacob," he said tentatively, like a man about to step into a puddle while wearing new shoes. Jacob looked up from his work. "Regarding our conversation the other day. About you needing a wife and mother for Joseph."

Jacob leaned back in his chair.

Abram cleared his throat again. "I don't mean to interfere…" He smiled. "Well, perhaps that is exactly what I mean to do. You'll have to forgive me." He eyed Jacob, looking for a reaction. Should he continue? Since Jacob gave no indication, Abram decided to plunge on. "In New York there is a woman, recently widowed, a young woman about your age. Her name is Rachel Hiebert. Do you know her?"

Jacob frowned and shook his head.

Abram babbled on. "She lives with her mother, Ruth Hildebrandt. She is also widowed. But that's another story. Not important right now. There are no children."

Seeing Abram's discomfort, Jacob broke his silence with a laugh. "Come now, Abram, are you trying to play matchmaker?"

Abram was a bit embarrassed but undeterred. "Hear me out, Jacob. And then you may do with it what you wish. Rachel is an enterprising young woman: strong and hard working, pretty, too. You haven't seen her on one of your visits to New York? They live at the edge of the village on the south end. She and her mother have been on their own for months now."

Jacob continued to be unhelpful.

Abram swam on. "No? Well, no matter. I think you should look her up. I think you'd like her. Would you like to meet her? I could arrange something for you."

Though he might have expected it, the suddenness of the question caught Jacob by surprise. To give himself time to sort out his response, he said, "Would she like to meet me? I'm the one with the child."

"Well, actually," Abram blushed, "I've made some enquiries. As a matter of fact, she would welcome a visit from you."

"Really." Jacob didn't know whether to be flattered or insulted. He wondered why she would she want to meet him of all people? Aloud he said, "Does she realize taking me as a husband means becoming a mother to Joseph on the same day?"

Abram was quick to retort, "You must understand she is in need of a helpmate as much as you are. Perhaps more so. It is very difficult for two women alone without a man in the house. And," Abram paused, "well, she has seen you from a distance if you have not seen her. I'm told she finds you," he paused and grinned, "mildly attractive."

It was Jacob's turn to blush. He thought a moment before putting down his pencil. "Tell me more about her," he said.

So Abram did.

June 1930

Jacob set out to meet Rachel Hiebert for the first time on a fine day in June. It was mid-morning when he left the smoking chimneys of Alexandrovka behind him. Despite the fact it was still early, the sun was already flexing its muscles in the pale blue Siberian sky, its rays warming his back and causing him to break into a light sweat. Or, perhaps, he thought, it was his nerves; Jacob felt like a teenager on his way to meet his date for the first time.

A brisk wind was blowing from the southwest. The spindly pines along the dirt path to New York rocked back and forth in the blustery squalls, metronomes keeping time with the dusty clops of Jacob's horse's hooves. When one or the other of the more exposed trees leaned dangerously far, Jacob wondered whether it would recover its head or be uprooted. He felt a bit like those swaying pines, his mind alternating between the desire to meet this intriguing woman and the urge to turn his horse around and rush back to the safety of his own home. With his eyes on the trees and a hand holding his hat firmly in place, Jacob making a mental note to be alert lest a tree should come down and end his journey before it had properly begun.

Jacob listened to the rush of air through the forest and took comfort in its strength. The wind was seen and heard only because of its effect on the trees. Such is love, he thought, though he knew he was getting way ahead of himself. We shall see if that emotion makes itself felt in the house of Rachel Hiebert.

Despite the mental games he played, Jacob knew there was nothing for it but to continue on. He had left Joseph in the care of Anna Hostetler. He dared not return without something to report from his meeting with Rachel. The fluttering leaves on the branches of the larch and birch trees seemed to beckon Jacob on, trembling fingers pointing the way to the house of two hopeful women, to Rachel and her mother. In the end, these encouragements combined with his own inertia ensured that Jacob's horse continued it slow plod northward. All things considered, it would be easier to face this music now than to avoid it.

The village of New York sat in an orderly array on the flat Siberian steppe, its rough-cut wood frame houses clustered along its main street like the pieces of a game of checkers lined up on either side of the board. As Jacob rode into the village he had the thought that, but for its name, this could be any other Mennonite village resting on the plain bordering the Amur River. From village to village, there was little variation in the design and construction of the pioneers' homes.

When Jacob entered the village, he counted the houses along the side of the road to his left. He noticed heads in the windows of more than one house he passed, which only served to increase his self-consciousness. He straightened his back and was relieved when he arrived at the fourth house. Jacob saw there was no fence, nor gate. On the edge of the front yard was a hitching post. It was positioned just far enough away from a large vegetable garden to prevent equine nibbling. Beside the post was a small trough filled with water.

Jacob dismounted and wrapped the reins around the post. He gave them a tug to make sure his knot would hold. The horse immediately bent its neck to drink and then began searching out blades of grass to chew, its velvet lips competently pulling them to its sharp incisors. Jacob patted the horse's rump and set his sights on the front door, chiding himself for the nerves that had set his stomach roiling.

Walking to the front steps, Jacob noticed his hands were moist from sweat. He wiped them on his pants and took several deep breaths to quiet his racing pulse. As he lifted his foot onto the step, Jacob saw his boot was caked with dried mud. He had just bent to give them a quick wipe when the front door opened. Startled, feeling he'd been caught in an act of mischief or social impropriety, Jacob quickly straightened up.

Not knowing what else to do, he held out his hand. "Hello, I'm Jacob Enns," he said a little too quickly, grateful his hand was clean—he'd not managed to begin wiping the dirt from his boot—and nervous lest she judge him for his dirty boots, thinking, why didn't I clean them before I left home.

Rachel took Jacob's hand, introducing herself. "I'm very pleased to meet you," she said, not mentioning that she had heard many things about Jacob, all of which had predisposed her to agreeing to their meeting.

Rachel stepped back so Jacob could enter her home. Jacob's eyes made a quick sweep of the room. Standing by the stove, he saw, was an older woman. Rachel introduced her mother, Mrs. Ruth Hildebrandt, which resulted in more handshakes and pleased-to-meet-yous followed by awkward silence.

Mrs. Hildebrandt was a small wiry woman. Her curly grey hair was swept neatly back from her forehead and pinned in a small bun. Ruth's dark eyes had searched Jacob's face when she held his hand. Jacob noticed her small hand held a strong grip; its rough skin gave evidence to years of hard labor.

"Thank you for inviting me into your home," said Jacob, trying to fill the vacuum that suddenly threatened to suck him out of the house and back into the front yard. He had the uncomfortable feeling he was somehow betraying his marriage vows with Naomi despite the fact death had separated them. His heart was still hers; what was he doing here in this house, accepting this invitation?

"May I take your coat? And your hat?" Rachel's question broke through the bars of Jacob's confusion and self-doubt.

"Yes, thank you."

"You've arrived just in time," said Rachel briskly. "We've prepared a lunch. You must be hungry after your ride from Alexandrovka. Was it long, the ride? Was it very hot? The winds are quite strong today, don't you think?" Realizing she was running at the mouth, Rachel wished she could stuff her hand in to stop herself. Taking a breath she said, "Would you like to wash up? There is a basin on the counter," pointing, watching surreptitiously as Jacob washed his hands and face.

When Jacob was seated, Rachel and her mother busied themselves setting the food on the table. Jacob furtively observed Rachel, not wanting to be glaringly obvious in his attempts to explore her person. Her dark hair was tied like her mother's in a bun at the nape of her neck, though a few strands had worked themselves loose and fell fetchingly about her oval face. Her nose was straight above her full lips that smiled easily as she chatted with her mother. Jacob saw how her almond eyes sparkled when she laughed at a whispered comment from her mother. Her hand was steady as she poured soup from the pot into a ceramic tureen.

"This was my great-grandmother's tureen," Rachel commented proudly when she saw Jacob's interest in it. "The colorful flower pattern on the white background is so intricate. When I was a child visiting her house, I told her that when I grew I wanted to have it. She gave it to me as a wedding present." Her voice faded and she blushed.

"It's beautiful," he said.

Mrs. Hildebrandt said the grace. Rachel spooned a thin bean soup into three bowls. "From our garden," she said. "Early green beans and carrots. They're a little small yet, but so tasty. I hope you like it." When Jacob nodded after his first sip, she added, "We grew the summer savory and dried it. I love the flavor it adds."

Jacob complimented Rachel on the soup. Ruth informed him Rachel had also baked the bread that accompanied it.

Aside from discussing the elements of the meal, conversation was stilted. Jacob and Rachel found that each thread they began had difficulty gaining traction. They spoke of the weather. Jacob talked about his son and both commented on the work they did for the collective. Neither asked about the other's deceased spouse, though both would have liked to, not out of morbid curiosity, but out of a desire to know and be known; their dead spouses were still part of both of their lives, for better or worse.

And though Jacob and Rachel were unaware of it, Rachel's departed husband Henry and Jacob's Naomi hovered restlessly in the small room, bound to the living by powerful, lingering cords of love that refused to die as easily as they had.

When their meal was done, Rachel's mother stood to clean up the dishes. Rachel started to get up to help, but Ruth gently pushed her down, saying she would look after the chores while her daughter visited with her guest. Rachel and Jacob, suddenly shy, glanced at each other, searching for words with which to begin their conversation.

August 1930

By mid-August, Jacob and Rachel were married. She chose the sixteenth of August, because it was the day her parents had married. It was a Saturday, hot and windy, with squalls kicking up little dust devils that threw about any detritus that happened to be lying in their paths.

The ceremony was simple, performed by a lay minister in the front room of Rachel's home and witnessed by Ludwig and Anna Hostetler. With shining eyes, Ruth Hildebrandt smiled widely when her daughter was wed, thinking the future looked brighter for both of them, a husband and a son-in-law.

There were those who, when they heard of the impending nuptials, suggested to each other that the couple should wait before marrying: Naomi's grave had not yet seen the snows of one winter; Jacob and Rachel had hardly allowed enough time to get to know each other. When the gossip reached their ears, Jacob and Rachel paid little heed. Drawn together by the mutual need of companionship and hope of love to come, they pledged their vows knowing they were still relative strangers.

Need drove the couple forward, for Joseph was constantly at the forefront of both of their minds. On this Jacob had been clear during their visits over the past two months. Joseph needed a mother; Rachel agreed that she would make the glad attempt to fill his need. Not having given birth to a child, she was readily prepared to accept Joseph as her own. Her own children would come in time, she had said with a smile. For the moment, they agreed their arrangement was more practical than romantic, and that the stirrings of mutual attraction they felt for each other was a good basis upon which to build their relationship in the future. Their strength, they also agreed, was that they shared a deep faith and enjoyed each other's company and conversation.

The prosaic nature of Jacob and Rachel's relationship did not stop Naomi Enns and Henry Hiebert from dancing an ethereal jig

132

on the occasion of the marriage. Freed from the religiously enforced cultural taboo that had constrained their earthly lives, they cavorted the joy they felt without inhibition seeing that their erstwhile spouses had opened themselves to the possibility of shared joy in the midst of their individual sorrows.

Following a simple marriage supper, the couple prepared to leave for Alexandrovka. The sensitive question of Ruth Hildebrandt's living arrangement had been settled in the days before their wedding. Though it was expected she, being an elderly single woman, would come to live with Jacob and Rachel at some time in the future, she insisted on remaining for the time being in her home in New York. "The garden is just coming into its own and there will be vegetables to harvest for a number of weeks yet," she said. "I am strong and can manage on my own. I'll stay at least until the snow flies. If I'm up to it, I may wait till spring. I know where you live. If I need help, I'll ask for it." And she'd chuckled, "The last thing you two need is for an old crone like me getting underfoot right now. As my mother used to say, 'There's nothing that spoils a good pot of borsht sooner than throwing an old bone into it.' No, you two need to some alone time to get to know each other better, and for Rachel and Joseph to figure things out." Which was a relief to Jacob because everything she had said was true.

Ruth's decision to stay in New York also gave time for an addition to be built onto Jacob's house. Before his mother-in-law could come to live with them, another bedroom would be needed.

When it came time to leave, Rachel packed her few belongings—her clothing, quilt, ceramic soup tureen, and some precious knickknacks and keepsakes—into a wooden box and bags. Jacob loaded them into his wagon. Rachel kissed her mother good-bye, promising to visit as often as she could. Joseph who, throughout the marriage celebration had regarded his newly acquired grandmother with quiet indifference, endured her parting hug and kiss on the forehead before clambering aboard. Jacob returned her embrace, feeling strangely thievish— he was taking a daughter away from her mother. He reminded himself that the separation of mother and daughter would be temporary. Promises had been made: they were committed to fulfilling their obligation by which an aged parent lived with her adult children, thus ensuring her care in her later years.

The sun was slanting toward the western horizon when Jacob clicked his tongue and flicked the long reins over his horse's back. In the spirit of the occasion, the horse pulled willingly and found its rhythm quickly, hauling the loaded wagon briskly down the road. The cooling breeze brushed the family's faces and tipped up the brims of their hats. Joseph sat quietly between Jacob and Rachel, though tucked more closely to his father.

Rachel sat straight-backed beside the boy, feeling very much the stranger, suddenly unsure of the commitment she had made. "There is time," she reassured herself as she watched the steppe roll by. "He will grow to love me." She was thinking of the son, but prayed her prophecy would hold true for both the boy and the man sitting on the wagon's seat beside her.

The sky had become a dark coverlet by the time their wagon rolled into the yard in front of Jacob's house. The dying rays of a fiery sunset had guided them through the last kilometers of their journey. As they drove through the village of Alexandrovka, kerosene lamps in windows had welcomed the newly-weds home. Joseph had fallen asleep where he sat, leaning on his father. Aside from commenting on the beauty of the burning clouds, Jacob and Rachel had ridden in silence. They were both thinking their own thoughts—thoughts of what was past, thoughts of what was to come.

Knowing Jacob needed to tend to the horse and wagon, Rachel offered to carry Joseph into the house. "I'm sure I'll manage," she said sensing Jacob's hesitation. She had not been in his home—her home—before. "Just tell me where I might find the matches so I can light the lamp."

"There's a lamp on the table. Matches are on the stove."

Jacob lifted Joseph down off the wagon into Rachel's raised arms. Their hands brushed lightly in the transfer, causing a spark of emotion to leap between them. Jacob watched as his bride carried his son to the house. Seeing her struggle with the door, he ran to open it, then went back to unload her crate and bags. He carried them to the house and left them on the porch. The horse needed tending to.

Jacob spent more time than usual brushing and watering his horse. Now that he was alone, without her sitting beside him, he needed to consider what he had done. He had remarried. It wasn't so much that he regretted or had second thoughts about marrying Rachel Hiebert. She was an attractive woman whose company he very much enjoyed. But now, as he thought about it, he was suddenly afraid that when he opened the door to his home, he would be met by visions of Naomi. He still often felt her presence at the most unexpected times and places. It wasn't that he saw her ghost—he didn't believe in ghosts—but every now and then she seemed to appear, like the fragrance of a flower carried on the breeze, or the call of a distant bird. She was there, yet she wasn't, in a moment lasting less than a heartbeat. How was he to give his heart fully to Rachel when he still loved and missed Naomi?

A tear escaped Jacob's eye. He rubbed at it furiously, ashamed that he should mourn Naomi at such an inappropriate time.

"It is too soon," Jacob said to his horse, rubbing her nose with one hand while offering her a handful of grain to nibble with the other. "I think I should have waited a while longer. What am I going to do?" In answer his horse tossed her head, impatient for another handful of oats. Jacob poured some into her trough. His horse dug in. For a few moments, Jacob stood and watched it eat, finding the familiar muted crunching sound of its molars crushing the grain comforting, as if the horse were grinding into paste and swallowing his questions and worries. "These are not thoughts I should be having on my wedding night," he scolded himself.

Jacob's belly was awash with butterflies when he closed the door of the stable behind him. Walking on the path to the house he saw a lighted lamp in the window. As he stepped up to the front door, it opened before he could put his hand on the latch. Inside, Rachel smiled at him. "I thought you might have decided to spend the night in the barn," she teased.

Jacob laughed softly. "The horse..."

"Yes, I know. You had things to do."

Jacob smiled gratefully.

"I didn't see a bed made up for Joseph," Rachel said softly. "I've laid out a sleeping place for him on the bench. I wasn't sure where you kept your extra blankets so I've used mine."

Jacob blushed, remembering her bags. "Oh! I'm sorry. I forgot about the. I should have brought them in for you."

"I carried them in while you were in the barn," Rachel smiled, enjoying Jacob's embarrassment, thinking her new husband was thoughtful, if also forgetful. "It's okay. Don't apologize. Joseph never really woke after the long day he's had, so I've tucked him in. I think he's sound asleep."

"Yes, thank you, Rachel." Jacob lowered his voice. "Since..." He paused, surprised at the emotion that was choking him, unable to get out the words. He tried again, "Since that night..."

Rachel was looking sympathetically at Jacob. She took his hand, the simple gesture giving him strength.

"Joseph has slept in my bed with me since, since that night." Jacob couldn't say Naomi's name; he already thought he'd sensed her presence in the house—most everything in it reminding him of her—and that would summon her for sure. "He has nightmares." Wanting to reassure Rachel that she had done the right thing, he added, "I'm sure he'll be okay there. It's time he slept alone." Feeling awkward he finished the thought "Now. With you here." And regretted the words the moment they were spoken.

"If he wakes and needs comforting, he can come sleep with us," Rachel offered quietly. She let go of Jacob's hand and busied herself with making tea. The kettle was already bubbling. "If there isn't room in the bed, perhaps I will sleep on the bench. Just until Joseph settles down. Until he gets used to me."

"I'm sure that won't be necessary," said Jacob, the denial a little more tentative than Rachel had hoped for.

Rachel handed Jacob a cup of tea. Since Joseph was using the bench by the table as a bed, they sat in chairs off to the side. Both studiously sipped their tea, grateful for the distraction. The silence between them lengthened. They listened as Joseph stirred, murmuring unintelligibly in his sleep.

Suddenly remembering, Rachel leaned toward Jacob and whispered, "I brought some cake that was left over from the wedding. Would you like some?"

And of course he did, which gave them a further distraction as Rachel plated two pieces and as they ate them.

"The cake is delicious," remarked Jacob. "Your mother is a wonderful baker."

"She is," affirmed Rachel with a grateful nod.

"Will you tell her for me?"

"I think you should tell her yourself, don't you?"

To which Jacob agreed, after which both again fell silent.

"So..." said Jacob, knowing something needed saying but having no way of expressing it, not knowing where to begin, nor where it would lead should he do so.

Taking his empty plate with hers to the sink, Rachel said, "I'm tired. I think I'll go to bed."

Jacob yawned in agreement.

"Do you mind if I put on my nightclothes in the bedroom while you wait out here?" asked Rachel.

"If you like." Spoken with some relief that didn't go unnoticed by Rachel. "I'll come in when you are under the covers."

"Which side of the bed do you sleep on?"

"The left."

When he heard the springs of the mattress creaking, Jacob knew it was safe for him to enter the bedroom. Rachel was lying under the covers on the right side of the bed, facing away from him. Standing on his side of the bed, Jacob quickly pulled off his pants and shirt, pulled on his pajamas. Nervously he climbed into bed: nervous because he knew what she expected of him, nervous because he didn't want to hurt this woman, nervous because he felt Naomi's presence the moment he settled his head between his pillow and quilt. He could smell her scent in the threads of the fabric of both as surely as he felt the threads of love still binding him to her.

Rachel turned in the bed to face him. When she saw that Jacob lay frozen beside her she murmured, "It's all right. I know you are struggling."

Ashamed, thinking, is it that obvious, Jacob moaned, "I, I can't. It is too soon. I'm not ready. I'm sorry."

"Don't worry," Rachel whispered, "I will wait for you."

It was then Jacob realized that if there had been any question of it in his mind before, she had answered it. Rachel loved him. Grateful for her love, humbled by her grace, he kissed her softly on the lips. "Good night," he sighed.

Jacob and Rachel turned to face the walls by their bedsides. She was soon asleep, tired out by the day's festivities. He lay long before sleep found him. Before it did, Naomi came to him like notes from a song fading into memory. "You must let me go," she insisted. "For all of our sakes, let me go. And for heaven's sake, you can begin by giving Joseph my quilt and using hers on your bed."

The next morning dawned clear, the pink wisps of cloud foretelling the heat that would soon enwrap the day and the days that followed, the August sunshine mixed with the occasional rainfall causing the myriad heads of grain in the collective's fields to stretch skyward, to swell and mature. The crop this year looked to be even better than last year's.

Grateful because she had been given time away from duties in the collective's gardens, Rachel spent her days adjusting to her new role as mother of a troubled five-year-old. Using her own intuition as well as lessons learned from conversations with Anna Hostetler, she patiently coaxed Joseph out of his hardened shell, surrounding him with crumbs of mother-love so that he could find no escape from her. Joseph responded sometimes by ignoring his new mother and at other times clinging fiercely to her.

One day Rachel found a large piece of paper that had come into the house as wrapping on a parcel. It had been folded and tucked away into a cupboard. Seeing that one side of the paper was completely unspoiled by any writing, she cut it into smaller sizes, gave Joseph a sharp pencil, and left him with instructions to draw what he wished.

While Rachel completed some household chores, she glanced frequently at Joseph, encouraged by what she saw. Each time she looked, his head was bent over his paper in serious concentration, his pencil moving methodically. When Rachel looked at what he had drawn an hour later, she was shocked to see a scene of graphic violence, many primitive figures holding guns outstretched, one figure lying on the ground. Rachel asked Joseph what his picture was about.

"Well," he said calmly, "the person lying on the ground there is my mother. That man," he pointed to another figure, "shot her. She's dead you know."

Rachel hid the pain she felt seeing Joseph's matter-of-fact explanation of the tragedy he was reliving. Wisely, she accepted the picture and its explanation, hugging Joseph to her while hiding the tear that slipped from her eye.

When Jacob returned home from work that evening Rachel showed him the tortured image Joseph had created. "Joseph explained it so casually," she said. "It broke my heart to hear such a little boy describing the violent death of his mother."

Jacob was shocked. He wondered if it was a mistake for him to have told Joseph how his mother died. "I couldn't keep the truth from him," he said sorrowfully.

"It was right that you should tell him the truth," Rachel said. "Even though he is so young, he needed to know. Children are quite resilient, you know."

Jacob realized it was not only he who was haunted by the death of Naomi. Joseph, too, was struggling to come to grips with his mother tragic death. "I should have known he would mourn for his mother, but I'm not sure drawing such pictures is good for him. Perhaps we should encourage him to draw what is good and uplifting, guide him away from dwelling on the evil that is past."

Rachel disagreed vehemently. "Joseph is drawing what is weighing him down, this violence that was done to his mother and to him. And to you," she added quickly. "These memories are shackles on you both. They are a festering boils needing to be lanced."

So they agreed Joseph should be encouraged to draw what he wished. Thus began his healing as day after day Rachel gave him another slip of paper and day after day he created an image of brutal violence and degradation. Many pictures contained a boat on which a soldier shot towards small groups of people hiding behind trees on the riverbank. Others showed many people crowded together in a box, or pushing the bodies of the dead out of a sliding doorway.

As the weeks passed, a sparkle slowly returned to Joseph's eyes. His periods of play became longer, and though acts of violence were still prevalent in his imaginings, his fits of temper became less frequent. He began to enjoy the company of other children more.

Joseph was becoming himself again, Jacob remarked as he and Rachel discussed his progress. "You've done wonders with him. He seems," Jacob searched for the word, "he seems happy! How have you managed it?"

"I think it's the pictures," Rachel reminded him. "Ever since he began drawing those horrible images he has begun to change. The boil is being lanced and squeezed a little bit every day. Each day I think the poison is less and one day it will all be gone. I think in his childlike way he is making peace with what he has experienced. With that dark turmoil gone from his soul and mind, he will have renewed courage to live in the present. We can see it already."

Rachel's optimism was infective. In the joy of the moment, Jacob embraced her. He kissed her warmly, surprising both of them. Bashful, feeling he had behaved out of turn he stepped back from her. Rachel smiled at his boyish behavior.

Guilt quickly followed as Jacob was reminded of his own struggle to let go of what was past. He thought of the firm grasp with which he still held on to Naomi's heel. "When will I have the strength to let go?" he wondered.

At Last, My Love

October 1930

It was toward the end of the month and Jacob was returning home from a meeting of farmers that had run late into the evening. The weather had turned cold and the clouds during the day had forewarned of snow. Jacob did not look forward to winter, the biting cold and the snow that made everything done outdoors a painful chore. In the afternoon the clouds had cleared, and now, as he walked, Jacob could see his breath like small white flags following along behind him.

The meeting had been its own chore. Jacob dislike meetings where emotions ran high and constructive solutions were elusive. A group of farmers had gathered together to express their growing resentment of the communist government's demands upon them. Like the year before, this year's harvest had been abundant, but so were the amounts of the quotas—meat, vegetable, and grain—the collective had to pay. As he walked through the darkened village, Jacob remembered the heated discussion.

One farmer's words had clarified the situation perfectly. "It's like we butcher a pig and all we're left with is the cracklings. Now, I love my cracklings, don't get me wrong, there's nothing like a thick smear of pork fat with bits of crisp meat on my bread for breakfast." At this there had been smiles and grunts of approval. "But it would be nice to be allowed some tenderloin or chops for a change. The Reds always take the best of what we have and leave us with what's at the bottom of the barrel." Another farmer jumped in, "Ha! You're lucky they left you the cracklings. I raised ten pigs this year. Thought I'd have at least one for the family. They took 'em all. Said they need them to feed the workers in the cities. Well, who's going to feed my family is what I want to know?" The mood in the room had quickly turned sour. "This place is perfect for farming," another farmer broke in. To be heard above the growing din of discontent, he had raised his voice and shouted, "It's the damn government that makes it near impossible to get ahead." After which another farmer cried, "With the crops we've been getting and the animals we've been raising, we'd be rich if we were allowed to sell what we have for a fair price. Instead, the commies give us peanuts and we must scrape by on the leavings for another winter." Which had elicited more angry murmurs.

Jacob shook his head in disgust. The farmers were right. The government made it impossible for them to get ahead. He looked up at the night sky. There was no answer to their problem there. But with no electricity in the village, no outdoor lights, the twinkling stars put on a dazzling display. He easily found the North Star, the Big Dipper, and the wash of light emanating from the Milky Way. It's so beautiful, he thought, so peaceful. In awe of nature's majesty, he had the thought that the stars he was observing had been seen in their places since time immemorial. "And they'll shine there till the end of days," he whispered in awe. The words 'solid' and 'immovable' came to mind. Our lives here are the exact opposite, he thought. We are fragile creatures; we are constantly having to adjust to what comes our way. Jacob longed for the stability he observed in the heavens. He wished he could provide that sense of security in his community, in his home.

Jacob thought of Rachel, now over two months his bride. She was proving to be a wonderful mother for Joseph. And a loving companion for him, he knew. Her patience and tenderness, her sense of humor and common sense had endeared her to him. Jacob had told Rachel he loved her, but he had yet to become intimate with her. His connection with Naomi had always stopped him. He could feel his failure becoming a dividing wall between them. Even as the memory of Naomi that had initially caused the rift was becoming less and less, the chasm between him and Rachel was growing larger. Jacob knew this must not go on much longer, but he could not think how to bridge the gap.

Coming to his house, Jacob saw a flicker of light coming from the bedroom window. The front window was dark. He opened the door and quietly stepped in. Scanning the shadows, he found Joseph asleep on his bench. Jacob hung his coat and hat on the rack by the door. He sat on a chair in order to remove his boots and winced as it creaked noisily.

Kneeling beside Joseph, Jacob straightened his covers and tucked them under his chin. The room was chilly. Jacob smiled as he thought of the healing from past hurts he had seen in his son, the sparkle that had returned to his eyes. He kissed Joseph lightly on the forehead. The boy stirred but didn't wake.

Jacob checked the fire in the stove. It was a glowing bed of embers. He threw a couple of pieces of wood in and waited a moment to see if they would catch. As flames began to lick their sides, he latched the door.

With a last glance at the room, Jacob went to the bedroom door. It was closed. He reached for the handle and paused for he thought he heard the trickle of water coming from the other side.

Pushing the door open, Jacob saw Rachel standing in the washtub. It barely reached her knees, he noted idly as he took in the whole scene. The flickering light of an oil lamp on a small bedside table framed her naked body in faint shades of gold. Rachel's shadowed back was toward him. Her dark hair was pinned atop her head, accentuating her slender neck and pale shoulders.

Jacob's first reaction was to apologize. "I'm sorry," he said, and quickly pulled the door closed. He felt he had intruded on a private moment, that he wasn't meant to see what he had seen.

"Jacob."

He heard is name called softly.

Jacob opened the door and stepped into the bedroom. Rachel turned slightly and looked over her shoulder at him. She smiled coyly. He saw she was holding a washcloth above her left breast, rinsing soap off her gleaming skin. One droplet of water, suspended briefly from the tip of her nipple, caught the light and magnified it, piercing his defenses and slicing through the last knotted cords that had been binding him to what was past.

Holding out the cloth, Rachel said, "Could you wash my back?"

Feeling dazed, aroused by her beauty, Jacob took the cloth and rubbed soap on it. Slowly he wiped his wife's back. His eyes were filled with the nearness of her smooth pale skin, her waist, her buttocks, her legs as he bent to wet the cloth in the tub and rose again to rinse the soap from her back.

Finished, Jacob stood for a moment, cloth in hand, unsure of what he should do next.

"I have a sore muscle in my back by my right shoulder blade. Could you rub it for me?" The words were soft, inviting.

Jacob placed his fingers on Rachel's back. She shivered.

"Your hands are cold," she scolded lightly.

Jacob blew on his hands to warm them. He placed them again on Rachel's back and began kneading the silken skin. With soft words, she guided him to the spot needing attention. She moaned with pleasure, "That feels so good!"

The kneading became caressing.

Rachel turned to face Jacob. Raising her arms, she removed the pins from her hair. Her lustrous curls tumbled to her shoulders. She stepped out of the tub. Pulling Jacob to her, she kissed him gently, then more firmly.

Haltingly at first, then eagerly, he responded.

Rachel looked into Jacob's eyes. "Yes?" she whispered.

"Yes," he answered hoarsely, without hesitation, knowing her meaning without doubt.

Rachel bent to the bedside and picked up a towel to dry herself.

"Let me," said Jacob.

Slowly Jacob patted the towel up and down Rachel's body. When he thought she was dry, he tossed the towel into the corner and kissed her again. With trembling fingers he began to tear at the buttons of his shirt. Rachel pulled his hands away.

"Let me," she offered breathlessly.

Slowly Rachel unbuttoned Jacob's shirt, then his pants. All the while she gazed into her husband's eyes.

Holding each other, Rachel and Jacob fell awkwardly onto the bed. The bed creaked loudly under their weight; like mischievous children, they tried to stifle the giggles that erupted in them.

Jacob pulled the covers over them for Rachel was shivering, whether from the cold, or desire, he didn't know. Feeling her strong, eager body against his, Jacob realized that he, too, was trembling and that he trembled from desire.

Excited by the urgency of their shared passion, Jacob felt the constraints of his past and the uncertainties of their future disappear. The heat of the present and of Rachel, the woman who loved him without condition—the woman he now knew he loved without condition—was all that mattered.

Afterwards, as they lay entangled in contented languor, Jacob whispered, "At last, my love, we are one." He was surprised when the words left his lips, for he was not sure he had meant to speak aloud what he was thinking. He marveled that he could say the words honestly, for at the same time as he said them he felt a twinge of grief for his lost love, Naomi. His heart swelled with gratitude that this remarkable woman had accepted him, that he and Joseph were no longer alone.

Half asleep, Rachel smiled and murmured her agreement.

Though his thoughts were far from issues of faith, Jacob was humming the tune of a favorite hymn the next morning when Abram Siemens arrived at the office. Jacob was tired—the night had provided much less sleep than he needed—but he was eminently happy. Jacob looked at the paper on the desk in front of him. Printed on it were some numbers he needed to balance. His mind refused to cooperate and he grinned as he remembered how Rachel had seduced him. Tonight, he promised himself, it would be his turn; he became aroused just thinking about the possibilities exploring the joys of lovemaking with her would bring.

Abram smiled a greeting after Jacob gave him a cheerful, "Good morning." It had been quite some time since Abram had seen Jacob as contented as he appeared to be this morning. Since Jacob and Rachel's wedding, he had watched him become more and more morose until one day Jacob had told him of his dilemma, of the knot that somehow still bound him to Naomi. Abram had reminded Jacob that the marriage vow held only until death. Jacob had agreed, but somehow the conversation had made little difference. Until now. Now, here was Jacob grinning like a Cheshire cat! He thought of Jacob's beautiful new wife, Rachel, and was sure he knew the reason for Jacob's good mood. There could be only one explanation for the sudden shift of spirit. "And it's about time!" he thought.

"Jacob," Abram said. "I'm glad to see you so happy this morning. But while we have some time alone, there is something we need to discuss."

Jacob put down his pencil. "Yes, certainly. What is it?" Leaning forward, he put his elbows on his desk and rested his chin on his right hand.

"I had a visit from Yevchenko yesterday after you'd left the office. He delivered a new directive."

"And what is it?"

Abram was silent for a moment. "Up until now Yevchenko has turned a blind eye to our house prayer meetings and teaching services."

Jacob had a sinking feeling. He knew where this was going.

"Well, he's laid down the law. Prohibitions against religious meetings will from now on be strictly enforced. Peter Federau will be arrested if he leads even one more meeting." Peter was the village's lay minister. Since there was no church building in Alexandrovka, the services were held in homes. "Anyone suspected of hosting a religious meeting will be arrested."

Jacob was quiet. Coming from Omsk where such services had long been forbidden, he had been surprised at the freedom they had been given to worship in their homes in Alexandrovka.

Abram continued. "I've come to realize it is futile for us to think we can make any kind of life here. They've taken all of our freedoms from us and for me, this is the final straw, this freedom is the most important." Abram's voice began to tremble with emotion. "If we cannot worship together and pray, if we cannot teach our children the faith that we hold dear, then there is nothing left for us in Russia. We cannot survive as a people if we are forced to deny our faith."

Abram leaned back in his chair and crossed his arms.

Jacob slowly nodded his head in agreement. "What are you suggesting?"

"I'm suggesting we do what you have been trying to do this past year and what others have succeeded in doing for years now. I'm suggesting we leave; we cross the river to China. And by God's grace hopefully we can somehow emigrate from there to a country that still values the freedom of its people."

Jacob watched as Abram stood and walked the few paces to the window and looked outside. After peering in all directions and seeing no one coming in the direction of the office's door, he returned to his chair.

"When were you thinking we'd make this crossing?" asked Jacob.

"As soon as the river is frozen strong enough to hold us."

Jacob felt a stirring of excitement. "How do we decide who goes and who stays?"

"You misunderstand," Abram said solemnly. "I'm not suggesting a few of us make this escape. I'm suggesting all of us go. The whole village. The whole collective. Everyone who wishes to join us."

Jacob laughed. "The whole collective! Are you crazy? What are we, about 500 people in the four villages? Six hundred? With the secret police living on our doorstep and with the river constantly patrolled by border guards there isn't a chance we could get that many people across the river without being noticed."

"Even so, I think we must try or die in the attempt. There is no other choice left for us. We cannot stay here and the consequences for those who choose to remain behind may well be dire. We must give everyone a chance to be part of it. Then, if they decide the risks involved in the escape are greater than the risks of staying, we will not be responsible for what happens to them after we're gone."

The depth of Abram's determination and the scope of his plan shocked Jacob. Not sure how to respond, he asked the next question that came to mind. "How will you keep Yevchenko's stooges in the villages from finding out what we intend to do?"

"We will tell a few trusted leaders in each village. They will be the only ones who will know what we are planning."

Jacob thought a moment. "I don't understand. How will you keep anything about preparing hundreds of people to cross the Amur into China a secret? Think of all that would need to be done to pull that off."

"Ah," said Abram with a smile. "That's the beauty of my plan. We'll make most of the preparations in plain view with the blessing of the local soviet council. Yevchenko's going to love it; he'll be crowing to Moscow what a wonderful collective we are."

"Okay," said Jacob skeptically. "Tell me this amazing scheme of yours."

Abram returned to the window for another look. The road was empty. Knowing they wouldn't be disturbed, he began to explain his plan.

The meeting at which Jacob and Abram broached the idea of a mass escape across the Amur River with the leaders of the villages of the Alexandrovka collective was held two days later. The men who were called together without advance notice and with no indication of the agenda to be discussed were not pleased to have been made to leave the comfort of their homes in the cold of an early winter afternoon. The lateness of the hour when the meeting would be finished only added to their exasperation—none looked forward to the long trip home in the frosty dark. The fact the meeting was held at Abram Siemens' home after a delicious supper served by Anna Siemens helped to mollify their resentment. During the meal, the new directive to be enforced by the GPU was discussed and lamented. There was much grumbling about other restrictions the soviets had placed on the collective that left everyone feeling like slaves to the communist state. Abram had carefully led the conversation so that, when their plates were cleaned away and coffee had been served, all were in a mood to hear what he had so mysteriously called them together for.

Not being a man to mince words, Abram began with what to those assembled seemed a startling introduction. "Gentlemen, I've called you together because I trust all of you implicitly." He paused for a moment as he let his words sink in for trust was absolutely vital to their success. He and Jacob with whom he had planned his approach studied each of the six men in turn. They were all looking at him, clear-eyed and expectant, if a little puzzled and surprised.

Satisfied by their response, Abram continued. "I want to invite you and the villages you represent to join in a venture that will change all of our lives forever." Abram knew he had their complete attention now as each of his listeners unconsciously leaned expectantly forward on their chairs. Abram paused briefly knowing that once he let this cat out of the bag, for better or worse, things would never be the same again. "I am planning to take the people of our village, those who are willing to join in, across the river after it freezes over. We're going to escape into China. From there, hopefully we will somehow be able to get to Canada or the United States. I'm inviting you to join us."

The six men sat up in stunned silence. Abram smiled, waiting for their spoken response.

Peter Epp from Friedensdorf leaned back in his chair. He frowned and said, "You're suggesting that four entire villages of people travel twenty kilometers over the steppe in freezing temperatures and then attempt to cross the river, unseen, into China?"

George Klassen of Halbstatt broke in, "How do you plan to get that many people across the river without being noticed by the border guards? It's impossible!"

"It's a ridiculous idea. Have you lost your mind?" Franz Willms from Friedensdorf bluntly spoke what more than one in the group was thinking.

When the naysayers stopped to take a breath, Abram said, "I am fully aware of the magnitude of what I am suggesting. Clearly, it will take some very careful planning and execution. This is not a venture for the faint of heart."

"It's lunacy," muttered Peter Epp making to rise from his seat. "I don't want to hear any more of what you plan. That way, when you're caught, I can honestly say I knew nothing about this absurd scheme you are suggesting."

Henry Klassen, George's brother, had sat in silence during the outbursts of the others. Now, he cleared his throat and quietly spoke. "I believe it is God's will that we should remain here in the Soviet Union. Our current circumstances are being put upon us by God Himself to test us and to strengthen our faith. With our strong work ethic, we are a testimony to our God in a godless land. Who are we to avoid God's heavy hand by trying to escape to another country?" George was speaking slowly, with conviction. "In His own time, God will ease the burden we carry. The Light we carry will win out in the end. For now, we must persevere."

Jacob was incensed. "How can you believe it is God's will that we should continue to suffer under Stalin's rule?"

Henry had no response. He shrugged and looked sorrowfully at his calloused hands resting upon the table.

"Well, I guess there's no arguing with what God wants then, is there," muttered Jacob sarcastically.

Abram's response was curt. "Jacob, it is not for us to judge what others have chosen in their hearts to believe. If that is the path Henry believes God has called him to follow, then he must follow it."

Uncomfortable with the conversation's turn, George piped in, "Anyway, it is too risky, what you are suggesting." And then, looking at his brother he added, "I'm sorry, but we must go. The hour is late and we have a long ride in the dark ahead of us."

George rose to leave. Henry followed. Peter Epp and Franz Willms were already reaching for their coats.

Peter Boldt and Isaiah Federau of New York looked at each other and remained seated. "We'd like to hear more," said Isaiah calmly.

Abram nodded appreciatively. He stood to shake hands with the four men getting ready to leave. "It goes without saying," Abram murmured apologetically, "that none of what you have heard here tonight will be repeated. Not even to your wives,"

"Of course," said Peter Epp.

The others nodded their commitment to silence. Each man thanked Anna Siemens for the wonderful meal before stepping out into the darkness.

The gust of cold air that blew into the room when the door was open during the group's departure brought a chill the small stove was not prepared to contain. Before seating himself, Abram stoked the fire with a couple of pieces of dry pinewood. They soon began to crackle and snap as flames licked their bark and ate into the cracks along their lengths.

The four men sat in silence for a time, listening to the music of the fire.

"I believe what we are hearing there in the stove is but a foretaste of what the future will be for our people in this land," said Abram quietly. He heaved a sigh. "It is for that reason we must leave."

The departure of the representatives from Friedensdorf and Halbstadt meant the group planning to escape across the frozen Amur River would be considerably smaller than at it might have been.

Abram remarked, "I'm glad we gave them the opportunity to join us. We needed to do that. I am responsible for what goes on in the entire collective; their refusal to join us has taken that responsibility out of my hands and placed it in theirs. I'm relieved there will be fewer of us. It's going to be hard enough for us to manage getting three hundred across the river without being discovered let alone six hundred."

Jacob nodded his agreement and thought, "Three hundred. Six hundred. Either way, we must be crazy to think we can do this."

Abram continued, "What we are planning may be called pure folly. Nevertheless, we will not be dissuaded." Looking at the three men remaining at the table with him he asked, "Are you determined to continue?"

Jacob knew what was coming and nodded quickly. Peter Boldt and Isaiah Federau paused a moment before Peter smiled and said, "Yes, that is why we are still here and not nudging our horses homeward with the others."

So Abram told them.

When he was finished, Peter said, "You're right. Your plan is insane!"

Isaiah shook is head in amazement. "Do you realize the risks involved?" When Abram Siemens only shrugged in response, he sighed, "Of course you do!"

Jacob smiled. He leaned forward in his chair, placing both elbows on the table. Abram nodded to him and he took up the narration. "Let me outline the risks: the first is that our real intentions are discovered while we're making our preparations; second, getting past the border guards undetected when we make the attempt; third, crossing the river without being seen;

fourth, avoiding falling into crevasses and holes in the ice that will be covered with snow; fifth, surviving the crossing in the coldest temperatures the Siberian winter may offer; sixth, having somewhere safe to go on the other side where hundreds people will need to be housed and fed after an ordeal that will have exhausted them; and seventh, avoiding the attention of the Russian border guards who like to keep an eye on China's side of the Amur as much as they watch their own side. They know Russian citizens regularly escape to China despite their best efforts to stop them." Jacob sat back in his chair and crossed his arms. "Have I forgotten anything?"

Abram smiled broadly at Peter and Isaiah, both of whom were morosely studying their hands. "Now tell me, what could go wrong?" he said.

"Surely, this is no joking matter!" hissed Peter.

"No, it is not." Abram quickly became serious. "Don't think we've not considered the consequences of what we're going to do. Once we are on the ice of the Amur, there will be no turning back. We must be prepared to accept the consequences of failure: imprisonment, exile to the work camps in the far north, death for those of us who planned it."

"It's crazy," said Peter, stunned by the boldness of what Abram suggested.

"So rash they'll never expect it," said Abram. "Who'd be so foolish as to plan the escape of hundreds? No one."

"So, correct me if I'm wrong," said Isaiah. "You're suggesting that while the authorities think we are preparing to go on a wood-cutting expedition, we will in actual fact be preparing our villages for a dash across the Amur."

"That's right," replied Abram.

"Have you discussed any of this with the people of your village?" asked Peter.

"Of course," replied Abram. "They have agreed to the logging expedition. But, aside from Jacob here, there are only a few others who know what we really intend to do."

"How do you know they'll join you in this insane venture when you inform them at the last moment?" asked Isaac.

"Those who wish to stay will have the freedom to do that," said Abram.

Jacob said, "I doubt there will be any who would choose to stay. We all can see the writing on the wall. This is our best chance to get out. It may be our last."

The four men were still for a few moments as each mulled over the magnitude of what they were planning. Each was asking himself, "Am I willing to pay the price?" The mood around the table changed as each came to the same conclusion.

"Okay," said Isaiah cautiously. "Let me get this straight. The first step is to get permission from our local soviet committee to cut firewood in the forests at Khabarovsk. Do you think they'll give it to you?"

Abram chuckled. "I've already had a conversation with the chairman of our local soviet, Comrade Petrov. I told him we didn't want to lie around all winter on our bearskin rugs being lazy and getting fat. I said we want to contribute to the welfare of our glorious communist state by supplying firewood for our comrade workers in the cities. You should have seen his face. Once he got over his surprise at our offer his smile alone was warm enough to light a Russian oven. He positively glowed with pride that citizens in his jurisdiction should be so patriotic and industrious."

"Boy, is he in for a surprise!" laughed Peter. The four men chuckled at that and then became silent as they thought about the repercussion their escape might have for men like Comrade Petrov.

"There will be hell to pay, I'd think," said Jacob. "I'm sure it'll be difficult for Colonel Yevchenko to escape having to suffer some sort of consequence as well. How will he explain the disappearance of hundreds of citizens in villages under his control?" He thought about how appropriate it would be if the colonel were to find himself in the crosshairs of his angry superiors. "It's time the bugger got what he deserves," he muttered to himself. "I'd pull the trigger myself."

Abram gave Jacob a sharp look but said nothing.

"Will Colonel Yevchenko agree to what you propose?" asked Isaiah.

Abram was confident. "I'm sure he will. He, too, benefits from our bold offer—such exemplary and loyal citizens we are."

"How far is Khabarovsk from here?" asked Peter Boldt.

"About eight hundred kilometers," Abram replied.

"Eight hundred kilometers!" Peter was aghast. "How are we to make such a long trip in winter weather?"

"But that's the beauty of it, don't you see?" Abram was excited. "It will give us the excuse to purchase strong sleds and more horses. And no one will think twice about all the food we're going to have to prepare. We'll be able to make all these preparations without raising the least bit of suspicion."

"All the same, Comrade Petrov must have a high opinion of our abilities, that he should agree to such an undertaking," commented Peter drily. "Eight hundred kilometers there in the snow and eight hundred kilometers back with loaded sleds." He shook his head. "It's almost as foolhardy as what we really intend to do."

Abram grimaced. "What does it matter to him if we lose a few men to the cold in the process? It would mean nothing. Regardless of how he feels about our collective, in the end we are all simply cogs in the soviet industrial machine."

"With Russia's millions, there are always more bodies to fill the empty spaces," Jacob added ruefully.

"So," continued Abram, "we're going to need to buy a lot of strong sleds as well as the horses to pull them. We should be able to find what we need at neighboring collectives. If not, we'll go to Blagoveshchensk. Meanwhile, a small mountain of food will need to be prepared. We already have as many sacks of flour as we'll need. We'll slaughter hogs and smoke the hams; some beef as well. The weather is already cold enough to freeze whatever meat we hang.

"Let me emphasize, none of this will raise anyone's suspicions because we have permission to proceed. Only when we begin to make final modifications to the sleds to carry passengers instead of logs will we need to be careful. And even then, most people will not be told the reason for the modifications. Then, when the day comes to leave, everyone will get a surprise and instead of traveling to Khabarovsk we'll use what we've prepared to get us into China."

"It's as simple as that," concluded Jacob.

"What about Yevchenko's stooges in your village?" asked Peter.

"We'll deal with them when the time comes. In the meantime, they'll be as much in the dark as everyone else.

Peter nodded, satisfied.

"One more thing," said Abram. "We're going to need someone to go to China to make arrangements for our coming. When we get there, we'll be cold and hungry. We're going to need to be fed and given lodging until we can figure out the next step." He grinned. "We don't want hundreds of people to arrive on someone's doorstep without some advance warning."

November 2, 1930

Jacob Enns stood on the bank of the Amur River examining its frozen, snow-covered surface. Beside him, Ludwig Hostetler did the same, while Alexander, their Chinese guide, looked at them impatiently.

"Why you stop?" asked Alexander.

Jacob ignored him, instead focusing his attention on the river. Except for places the ice had risen up and piled upon itself, it appeared to be as solid as the earth beneath his feet. But Jacob knew, when it came to the river's ice, appearances could be misleading. They would need to tread carefully as they made their way across it. Fortunately, Abram had arranged for Alexander accompany them. He knew the territory and would take them safely across.

Alexander was a Chinese trader who grew up in a village on the Chinese side of the Amur. As a young child he began accompanying his father on his trading forays in the Russian villages across the river where he was proudly introduced to customers as Yu Hua. Hua was a clever lad and over time developed some fluency in speaking Russian. When his father's health declined, Hua continued trading on his own. Somewhere along the way, his customers began to call him Alexander: the name was easier for them to pronounce. When the German-speaking newcomers arrived, Alexander expanded his trading routes to include their villages. At one time or another, he had done business with most of the settlers of Alexandrovka. They had found him to be an honest man whose word could be trusted. Happy to accept Russian rubles for a bit of guiding, Alexander had readily agreed to take Jacob and Ludwig on their scouting mission across the river.

"Why you stop?" Alexander asked again. "Come, we go." He pointed in the direction they must travel.

"In a minute," Jacob said, annoyed that he was finding it hard to keep up to Alexander's energetic pace.

Beside Jacob, Ludwig Hostetler snapped a twig from a dead willow branch. Jacob jumped at the sharp sound. Ludwig took no notice. He began to chew on the twig thoughtfully.

Whereas Alexander looked like he had been out for nothing more than a morning stroll, both Jacob and Ludwig were hot and tired after the long walk from Alexandrovka. Since leaving home that morning, they had come almost twenty kilometers, traveling roughly due south over the steppe. They had avoided the Russian villages along the way by tramping through fields and gullys. Despite the chill in the air, their wool coats were unbuttoned and their gloves were stuffed in their pockets.

"What do you think?" asked Jacob.

"It's early in the season," said Ludwig noncommittally.

"Looks pretty solid," suggested Jacob.

"Uh-huh."

"Ice is good," said Alexander. "Hard." He stamped the ground to illustrate his point. "We go now."

"We'll need to avoid those areas," said Jacob, pointing out dark spots where the river's current had as yet prevented ice from forming.

"Yes, yes," agreed Alexander.

Looking around, Jacob spied a straight branch lying amongst the bracken. He picked it up thinking it would be long enough to serve as a walking stick.

Despite Alexander's confidence, Jacob and Ludwig were silent as they weighed the task in front of them. Not only would they need to elude the guards patrolling the river. Despite Alexander's reassurances, they'd also be making the crossing while unsure of the strength of the river's ice. It had not yet been cold long enough for the river's ice to have fully formed. Their eyes stretched across the river to a flat, tree-covered island lying between them and the far shore. Their destination, the Chinese village of Kani Fu lay beyond the island, though they could not see it. Above the island, the blue mountains of China floated shimmering in the distant air, disconnected from the land by a haze of low-hung cloud.

"How far across the river, do you think?" asked Jacob, squinting to protect his eyes from the glare of the noonday sun on the snowy landscape.

"Not far!" said Alexander, wondering what these two farmers were concerned about. He had been across the river a number of times since the ice had begun to form over the last couple of weeks.

"About two kilometers. That's what Abram said it'd be," Ludwig added drily.

Standing on the riverbank, Jacob reminded himself of how he had gotten there. When Abram Siemens asked him to make the journey to Kani Fu, he had not hesitated. Nor had Rachel offered any argument when he later told her. They were both aware of the dangers involved in what was being planned and they were resolute in the face of them. It was still dark when he had departed that morning. He had kissed his sleeping son's forehead and straightened the blankets around him. Outside on the landing, he and Rachel had clung to each other in a desperate embrace. "You make sure you come back, Jacob Enns," she had scolded him tearfully as she handed him a sack of food enough for a days journey. Jacob had promised to return as soon as possible, though he knew that keeping the promise was not entirely in his hands. Ludwig Hostetler was a shadow beside the road when the two men had met a few minutes later.

"Your mission is simple," Abram had said when he had briefed them. "Arrange board and room for up to 400 people." And then he had smiled, "Well, maybe not so simple. But from all I've been told, the people of Kani Fu are plain, friendly folk who will put themselves out if they see a profit in it. Assure them we will pay for any services rendered. And that it'll only be for a night or two."

And now, here they were by the frozen Amur, about to make the crossing that twice before had eluded Jacob. He chuckled quietly. "I feel a bit like one of Joshua's spies sent to check out the Promised Land, getting ready to cross the Jordan River."

"Except this time, hopefully there won't be any walls falling down," chortled Ludwig.

"And no bloodshed," Jacob quietly agreed.

"We're not going over there to conquer anyone. We just want some help along the way as we pass right on through."

"All the way to America," added Jacob softly.

"Well, we aren't going to get there by philosophizing here on the riverbank," said Ludwig. "It is time we get a move-on. The guards should be enjoying their lunches right about now and the sun's bright enough, they won't see us for the glare."

"Whose idea was it that we go in broad daylight?" asked Jacob. "Maybe we should wait until tonight and cross in the dark."

"No," protested Alexander. "We go now. Guards not see us. Too bright."

Jacob looked back in the direction from which they had come. Through the trees he could see their tracks. The snow was not deep, a few centimeters only, but enough to betray them should a border guard happen upon them. "It'd be nice if was snowing," he suggested. "Cover our tracks."

"Well, we can't sit here waiting for the guards to find them," said Ludwig laconically.

"True," replied Jacob, "and despite what Alexander says, I don't think the ice is really set yet. We'd have a harder time avoiding the dangerous spots in the dark." Both men took another look at the frozen river. "Anyway, I've heard of people successfully crossing the river during the day when the sun is highest in the sky. The glare does make it hard for the guards to see."

Ludwig shrugged. "All right, then," was all he said.

Jacob and Ludwig each took a linen bed sheet out of their bag. At one time the sheets had been white. Repeated washings had turned them a light grey. Opening the sheets up, they wrapped them over their heads and tied two corners together by their chest.

Alexander had no need of camouflage. His padded pants and jacket were of a faded hue that would more easily blend in with the winter landscape.

"Aren't we a fine-looking pair," chuckled Jacob.

"If there are any guards who are feeling extra zealous today, this should keep us away from their prying eyes," said Ludwig. It was Anna who had suggested they take along the sheets.

Jacob and Ludwig looked at each other from behind to make sure there was no dark clothing showing that might catch the attention of a guard. Satisfied, Jacob eyed the three-meter drop to the river. "Right," he said, "let's be off," and plunged down the bank to the surface of the river.

Alexander seemed to skip down the steep slope while Ludwig slipped halfway down, sliding the rest of the way on his bottom. "Not a very auspicious start," he grumbled, brushing the snow from his pants.

Jacob made sure Ludwig's bed sheet was still properly in place. He listened for any sounds that might suggest an approaching guard. There was nothing but the whisper of wind through the willows and the far-off croak of a raven.

Without a backward glance, the three men ventured out onto the ice of the Amur River.

It wasn't long before Jacob, Ludwig and Alexander were well out on the river. As they walked, they occasionally paused to look back along the riverbank. Worrying questions were ever present in their minds: Was anyone there? Could they be seen from the shore? But they saw no one.

Looking along the shoreline, Jacob thought he recognized a particular bend in the riverbank, a little bay where the willows grew low against the waterline. He told himself he couldn't be sure and put it out of his mind.

When Alexander judged that they were far enough from the shoreline, they stopped looking back. They had reached the point of no return: any shout they might hear would mean the border guard was on the river himself, and that would mean a race to the Chinese side, or a bullet in the back.

Alexander seemed completely at ease on the river ice. He led them on a sure path toward the island that steadily grew larger before them. Even so, for Jacob each step was a test of faith. As much as he could, he placed his boots in the spots where Alexander had stepped. Ludwig followed behind, placing his feet where Jacob had trod. Eventually, following the sure-footed Alexander, they grew more confident and walked side by side.

They did not talk, for except to voice a warning there was nothing needing to be said. Rather than speak, they listened. At first they listened for a distant shout of alarm. As the distance between them and the Russian shore increased, the fear of discovery diminished and they relaxed their vigil. They began to notice ambient sound, the crunch and squeak of their boots on the snow-encrusted ice, the occasional call of a raven. Eventually, they began listening to the river itself, for they realized the river had much to say. Its ice was alive with a wide vocabulary of sounds: high sounds and low, glugs and gurgles, snaps, crackles and groans, and sounds for which they could find no words of description, sounds of mystery and of solitude. They became aware of the sounds of flowing water imprisoned under ice fighting against its burden, attempting but failing to throw it off, sliding underneath, ever searching and ready should a way of escape be discovered. And always above the river, the whisper of the wind as it curled and twisted its way from China to the Soviet shore.

They reached the north shore of the island in the middle of the river. Carefully, they climbed its icy banks. Without a word, Alexander led them on a winding path through bracken and a thick growth of birch and larch trees. Jacob had been told there were people living on the island, but they met no one. Nor did they see any sign of habitation. Eventually they found themselves descending the island's southern side and soon they were back onto the frozen Amur.

As he walked, Jacob became mesmerized by the seemingly endless expanse of snow and ice and the brilliance of the sun's reflected light, against which he constantly shielded his eyes. Worn down by tension and the drudgery of the long trek, Jacob began to daydream. In his mind's eye he found himself again on the river, but this time in a boat. He felt the smooth wood of the oars in his hands and heard the splash they made when he tried to wield them. He saw Naomi and Joseph sitting in the stern, their eyes suddenly wide with terror as a motorboat with a bright searchlight bore down upon them. He heard the shots of a rifle and felt again the panic and the horror of his wife's warm blood flowing from her. He felt her body grow heavy in his arms and groaned at the memory. He stumbled as he closed his eyes and shook his head to somehow rid himself of the nightmare that had appeared unbidden to haunt him.

Ludwig heard the grief in his friend's cry and saw him stumble. Somehow he knew immediately the reason for Jacob's distress. He called out to Alexander to stop.

Seeing they were well away from the island with perhaps another kilometer to go until they reached the Chinese bank, Ludwig put his hand on Jacob's arm. Thinking to divert Jacob's tortured mind he said, "Let's stop and rest a bit, Jacob. It is long past lunch and I'm hungry." Looking around, he saw a spot where the river had heaved up a large pile of ice-chunks. "Let's sit down over there. It's sheltered from the Russian side. We can have a bite to eat."

Freed from the memories that had so unexpectedly gripped him, Jacob gladly agreed. While Alexander squatted beside them, Jacob and Ludwig sat down on the ice. Legs stretched out, they leaned back against the pile of ice-chunks Ludwig had chosen. Its hemispherical shape was so evenly constructed, it could have been mistaken for a beaver lodge. Like schoolboys at lunchtime, Jacob and Ludwig brought their bags to their faces where they could peer inside and pulled out the meat and buns their wives had prepared for them. Alexander found something to eat in his pocket and nibbled at it slowly. Munching their meal, Jacob and Ludwig eyed the far shore.

"We should be there in time for an early dinner," said Ludwig, making light and avoiding the subject of Jacob's painful memories. "I wonder what'll be on the menu." He sniffed and swallowed. The cold wind was making his nose run. Looking at Alexander he asked, "What do the people of Kani Fu eat? Not borscht, I'm guessing."

Jacob chuckled.

"No. Not borscht," grinned Alexander.

The three men lapsed into silence as they finished their meal. As he sat, Jacob became aware of a deep thrumming sound coming from below him, like the sound of his pulse he sometimes heard in his ears, though slower in its repetition. Surprised, he leaned over so that his head was nearer the surface of the ice. He listened for what he'd imagined he'd heard. But instead of sound he became aware of movement. The ice upon which he was resting seemed to be slowly rising and falling. For a moment, he imagined himself sitting upon the chest of some immense recumbent dragon, feeling its chest rise and fall as it slowly, rhythmically, breathed.

The thought brought back to Jacob something he had once been told. "One of the Chinese traders who came to our village once told me that the Amur River is a great black dragon. Is that right, Alexander?"

"Yes, I've heard that," Ludwig said, picking at a piece of gristle that had lodged between two of his teeth.

166

"The people worship river as a god to be feared," replied Alexander. "They believe it control weather."

"Do you believe that?" Ludwig asked.

Alexander merely shrugged.

"Superstitious nonsense," muttered Jacob. As he spoke, they heard a loud, sharp crack. The ice upon which they were sitting seemed to buck and strain against their weight. The men looked at each other in alarm. They jumped to their feet. Picking up their belongings, they quickly moved away from the spot. Without warning, the ice where they had been sitting began to buckle and heave. Alexander, Jacob and Ludwig turned and ran.

When they were some distance away and felt they were no longer in danger, the men stopped and looked back. They saw a crack had appeared. A large section of river ice had broken away and was slowly being pushed downstream. As its vanguard met with the resistance of the sheet ice it encountered, great chunks were being piled together in a long jagged line of frozen destruction.

Jacob and Ludwig looked at each other and shook their heads in wonder. Ludwig grinned and said, "That was close."

"No problem," exclaimed Alexander.

"I hope the ice is more stable by the time we're heading back," Jacob said, as they again turned their eyes toward China.

They had not walked very long before Alexander, who was again in front, stopped. He held up his hand in a signal to Ludwig and Jacob. "Listen. Do you hear it?" he asked.

Ludwig stood still. "What?"

"I hear it," said Jacob. "A faint gurgling sound."

Looking in the direction they needed to go, Jacob saw only an unbroken expanse of white. Moving cautiously forward, he began to tap the snow-covered ice with his stick, all the while ignoring Alexander who was exclaiming, "No! You no go there!" Almost immediately, Jacob's stick met with no resistance. Unprepared, he almost lost his balance as the tip of his pole plunged into running water. Using the stick as a hammer, he quickly exposed a spot where the strong current had prevented ice from forming. Jacob continued whacking at the thin crust of wind-blown snow with his pole until a large piece of the crust broke off. It quickly disappeared into a breadth of open water large enough to swallow a horse and rider.

"Nice work!" said Ludwig, as they carefully skirted the hole in the ice. He chuckled, looking at Alexander, "This river dragon of yours certainly has his tricks."

Alexander's face was stern. "You no make fun of River Dragon."

"The sooner I'm back on solid ground, the happier I'm going to be," said Jacob.

They saw the smoke rising above Kani Fu before they saw the village. The wind had died and the plumes of a twenty or thirty cooking and heating fires rose above the thickets of trees and into the sky like Corinthian columns supporting the thick blanket of grey cloud that had formed above them and held in place by a trick of the air currents above.

As Jacob neared the flat riverbank, he noticed the many white lumps clustered along it that he had thought from a distance to be large boulders were actually boats. Many of them were lazily leaning on their upturned hulls like so many beached beluga whales, a fat eiderdown of snow capping them all. "It'll be a long while before they're back in the water," Jacob thought idly. Which led him to think of his own boating experience, at which point he soundly scolded himself: he had enough to think about in the present without constantly dwelling on the past.

Alexander led Jacob and Ludwig across the ice to a place along the bank where a small bay had been carved out by the river's current. There, a gently sloping track led from the river up the bank into a small wood. On either side of the track grew a tall stand of larch. Their naked, tawny branches created a bristly screen that hid from view the modest village sprawling behind them.

Looking at how the village was accessed from the river, Ludwig said, "Looks good. Perfect for horses and sleds. Fortunate too, for by the time we get here, the horses will be pretty much done in."

"Getting off the river here is certainly better than getting onto it from our side," observed Jacob. "I don't know how we're going to manage that drop down the embankment with horses and loaded sleighs."

The road they followed was a narrow, uneven track. Broken bits of ice lay in wheel ruts where long thin puddles had frozen and been broken by the next wagon to drive through. Streamers of snow lay where the road's diminutive ridges and valleys had caught the crystals.

The first house they came upon was within calling distance from the river. It was a small, simple shack, its front door facing the road. Long-stemmed steppe grasses and the latticework of thin poles holding them down poked here and there out of the wind-swept snow covering its thatched roof. Weighed down by the collected burdens of its past, the eaves of the roof slumped shoulder-like over the tired adobe walls, a portent to any who would see the consequence of time and age. The house was surrounded on two sides by a warren of flimsy fences constructed of thin sticks and branches. There was no sign of a shed to house whatever animals the fences were meant to contain.

Jacob said, "It wasn't so long ago that the first settlers of Alexandrovka all lived in adobe houses like this."

"A few of them still do," said Ludwig.

Alexander said, "Many peasants and animals live together in same house. They very poor." He grimaced to show Jacob and Ludwig that he disapproved of the practice.

An old crone appeared in the doorway of the house and stared at the three strangers. She was bundled in a thick, padded cotton coat the color of wet earth. It hung below her knees and was tied at her waist by a strip of dun-colored cloth. Her legs, what he could see of them, appeared to be wrapped in cloths of the same nondescript color. A wide-brimmed conical straw hat held in place by a rag knotted under her chin shadowed her dark face. Jacob nodded a greeting as they walked by. Her wrinkled face did not break from its stolid stare.

They continued following the rutted track and soon left the woods behind. With the larches at their backs, the village of Kani Fu opened up before them. Jacob saw that all of the houses, similar to the first they had seen, were crowded up against a road wide enough to only accommodate one horse-drawn sleigh. Their sulking salt and pepper roofs and brown windowless walls gave them the appearance of a crowd of dispirited senior citizens waiting together in a huddle, perhaps in a breadline, or in waiting for an important personage.

Everywhere Jacob noticed the same rickety old fences. In some yards he saw a few chickens, their feathers puffed out against the cold, scratching away the snow, busy with the work of pecking for whatever could be found to eat in the exposed dirt. Other pens contained ducks huddled together for warmth. Some fences corralled a pig or two. These were attached to more substantial houses, some of which were constructed of wood. Overall, it was obvious that Alexander had spoken rightly; the people of Kani Fu looked to be, for the most part, a very poor folk.

Seeing the three strangers in their village, a crowd soon gathered around them. Many were children who looked at the two white-skinned strangers shyly. Like the old woman, the children were bundled in thick cotton padded clothing. They reminded Jacob of large-eyed, black-haired muffins. A few of the braver ones chattered to each other and drew closer, hoping to touch the visitors. It was obvious to Jacob that the children had seldom seen a person like him.

Alexander quickly lost patience with the sideshow. He urged Jacob and Ludwig to hurry after him toward the village center. There they came to a building perhaps half again larger than those clustered around it. Its peaked, thatched roof was a bit higher than the others, with a slight upward curve along its eaves giving it a jaunty look beside its lethargic neighbors.

"This is village inn," Alexander announced. "You stay here for night. You sleep here," he repeated, in case they had missed his meaning the first time.

Stepping into the inn, Jacob saw it was one large room. The open-beamed ceiling was supported by a row of four stout posts running down the middle of the room. Pegs on the posts held a hodgepodge of saddles, horse blankets and other personal belongings. At their ends, the beams disappeared into the stout adobe walls. The wide sills of the room's single window—boarded up on the outside—set in the heavy walls revealed their thickness that provided insulation from the heat in summer and the cold in winter. The inn was lit by the soft glow of a bowl-shaped oil lamp hanging from a beam at its center.

What Jacob found curious, though, was a large brick platform a little more than half a meter high that ran the length of the room from one end to the other. It rose out of the neatly swept dirt floor in the middle of the room and stretched to the wall opposite from where he was standing. Sitting upon the platform on an assortment of thin mattresses and blankets were six Chinese men. One of them was reclining on his elbow, smoking a long pipe. Another seemed to be sleeping. Jacob saw the other four men were engaged a game with cards he did not recognize. They were talking in loud voices and laughing as they played. The platform was wide enough so that as the men lay with their heads close to the outer wall their feet were still well on top of it.

While Jacob was taking in the room, the innkeeper hurried over to where they stood. He was dressed in a thick cotton top and loose cotton pants. In the dim light Jacob could see that the man's clothes were of an indeterminate color. His unruly black hair poked out from under a bowl-shaped cloth cap.

Alexander spoke with the innkeeper. The man's eyes lit up when Alexander told him the Russian guests wanted to stay for a few days, maybe a week, and they would be paying in Russian rubles. Yes, there was room for them. It would be his honor to serve as their host. The innkeeper bowed in Jacob and Ludwig's direction as he said this. And yes, supper would be served shortly. A price was haggled and matters were soon settled.

Alexander, Jacob and Ludwig found a space on the platform next to the noisy card players. They removed their coats, hanging them on pegs on the post nearby. They left their boots at the base of the platform on the clean swept earthen floor beside those of the other guests.

Jacob and Ludwig stepped up onto the platform. With the open beam ceiling, there was room enough for them to stand without worrying about hitting their heads. A thin cotton mattress lay on the platform for each of them. When Jacob sat upon his, he was surprised to find it was pleasantly warm. He lay down, allowing the heat rising from the platform and through the mattress to soak into his chilled flesh and bones.

"Ahhh, Ludwig, but this is nice," Jacob said with a tired grin.

Leaning back, Ludwig nodded in agreement. "But what is this thing?" he asked Alexander.

"It is called *kang*," Alexander smiled. "All Chinese house have one. Heat and smoke from cooking fire flow through inside kang. Heat whole house. Chimney let smoke out outside. Very..." he thought a moment, looking for the right word, "useful."

"Yes it is," said Jacob, feeling suddenly sleepy after their long cold trek. He closed his eyes, ignoring the curious stares from his neighbors a mere arm's length away.

Almost immediately, Jacob heard himself snore. Then, despite the raucous commotion going on beside him, he heard no more.

Jacob had not been asleep long when Ludwig elbowed him awake. "Supper," was all he needed to say to get Jacob's full attention.

Jacob sat up, rubbed the sleep from his eyes and realized he was ravenously hungry. At the far end of the room, he saw a woman working at the stove. Her black hair hung down her back in a long braid. In the semi-darkness, he could see that, like the innkeeper, she was wearing dark cotton pants and a simple cotton blouse tied at the waist with a cloth. Jacob watched as the woman he decided must be the innkeeper's wife ladled something into a collection of white porcelain bowls. Placing each bowl on a large wooden tray, she carried them along the length of the *kang* so that each guest could take one.

Using the porcelain spoon the woman gave him, Jacob dipped it into the steaming gruel and took a sip. "Hmm," he grunted looking suspiciously at the grainy soup. "Hot, but definitely not borscht."

"Millet mush," said Ludwig. "Not bad," he added, chewing on a bit of pork he'd found in his bowl. "Do you have any more of Rachel's buns in your bag?"

Jacob shook his head. He looked again at the thick liquid in his bowl and decided to make the best of it. "Not bad, once you get used to it," he muttered after swallowing a few mouthfuls.

As it turned out, millet porridge would be the mainstay of their menu for the week. The small seeds cooked and seasoned with dried herbs were what most people in Kani Fu ate every day through the long winter. The few pieces of pork the men occasionally discovered in their bowls were a luxury few could afford.

As soon as their bowls were empty, the innkeeper's wife collected them. She returned to the stove where another pot was billowing steam. Again she became busy, ladling something into each of the bowls.

When she returned the bowls to her guests, Jacob wondered what she had conjured up this time. "Looks like dumplings," he said hopefully.

"Yes, dumplings," smiled Alexander, holding his bowl close to his chin and using his chopsticks to tuck one into his mouth.

Jacob preferred to use his spoon. Biting into the dumpling, he found it was filled with seasoned pork. "Delicious," he concluded.

The innkeeper came by, bowed and rattled off some words Jacob couldn't understand. "You honored guests," Alexander translated. And then he added in Russian, "You pay much money for little dough pockets. Very expensive." His comment did little to curb Ludwig's appetite as he asked the innkeeper if there were more dumplings in his wife's pot.

There weren't.

When dinner was finished, the card players on the *kang* beside Jacob leaned back against the wall. Each pulled a pipe out of his bag of possessions. They busied themselves with their pipes, stuffing tobacco into the bowls, tamping it down and lighting it. Ignoring Jacob, Ludwig and Alexander, they puffed contentedly, the smoke curling delicately from their nostrils. Soon a grey cloud began to envelope everyone close by. Jacob and Ludwig reclined on their elbows in order to breathe the less smoky air below the rising fumes.

One of the men belched and sighed contentedly. He was small and wiry. A sparse beard straggled his chin and a thin mustache sprouted about his skinny lips. When he smiled, his missing front teeth gave him an impish look. By the deference he was being shown by his companions, Jacob concluded he was the leader of the group. The man removed the pipe from his lips and spoke to Alexander.

After what seemed to Jacob to be a prolonged conversation, Alexander turned to him and said, "These men horse traders. Cross river many time. Buy many Russian horses and bring them to China."

"Can't they get horses here?" asked Jacob.

"No, villages here too isolated. Too many mountain roads to bring horses from south. Too expensive. Easier to cross river. Much cheaper, too."

Both Jacob and Ludwig knew that cross-border trade was illegal. The border patrols were not only there to keep people from leaving the Soviet Union. They were also there to keep people out. Jacob looked at the four men with newfound respect. These were fellows who knew how to avoid detection.

Hoping he wouldn't offend their guide, Ludwig said, "I know that you are good at evading border guards, Alexander. But can they also give us some suggestions for avoiding the patrols?"

"Yes," said Jacob, "do they know their routines, when they're more likely to be out, what time of day is best for avoiding them?"

"Is one place better to cross than others?" added Ludwig.

Alexander turned to the horse traders and began speaking. Occasionally he stopped to listen to a reply. They looked incredulous when Alexander told them he and his companions had crossed the river in broad daylight.

"No, no! You crazy?" said the leader emphatically. "Best time to cross is night!" He proceeded to give Jacob and Ludwig a lesson in how best to elude the Soviet border patrols.

The next morning dawned bright and clear. After a breakfast of more boiled millet Alexander announced that he would take Jacob and Ludwig to see the village headman. "Village chief very important person. Very old. He the man to talk to. If he agree to help, then village help. If no, then no."

It was mid-morning when Jacob and Ludwig stepped outside. After spending so many hours in the shadows of the gloomy inn, they were momentarily blinded by the brilliance of the day. As they walked along the road to the village chief's house, here and there they saw people—old and young alike—seated on stools in the sunshine. It had warmed during the night. Jacob thought at first they were simply enjoying the reprieve from the gripping cold. Then he noticed most of them held a garment in their hands—shirts or pants—and they were studiously picking at the seams.

"What are they doing?" Jacob asked Alexander.

"Oh, they pinching lice. Lice big problem. Live in seams of clothing. Bother people at night. They try to get rid of pests." He shook his had and laughed, "Never possible. Lice like Chinese family, always there no matter what."

Jacob felt a little crawly at the thought of the vermin living in his clothes and feeding on his blood. He thought of the sheets he and Ludwig had brought from home in which they had wrapped themselves as they slept. Were lice already infesting his bedding? He made a mental note to give it a good shake before laying down that night. "If we make it out of here without our own little infestation, it'll be a miracle," he croaked.

Ludwig chuckled.

Jacob found himself scratching at his armpits.

Taking a small path off the road, the trio soon came upon a humble house. There was nothing to differentiate it from those gathered about it. They all had the same tired look.

"This is village chief's home," Alexander said. He knocked on the door.

A wizened old man hardly taller than a pubescent child answered. Opening the door a crack, he looked up at his visitors. The skin of his face was more wrinkled than Jacob would have thought possible, shriveled and pinched as if the man had spent a lifetime under water. His beard was so thin Jacob thought he could easily count the hairs if given the opportunity. The man's eyes were guarded slits, his thin mouth cautious. Alexander explained who they were. After a moment of thought, the door opened wider.

Stepping into the simple adobe house, Jacob quickly saw it was a miniature version of the inn. Here, too, a *kang* took up half of the floor space. It was piled high with bedding and clothes. What struck Jacob as unusual, though, was that the sides of the *kang*, the walls and the ceiling of the home were completely covered in newspapers and colorful calendars, every square centimeter stuck on like wallpaper. Jacob had never seen anything like it. He tried not to stare lest he offend his host.

In one corner of the dwelling, Jacob saw an ornately carved wooden box on a stand. Its small doors were open. A tiny bowl rested on a raised surface within the box. Later Jacob asked Alexander about it and was told it was a shrine to the Black Dragon.

"Every house have shrine," Alexander would explain.

Alexander, who seemed to know the old man, proudly introduced him to Jacob and Ludwig. The introductions were formal, using only surnames, host first, then guest. Looking at Jacob and Ludwig he said, "This is Mr. Wang." While they each shook his hand, he gave Mr. Wang Jacob and Ludwig's names. "Mr. Enns and Mr. Hostetler," he said, though he made a complete bungle of pronouncing Ludwig's foreign-sounding surname.

A simple grate at one end of the *kang* served as Mr. Wang's stove. A door in the *kang's* wall beneath the grate signaled the fire pit. A kettle was singing on the grate. Indicating a couple of simple wooden chairs beside a rickety table, the chief gestured for his guests to sit while he busied himself with making and serving tea. Alexander moved some clothing aside and sat on the edge of the *kang*. Jacob and Ludwig settled themselves upon the chairs. The man smiled with pleasure as each guest accepted his porcelain cup. His parted lips revealed a mouthful of blackened stumps, the sad remnants of his broken teeth.

Mr. Wang sat beside Alexander. As they sipped their tea, Alexander explained the purpose of their visit: they wished to make arrangements for the housing of a few hundred German-speaking Russians. For one or two nights. Three at most.

The chief laughed loudly at the request. In his small village? There were not enough houses to provide shelter for so many, he assured them. Mr. Wang feigned incredulity even as he quickly considered how many rubles he might squeeze from these *laowai*, these foreigners.

After a few more protestations, the bargaining began. In moments it became serious. It took only two more cups of tea before a deal was struck. The people of the Alexandrovka collective would have beds and food waiting for them when the time came that they should cross the Amur River into China. Kani Fu would be honored to have them as its guests.

From the ice of Amur River, Jacob looked back at the riverbank, beyond which he knew Kani Fu lay. It was night. The light of the full moon painted a soft blue-grey glow upon the snowy landscape. Beyond the shadowy curtain of trees, Jacob knew life continued in its routines established over centuries. And though he had appreciated the hospitality of the village's residents, he was happy to finally be making his way home.

For a few days after their arrival in Kani Fu, the weather had been unseasonably warm. Alexander had worried the river's weakened ice would become too unpredictable, rotted by the warmer temperatures, so they had been forced to delay their return to Alexandrovka. Jacob and Ludwig spent their days exploring the hilly countryside around the village. Though they were in a foreign land, they had felt right at home amongst the trees, bushes and hillocks, for nature has no regard for the divisions created by political borders. The flora around Kani Fu was much the same as that of Alexandrovka.

A few of the villagers, growing accustomed to the presence of the *laowai* amongst them, had eventually dropped their reserve. After some initial, hesitant smiles, they had invited Ludwig and Jacob in for tea. Over the steaming cups, mutual curiosity about the other could be somewhat satisfied, even if attempts at conversation inevitably were brief and ended in self-conscious laughter. And in the end, the visitors had found the villagers to be a friendly, cheerful people for whom poverty was an accepted fact of their existence to be lightly borne; it did not stop them from sharing what they had.

Finally the weather had turned. The frigid nights returned. Alexander judged the ice likely to be sturdy enough.

Standing on the riverbank that afternoon, Jacob had stared long at the ice covering the river. Like the water beneath, it was a living thing. The ice moved. It drifted, heaved, buckled. In places the river simply refused to be encrusted, choosing instead to keep open niches where the fingers of light and air could brush its back, even in the coldest hours of winter. Jacob thought about the Black Dragon the villagers of Kani Fu believed the river to be, their explanation for the forces that ruled their lives.

Turning to look in the direction they must go, Jacob adjusted the pack on his back. It was filled with silk fabrics and various trinkets. More awkward than heavy, in the cold of the night it was an annoyance to be managed. In order to throw off suspicion, should border guards discover them upon the river, Alexander had insisted they purchase supplies that could be sold in their village. As far as the patrols were concerned, they were simple traders going about their business. In addition, he had said, a small bribe would probably ensure their freedom and safety.

"Come," said Alexander, impatient to get started. "We have far to go. No time to stand and look."

Jacob nodded. It would be a long walk home. Waiting there were Rachel and Joseph. His heart leaped at the thought.

The boat is small. Its lines are sturdy but sleek. He suspects it is a rowboat, though he can't be sure for there are no oars or oarlocks. He is sitting on the wooden center seat. Beside him is Rachel. He does not see her but feels her presence. He knows she is there.

The water is calm, the air still and warm.

There is no sense of sound. There is no lapping of wavelets upon the bow. The ringing in his ears that accompanies his every waking moment is not there. He cannot hear himself breathe, is not aware of the need of breath.

There is no sense of movement, no rocking or swaying. No one is pulling at oars. No one is controlling the direction in which the bow is pointing. They are a still life on canvas painted in hues of beige and grey.

Without warning, in the blink of an eye, the boat is filled with water up to the tops of the gunwales. It was dry; now it is swamped. There is no explanation, no reason for the transmutation. The boat had seemed sound. Now, it falls away like a withered leaf in autumn and is gone.

Jacob is in the water. He is weightless. The water has no form or substance. It is neither cold, nor cool, nor warm, nor hot. It is as if Jacob is floating in space, in a vacuum. He does not know if he breathes or if he holds his breath. He knows only that time has stopped and there is nothing beyond this vacant suspension.

To his left, Jacob sees Rachel. She is close by. He can see she is facing away from him, but his vision is clouded, the cream-colored space between them blurred silt-like. Effortlessly, Jacob moves toward her. He notices she is wearing a favorite purl knit sweater. She is floating in the water below him, her legs drawn up like she's seated in a chair, as if her body has not had time to adjust to the absence of her seat in the boat. Her hair floats freely around her head. Her elbows hug her sides. Her hands are closed into fists in front of her. She is not moving. Jacob reaches for her, grabs her by the arm and kicks toward the surface. He hears Rachel scream through her pinched mouth as they rise together toward the light. Their heads break the surface. Rachel gasps, filling her lungs with air.

Jacob woke with a start. He reached for Rachel lying beside him. Her back was to him as she lay on her favored left side. Disturbed in her sleep, she scooched backward while he slid toward her; they met in the middle of the bed. Hugging her to him, her back warm and comfortable, smelling her hair pressed into his face, Jacob remembered the dream he had just had. What did it mean?

Jacob had arrived home in the hour before dawn when the stars begin to fade and all that live upon the land hold their breath in anticipation of the coming day. Knowing his family would be asleep, he tapped lightly on the door before opening it to warn Rachel of his approach, letting her know the one entering her darkened home did not do so with ill intent.

As it happened, Rachel was sleeping lightly and woke at his knocking. As the days had followed each other since Jacob's departure, she had become increasingly concerned that something had happened to him. Why was he so long in returning? Had the border patrol found him? Had he fallen through the ice on the river? Was he injured? Imprisoned? Was he dead? Her mind had taken her on a roller coaster of worry, her nights full of persistently irrational thoughts. Stepping through the door, Jacob had whispered, "It's me. I'm home." Seeing her husband standing in the entryway Rachel had flung herself at him, wetting his cheeks with her tears.

They had talked in hushed tones, lying together under the covers of their bed while dawn lightened the shadows of their room. He told her some of what he had seen and done, but soon was unable to continue. As the adrenaline of his homecoming wore off, Jacob's teeth began to chatter. Chilled from his long hike, his exhausted body began to tremble. Rachel held him tightly to speed his warming. As the neighbor's rooster crowed a greeting to the new day, he had fallen for a while into an exhausted sleep and dreamed of water.

Jacob had not been awake long when he heard the rustle of bare feet on the wood floor. Raising his head, he saw Joseph standing at the foot of the bed. He was wiping the sleep from his eyes with his small fists. When he saw his father lying before him he cried, "Daddy!" and leaped onto the bed.

Jacob put his finger to his lips to forestall further exclamations. "Mommy is sleeping," he whispered, as Joseph happily tucked himself in beside his father.

"No she isn't," said a sleepy voice. Rachel rolled over to better give her attention to her family while Joseph climbed over Jacob in order to bask in the warmth of the love he felt when lying between his parents. He smiled broadly and gave a contented sigh.

It was not long before Rachel broke the spell. "Jacob, I forgot to bring in water last night. If you could go get some from the well, I'll heat it for you. You need to bathe, because you smell."

And Joseph giggled at his mother's impertinence.

November 10, 1930

The evening after Jacob and Ludwig's return, Peter Boldt and Isaiah Federau of New York came to Alexandrovka in response to Abram Siemens' summon. The five men met after dark, in secret, at the Siemens' home. Jacob and Ludwig spoke of what they had seen and the arrangements they made in Kani Fu.

"So, just to be clear," said Abram summing up, "the people of Kani Fu have enough room to accommodate upwards of 400 people for one or two nights? Longer if needed?"

"That's what their village chief says," Jacob said.

"Such a small village," said Peter Boldt hesitantly. "It will surely be terribly crowded."

"Yes," added Isaiah. "They may be willing to house us if we pay them. But is their desire for our rubles clouding their judgment?"

Remembering the size of the village and the houses he had visited, Jacob knew Peter and Isaiah had a point. "Yes, it will be crowded," he said matter-of-factly.

Ludwig said, "There is another village close by. It is called Chikade. It's bigger than Kani Fu. If we find there is not enough room in Kani Fu, perhaps some of us could go there."

"It's only another half-hour up the road," added Jacob.

Abram nodded solemnly. "Good. That sounds reasonable. Whatever else happens, we will have refuge when we arrive in China. We can put up with anything for a night or two, as long as we are warm and dry." The two leaders from New York were nodding their heads in agreement.

Abram paused. "So then. With that in mind, are we agreed we will carry on with our plan?" He looked around the table from one man to the next. "Once we inform everyone in our villages that our real intention for the preparations they have been making is not to cut wood in Khabarovsk, but to attempt an escape over the Amur into China, there will be no turning back.

185

Should the GPU learn of our plan, we all know the consequences we five will suffer."

"You mean we'll all get to meet Jesus sooner than we'd expected?" said Jacob with a wry smile. Ludwig chuckled. Peter looked disapprovingly at Jacob while chewing on his bottom lip. Isaiah stared at his hands folded on the table before him with the stern concentration of a levitationist. Each in turn gravely nodded his agreement.

"Then it's settled," said Abram quietly, ignoring Jacob's poor attempt at levity. He paused again as the gravity of their decision began to sink in. "The next question then is, when. When shall be go?"

"May I suggest mid-December?" said Peter.

"Winter will have settled in, the river's surface will be frozen solid by then," Isaiah said. "Besides giving us a month to make final preparations, a date in mid-December will give us time to sell any grain or flour we have left over. We will need every ruble we have in China. There will be living expenses, fees to be paid in order to emigrate America. We'll need money to begin our new lives in Canada or the United States. We don't want to arrive there as paupers." His face became animated as he grew excited at the thought of the grand possibilities escape from the Soviet Union would offer them.

"And, if we leave empty bins the Soviets won't benefit from our hard work. They rob us enough as it is," added Peter bitterly.

"Good idea," said Jacob. "We should do the same. We'll need to be careful we don't raise any suspicion as we do it, though. Sell small amounts at a time; spread the sales around to different villages. We don't want to attract unnecessary attention."

Abram said, "I agree. So then, let's set December 15 as the date. Are we agreed?"

In turn, Jacob, Ludwig, Peter, and Isaiah firmly said, "Yes."

"Good," said Abram, satisfied.

Peter said, "The river's ice can be unpredictable. We will need a guide."

"Alexander knows his way around," said Jacob. "He didn't miss a beat taking us across."

"Can he be trusted?" asked Isaiah.

"He's never done anything to cause us to doubt him," Ludwig replied. "And anyway, who else is there?"

When no one could suggest anyone else to guide them across the river, Abram said, "Fine. I'll talk to him."

"When do we tell everyone what we're planning?" asked Peter.

Abram looked at Ludwig. "How long do you think it will take to retrofit the sleds to accommodate passengers?"

Ludwig thought a moment. "I'd say we should allow two weeks just to be sure."

"Alright then," said Abram. "Let's tell everyone on the first of December. Are we agreed?"

When everyone looked satisfied, Abram asked, "Is there anything else we need to discuss?" Following a moment of silence, he placed both his hands on the tabletop and stood. "Gentlemen, our course is set. There is much to do before we leave." He paused briefly. "And may the grace and mercy of God go with us."

A formal prayer closed the meeting. As they left the Siemens' home to go their separate ways, the hearts of the five leaders grew heavy as the magnitude of what they intended to do settled upon them.

December 1, 1930

There was a collective leaping of hearts when the people of Alexandrovka and New York learned what their leaders had planned for them. Some were openly incredulous at the shameless audacity of the plan. Others didn't trust their ears and asked for the news to be repeated. Some set their jaws in glad determination. Others felt their legs weaken as fear of the dangerous unknown took hold. But none questioned the wisdom of the decision. Rather, their hearts rose together in harmony like a symphony in which the players reach the one note that resolves all the tension the musical score has created until that point.

Except for the children. They were told nothing. For the younger ones, life continued as it always had. For the older ones whose greater awareness perceived more, questions arose which were either left unasked or if asked were left unanswered. And those who guessed were given stern lectures on the imperative of secrecy.

Behind closed doors family members hugged one another in joy, in fear, in comfort, in support. Children looked on as parents embraced. They wondered at the sudden shows of affection by people often too reserved for such public shows. Their experience of the Ecclesiastes' message, "There is a time to weep and a time to laugh; a time to mourn and a time to dance," had in Stalin's Russia for too long been dominated by weeping and mourning. For some, there had never been any other time.

However, the joy felt at the thought they would soon be freed from the oppression of their communist masters was short-lived. The reality of their situation coated their spirits like freezing rain, weighing them down and burdening them. How could they accomplish everything required in the two weeks remaining without Colonel Yevchenko and the GPU finding out?

How could the truth be kept from his two stooges, Peter Dyck and Gerhard Wieler?

With hearts quaking but determined, preparations began in earnest.

On the sly, sleds that had been purchased to carry logs were modified to carry people; seats and backs were needed for the women and children who would ride in them. Where there was no room to hide their work in barns, piles of straw in front yards became shields behind which men sawed boards and hammered them into place. Men skilled in working with leather fashioned extra harnesses and straps as replacement parts, should they be needed on the river. Horses were fed extra rations to build their strength.

At Abram's direction, Jacob oversaw the distribution of sacks of flour and jugs of sunflower oil to each of the families of Alexandrovka for use when they reached China. Pigs were slaughtered, their hams hastily smoked and cured. Cattle were butchered, their meat cut up and stored where it would freeze before being dispersed to all who would need it.

Villagers were given permission to take personal items of value that could be sold without raising suspicion to markets in nearby villages. In the end, few took advantage of the offer. The risks involved seemed too great. They could not face more unknowns, since the unknown before them was already larger than many could bear.

The weight of the deception they lived became a menacing force, driving them indoors where the walls of their homes prevented them from screaming to the heavens in acts of self-betrayal. For a people for whom truth-telling was ingrained from birth, living in deceit was as unnatural as breathing underwater. But, though living their lie went against everything their faith taught them, life in the Soviet Union had prepared them for this communal act of dishonesty; for years now they had been risking arrest by secretly worshipping their God in the privacy of their own homes, windows shut and curtains drawn. Prevarication was not new to them. Though it went against their nature, they had had to learn to swim underwater and to come up for snatches of air before disappearing again below the surface.

As the days passed, the time of departure drew nearer. Together with its approach, fear crept unbidden into the houses of Alexandrovka: fear of discovery, fear of betrayal, fear of failure. It began in fits and starts, then deepened and spread among the people like a plague. People who had always prayed prayed more frequently and more fervently. People who did not pray because they had forgotten how found their knees bent in supplication, begging the God they had ignored to protect them and to bring them safely out of this slavery into the Promised Land of milk and honey. Those who could not pray let their yearning silence speak for them.

And so the tension built in the community. Sleep became difficult for some to find as they lay awake turning plans and possibilities over in their minds. They tossed restlessly as their weary minds refused to let go of the "what ifs." Others ate little, finding the thought of food distasteful. Their stomachs roiled with worry.

For the whole community, Colonel Yevchenko's spies in Alexandrovka were a great source of anxiety. However, the apprehension their presence in the village caused was far over-blown. Given the ease with which the two men could be misled, it seemed the colonel had quite overestimated their usefulness.

Throughout the closing weeks of November and the first fortnight of December, Teacher Wieler spent his days teaching in the school as he always had. He had no interest in embarking on an eight hundred kilometer wood cutting expedition; nor was he invited to participate. Disinterested, he remained oblivious to what the parents did while he reviewed with their children such things as addition and subtraction, vowels and consonants, and the duties owed to the communist state by a good soviet citizen. He spent much time on the last for indoctrination in civics was high on his list of priorities; he would make good communists of these German Mennonite children.

As for the carpenter, Peter Dyck, Abram Siemens saw to it that he was given a large project that would keep him busy in his workshop. Abram called him to the collective's office one day and showed him the primitive desks being used and the open boxes stuffed with official papers. "It's time we had proper desks to do our work on, and cabinets in which to store our important documents, don't you think?" he had said to Peter. "We are a model collective. It is not fitting that we should still be using old doors as desks." Peter Dyck had readily agreed. "With your carpentry skills I'm sure you will build fine pieces of furniture that even our great leader, Comrade Stalin, himself would be proud to display in his office." Peter had glowed with the praise and promised that Abram would not be disappointed. He had not been seen since.

Colonel Yevchenko continued to appear at the collective office for his regular weekly visits. But he rode through the village with blinders on. He saw nothing because he was looking for nothing. He made no attempt to peer behind the straw stacks and barn doors. His visits were short. After a perfunctory conversation and a few questions about their preparations for the journey to Khabarovsk, he would mount his horse and leave. He had been completely disarmed by the collective's offer. In their socialistic zeal, they had proven themselves to him to be beyond reproach.

The colonel, though, seemed to Abram and Jacob to be preoccupied and fatigued. They speculated together about his health. But they could not have guessed at the source of the GPU commander's demeanor. What they did not know was that he had taken to riding the dyke alongside the Amur River at night. With the increase of attempted escapes over the border, now that the frozen river had become a tempting passageway to China he had taken it upon himself to patrol its banks himself. The border guards were, in his estimation, useless. In the cold and dark of the Siberian winter night, he was convinced they too quickly retreated to their fires and their vodka.

What Yevchenko looked forward to most during the tedium of his day was the hunt. Each night he put on his greatcoat and quietly rode his horse along the icy embankment. Sipping his vodka to light a fire in his belly when he became chilled, he looked for signs of those who would flee his country for a life elsewhere. To him they were all traitors: the penalty for treason, death.

While his thick moustache grew icicles in the frigid night air, the colonel rested his loaded rifle in front of him on his saddle in readiness. He remembered his time on the front lines of the civil war, hunting the hated White soldiers—scum finally defeated barely eight years ago; oh, how he missed those days—finding them in his sights, breathing softly, pulling the trigger. He imagined his prey on the ice, trying to slip away toward China. He imagined what he would do when he found them.

When he found them, he would stop them. He knew that one night he would be lucky. It was only a matter of time.

December 15

On the day of their departure, the sun set just before 4:30pm, not that its descent had been witnessed. A low-hanging layer of thick grey clouds had prematurely darkened the village. Like so much else that had been robbed of its beauty by the unrelenting Siberian winter, the fiery display played itself out above the village unnoticed. All day, temperatures had hovered around -30 Celsius. The night promised to be much colder.

At a clandestine meeting early that morning, the people of Alexandrovka had been told to be ready to depart at 9 o'clock that evening. The convoy of sleighs from New York was expected at that time. Without delay, they would depart for the Amur River in the dark.

Exhilarated by the imminence of their departure, Jacob left the meeting with no idea that his feet would turn toward the forest of pine trees near the village. As he walked, he became lost in thought at what yet needed to be done. Ice crystals floated in the air around him, catching random bits of the morning light and winking like fireflies. Before he knew it, the forest stood tall before him. As though answering a call, he chose a path that led to a place he had not visited since the previous summer.

When he arrived in the glade, Jacob gazed about him. Unlike the last time he had been there, the birches were now naked. The vibrant greens of the pines were dulled in dormancy. Snow was mounded around the undergrowth with bare branches protruding here and there like knitting needles from skeins of wool. The ground was covered in white. It hardly seemed the same place where he had laid to rest his beloved Naomi.

Knowing what he must do, Jacob found a couple of suitable branches. After breaking them to the length he wanted, he dug in his pocket and found a length of string. Carefully he tied the branches together in the shape of a cross. Estimating where Naomi's grave must be, Jacob knelt in the snow. He knew the

193

ground was iron hard from frost, so pulling the snow together he formed a foundation in which he planted the cross. But in the dry cold, the snow held no moisture and therefore could hold no shape. When he stood, the snow crumbled and the cross fell over. Jacob was forced to content himself with laying the cross upon the grave.

Jacob stood for a moment with bowed head, looking at what he had done. "Naomi," he said. "You have lain here until now unmarked. But you have not been forgotten, nor will you ever be." He paused as memories—some sweet and some heavy—filled his heart. After a moment he said simply, "We are leaving this land today, and Joseph will have the bright future you hoped for him. Rest in peace, my love."

Jacob said a prayer and without looking back, left the glade.

As Jacob and Joseph sat down at their kitchen table for a last meal before leaving, his mother-in-law helped Rachel serve the meal. Ruth Hildebrandt had arrived at their house the day before. Among the few belongings she'd brought was her sewing machine. "We'll need it to mend our clothing!" she had said indignantly when Jacob delicately suggested it might be superfluous baggage adding needless weight to the load their sleigh would carry. "We must be ready for anything, on this adventure we're undertaking," she had scolded. Watching her place a basket of buns on the table, Jacob smiled as he remembered her calling what they were about to do an "adventure." Their reunion had been happy but, in the circumstances, subdued. While Jacob and Rachel were all nerves over what was coming, she did not seem in the least bit afraid. "I've lived long enough in this god-forsaken country. It's time my feet walked on better soil, whether it be in China here below or heaven above." She had spoken matter-of-factly, without a hint of misgiving. Jacob admired her feisty nature, but her bravado did little to steady his own misgivings.

The aromas of borsht, roast beef and fresh baking filled the room. Jacob took in a deep breath, relishing the smells. His mouth began to water in anticipation of the feast. Rachel and Ruth had spared nothing in the preparation of this meal. "We're leaving," Rachel had said. "Anything we're not taking along is being left behind. I don't want to think about what will happen to our things, but I'm not leaving food for the mice to chew." With the coming of winter, a family of mice had moved into the house, with which she had been skirmishing ever since. So far, there had been no casualties.

Jacob could not restrain a compulsive glance at the few bundles of personal possessions lying ready by the door. He thought, "Is there anything else we should be taking?" Knowing how laden their sleigh would be, Rachel had been careful in her choices of what to take along: extra clothing, a toy for Joseph, her knitting needles and yarn, a couple of precious small knick knacks, all wrapped tightly in blankets and tied with rope. The quilt from her bed lay atop the bundles. It would be used to keep them warm during their flight.

They would be traveling in their good friends, the Hostetler's sleigh. Their food allotments were already at the Hostetler's house. Together with the two households' belongings, Rachel, Ruth, and Joseph would ride with Anna and her children. Jacob would ride his horse. Ludwig would drive the sleigh.

The meal lay steaming hot on the table before Jacob and his family. Bowing their heads, they thanked God for the bounty of their meal and once again implored Him for their safekeeping in the hours to come. Even as he spoke the prayer, Jacob recalled a similar prayer a few months earlier. He could not hinder the thought, "And look how that turned out," from entering his mind.

Taking up the carving knife, Jacob cut into the roast. It was juicy and tender. "Perfect," he said with a smile. With deliberate formality, Jacob placed a thick slice on each plate. As the plates were placed in front of each one at the table, Ruth ladled soup into bowls. Rachel buttered a bun for Joseph and cut up his meat.

As Jacob looked at all the food before him, he said, "What a feast for our last supper in Alexandrovka!" He lifted his spoon to try some borscht. Sipping it carefully—he didn't want to burn his mouth—he found it tasted nothing like he expected it to taste. He put down the spoon and tried a forkful of beef. It was so tender it practically melted on his tongue, but he had difficulty swallowing it. Jacob realized that, despite the hour and the delicious food, he had very little appetite. His anxious stomach seemed to be occupied with thoughts of its own, leaving little room for food. Nevertheless, he forced himself to eat. He would need all his strength for the crossing.

When supper was cleared away, Jacob bundled himself in his winter coat and put on his padded boots. He kissed Rachel, saying he would soon return. There was something he needed to attend to. When Rachel asked where he was going, all Jacob would say was "Don't worry, I won't be long."

With determined steps, Jacob walked the darkened road of Alexandrovka toward the home where a carpenter lived alone with his conscience. When he arrived there, Jacob saw three men were waiting for him on the pathway in front of Peter Dyck's house. One was carrying a coil of rope.

"Good," Jacob thought. "They're all here. We can get on with business right away." He was not looking forward to the coming encounter.

When Abram Siemens suggested this assignment, Jacob had asked to visit the Teacher Wieler instead. He would have liked to see the look on his face. But Abram wouldn't agree. "For you, Jacob, it is personal between you and Gerhard Wieler. I understand that. But there is no room for grudges in what we will be doing." Jacob had had to acknowledge the truth in what Abram decided.

After silent nods of greeting, the four men filed onto Peter Dyck's porch. Jacob knocked and heard a faint reply. The door was not locked so he opened it and stepped inside. His three companions quickly followed. Peter was sitting at his table. A kerosene lamp burned brightly at its center. His Bible was open before him. He looked up, a puzzled look creasing his face.

"What..." the carpenter began, but Jacob interrupted him. "Good evening, Peter." Peter Dyck looked from one man to the next. The firm set of their faces lit a tinder of fear in his belly.

Jacob got right to it. "We have long known that you are a spy for the GPU." When Dyck made to disagree, Jacob waved his objection aside. "Do not even try to deny it."

"But," gasped Dyck, "I..." His flailing thoughts refused to coalesce. The dread that gripped him blossomed in his face like spilled paint running along the floor. He had often wondered if such a day as this would come, and here it was.

Peter tried to stand up, but one of the men pushed him back down into his chair. What were these men planning to do, Dyck wondered in growing panic. He stared at the rope hanging loosely in the hands of one of the men.

"We have come here to give you a choice, Peter," Jacob continued. "So listen very carefully. We are leaving tonight. The whole village. Everyone." As he spoke Dyck's face became a mask of shocked bewilderment. "We have been preparing for this night for months." Jacob couldn't help himself, "And you didn't know." He chuckled maliciously. "Some spy you are, Peter. Your boss, Yevchenko, would be proud." Dyck's blank look told Jacob he'd missed the sarcasm.

Jacob shook his head in disgust. He did not like this man. Knowing he was a spy, the people of Alexandrovka had always had to tiptoe around him. Fortunately, no harm had as yet come to anyone as a result of his collaboration.

"The whole village is escaping across the Amur into China. You have a choice to make," Jacob said. "You can come with us, peacefully—mind you, no shenanigans. Or, if you prefer to stay, we'll tie you up here in your house so you can't warn your Soviet friends about what we're doing. We'll leave you behind for the GPU to find. Or maybe they won't find you." He let Peter's imagination work on that for a moment. "What is your decision?"

Peter looked rapidly from one man to the next, his mind reeling. He found his tongue. "You're leaving?" he said incredulously. "Escaping to China? The whole village?" He was having a hard time believing what he'd been told. Was this some sort of trick?

Losing patience, the man with the rope said, "Let's just tie him up and be done with it. Serves him right." He started uncoiling the rope.

"I'll come. I'll come with you." Peter's words were loud and sharp, as if he was speaking to someone hard of hearing. "I'll come," he repeated, his hands in the air in front of him in a gesture of surrender. Then more softly, "I don't want to stay. I hate what this country has become. What it has done to me. I won't make any trouble. I promise."

"It's more than you deserve," said the man with the rope. The others stared silently at Dyck, judging the sincerity of his words.

Jacob said, "Pack a few things. Be ready to leave at 9:00 o'clock. You'll be called when it is time." And as an afterthought, he said, "Bring your horse."

The other collaborator, the teacher, Gerhard Wieler, also received visitors that evening. He, too, quickly agreed to join the villagers in their attempt to escape into China.

Jacob had been home only a few minutes after his business with Peter Dyck when a runner appeared at his door. "Abram Siemens wants you to come to the collective's office. He wants you to hurry!" he said breathlessly. It was just after 8 o'clock.

When Jacob reached the office, he saw Ludwig Hostetler coming from the opposite direction. Jacob paused at the door for Ludwig to catch up. "What's this all about?" he asked. Ludwig shrugged and shook his head. They climbed the steps and entered the office.

Peter Boldt and Isaiah Federau were seated in the room. Two other men from New York stood to the side. Jacob had seen them before but could not remember their names. They were all heavily dressed to ward off the cold, but none had removed their thick coats. Abram Siemens sat behind his desk with an unhappy look on his face.

The air in the room was thick with emotion. The frown on the face of the General Secretary of the Central Committee of the Communist Party of the Soviet Union, who despite his disembodied state seemed to be of the opinion he was chairing this meeting, was more menacing than usual.

"New York is not ready to go," said Abram crisply, without introduction. "They want to postpone for a week."

Jacob was stunned.

"Let me explain," stammered Peter Boldt. "We have been unable to sell all of our flour. We need the extra time. We held a meeting in the village. Everyone agreed."

"It's out of the question," said Jacob. "The danger of discovery increases with each day we delay."

Ludwig grunted his disgust at the idea of waiting. "You'd endanger all of us for the sake of a few more rubles? You must be joking!"

Peter would not be moved. "I'm sorry, but that is the decision of our village. We need time to sell our surplus grain." He added firmly, "We are prepared to go next Monday."

"You go next week. But we're ready to go. We'll go today." Abram was adamant.

Peter looked uncomfortable. "We thought that would be your answer." He paused. "If you go today, the authorities will be on high alert next week. It would be too risky for us to make the attempt. I'm sorry, but if you will not wait, then we'll have no choice but to report you to the GPU."

Abram, Jacob and Ludwig were aghast. "You'd betray us?" Jacob cried, dumbfounded.

"We must look out for the interests of our people," Isaiah said defensively. The whine in his voice made Jacob feel sick to his stomach.

Abram voice was terse. "Then you leave us no choice. We will wait."

"A wise decision," said Peter, trying to hide the relief he felt. "We understand how hard this must be for you. Your people will understand, once you explain the situation to them."

"And, to make sure you don't change your mind," said Isaiah, his voice thin and prickly as a blackberry bush, "two of us will remain here in Alexandrovka to watch you. We wouldn't want you to break your word by sneaking off on your own."

Peter said, "We apologize for the intrusion, but it is necessary."

As Peter and Isaiah stood to leave there was no shaking of hands. That formality, after what was being done to the people of his village, seemed to Abram hollow and meaningless.

After the delegation from New York had left the office, Abram was irate. "Inform everyone that we're not going tonight." Then, in a quiet voice, in case someone might be listening at the door, "Tell them to remain at the ready. We are not going to wait for these jokers from New York to sell their precious flour. The first chance we get when they're not looking, we're going."

December 16, 1930

It wasn't until the early hours of the next morning that the two observers from New York returned to their homes. Chilled to the bone, they hurried to their home fires, confident there were not enough hours of darkness left to attempt a crossing. Their presence in Alexandrovka was no longer required. Others would return to take their places that evening.

But after the New Yorkers had gone, a meeting of Alexandrovka's villagers was called. It was held in the only indoor space big enough to hold them all, a large empty barn. Emotions were high, swirling about with the chilly drafts coming in through cracks in the barn's wooden siding. People huddled together for warmth and comfort, moaning their despair in an anxious chorus of fear: we will be discovered if we tarry. There was little debate for the dam that held them in Alexandrovka as prisoners to the communist dictatorship had been breeched. Their hearts were already crossing the ice into China. It was quickly decided that Abram had not spoken out of turn in his instructions to Jacob and Ludwig. Despite being a people for whom their word was their bond, in this instance they agreed, they would not bide by the promise of their leader. The danger that accompanied waiting was too great, the desire to escape too pressing. They would leave at the first opportunity.

That afternoon, just as darkness was falling, a trio of New Yorkers rode into Alexandrovka. Their faces revealed none of the embarrassment they felt. This had not been an assignment of their choosing. Yet, too, they were determined to join the escape into China, and if that meant a delay of a week, then so be it. In times like these, trust was a sharply honed blade: one could be easily cut with the slightest of motions. They would watch and ensure that the people of Alexandrovka did not slip away without them.

The New Yorkers patrolled the streets of Alexandrovka, looking in at homes, checking for activity in barns. The villagers they watched greeted them stiffly, with a cold formality that hid their true feelings of anger and resentment. When the watchmen walked on, the people continued their interrupted preparations. Nothing would dissuade them from their goal.

And for once, the foul weather seemed to favor Alexandrovka, for the mercury dipped and dipped further, from -30 to -35 to -40 to -45. The New Yorkers, realizing they risked serious frostbite should they remain outdoors, decided no one in their right mind would attempt a crossing in such conditions. Sure that the people of Alexandrovka would stay close to their fires, by 10 o'clock that evening, the watchmen decided to head home.

Faces hidden behind curtains in the homes of Alexandrovka watched as the wardens rode out of their village. They took the north road that wound its way through forests of sleeping pine, birch and larch and alongside frozen ponds and marshes toward their village. Those who watched worried all the while. Were the New Yorkers really gone? Would they return? There might be indecision amongst them, they thought, and perhaps they would come back.

In the meantime, Jacob, living at the southern edge of the village, was asked to watch the road to see if anyone might be coming from that direction. Konstantinovka lay a few kilometers to the south, where the GPU had their regional office. When the time came to muster all the loaded sleighs, it would not do to be surprised by an unexpected visit from the secret police.

Bundled in his warmest clothes, Jacob walked along the road away from Alexandrovka before stopping and listening. The frigid air was completely still, so though he could see little for the darkness, he could clearly hear any sounds coming from the village and across the fields.

Jacob was about to turn back toward home, when he noticed a faint scraping sound coming toward him from the south. He knew that sound. As it grew louder, Jacob knew a sleigh was coming at speed. Whoever rode in that sleigh was in a hurry.

Jacob's heart began to race as he considered the possibilities. Was it the GPU? Had Alexandrovka been betrayed?

It was not long before the sleigh swished by where Jacob stood by the side of the road. Jacob glimpsed the people in it, two men and a woman. Not GPU, from the clothing they wore, he thought with relief.

Breathing through his nostrils to warm the air he took in, Jacob ran after the sleigh, if the hobbling he did in his thick clothing and boots could be called running. Coming into the village, he saw the sleigh stopped in front of the collective office. The three passengers had climbed down. Abram Siemens was talking to them.

As it turned out, one of them had been hiding in Abram's barn. Divining that the escape would happen that night, he had gone to Friedensdorf and returned with two of his relatives. When Jacob joined them, they were begging Abram to be allowed to join the crossing.

"You are welcome to join us, Mr. and Mrs. Friesen," said Abram grimly, "the more the merrier."

Seeing Jacob, Abram said, "Ah, Jacob. Spread the word. We leave in an hour."

Assignments had been given to some men while final preparations were being made. Abram had hastily called them together. Jacob was among them. They would be needed as outriders, he informed them, watching for border patrols and forming a web of protection around the train of sleds that would carry the villagers to safety. The men in the train would be too preoccupied with managing the sleighs and horses to look beyond them to see what might be there. Some of the outriders would go beside the train, a few behind, and some would ride ahead.

Jacob was asked to follow the convoy and look behind it. "We will leave a trail any child could follow," said Abram. "The most slow-witted of guards will realize its meaning and raise the alarm. You must keep a sharp lookout for them."

"Do you have weapons?" Abram asked the outriders. Some carried their rifles used for hunting or the job of butchery. Knowing Jacob had no gun, he handed him a revolver. It was clean, polished, and smelled of gun oil. In answer to Jacob's surprised look, Abram said, "It's a Webley. British. I got it in Slavgorod. The British Expeditionary Force brought them in 1918 when they came to try and stop the Bolsheviks." He did not say how he had come to own it.

Feeling uncomfortable, Jacob asked, "And what am I to do with this?"

Abram looked at him with a stony face and said, "You'll know what to do if the time should come that you must use it."

Taking the gun back, Abram pushed a small lever beside the handle grip with his thumb. The revolver flipped open. "See," Abram said as he showed Jacob. "Six bullets. That's all I have left." He pulled the barrel up so it clicked into place. Handing the revolver back to Jacob, he said, "To shoot, you have only to pull the trigger. But be careful. It has a good kick!"

Jacob lifted the gun and sighted along the short barrel. He wondered how in the world he'd be able to hit anything with it even if he found the courage to pull the trigger. Putting the gun in his coat pocket, Jacob hurried home where his help was needed. The unfamiliar weight bumped against his thigh as he strode along.

In their final preparations for departure, families carefully packed their sleds with foodstuffs and possessions, some necessary and some too precious to be left behind. Before they walked away from their homes, some shed tears at the thought of other items equally as precious that were being abandoned. There simply was no room for their ornate pieces of furniture, their large oil paintings depicting scenes of beauty, portraits of parents and grandparents hanging in places of honor, and other heirlooms passed down through generations resting where they always had upon shelves and bookcases.

With mechanical care, clocks were wound, the better to mark the hours of their abandonment. Some in the final rush to depart left food uneaten upon the table. Some left lamps burning, casting a pale light on what was and would be no more, lighting the way for the vanguard of those who might come thereafter.

An earthquake was rocking the village of small familial worlds, creating a chasm that would separate them from all they had ever known, all they had loved and come to call Home.

While the women wept in their front rooms, touching and caressing memories and objects of worth, the men went into the barns and wept, too, as they unlocked the wooden stanchions that kept their cows in place, gentle beasts whose teats they had stroked morning and evening without fail, taking the warm buckets of life-giving milk for their families' gain. Gates in pens holding beef cattle, sheep, pigs, chickens, and geese were left open. The animals would need their freedom to forage for feed. Aisles and pens were stuffed with hay; buckets of water were filled for drinking. In the farmers' hearts was the knowledge that their animals' chances of survival were greatly diminished by their absence. They felt the desertion of their beloved livestock in their very bones.

With ever more rapidly beating hearts, the men of Alexandrovka harnessed their workhorses to the sleds. Two horses would pull some sleds. Teams of three would pull other sleds. Riding horses were saddled and made ready.

Wrapping themselves in layers of thick clothing, the families closed the doors of their homes and walked into the street. Knowing that in the frigid temperatures wet cheeks would freeze quickly, they wiped their faces dry of their tears.

As they climbed onto the sleighs or mounted their horses, some gave thought to what would become of their discarded homes. Would they be inhabited again? By whom? Russians? By other German Mennonites? Only God knew. In a move of tender hospitality, Rachel had written a note in German and Russian welcoming whoever entered her home and wishing them well with what they found there. She had left it where it would be easily seen on the kitchen table. A few gave no thought to the future of the wood framed buildings they had lived in and called home. To their minds, they were taking Home with them: a few possessions and more importantly, the people they loved. What they were leaving behind was merely a shell they had occupied for a season.

Others, had there been any dust to be found beneath the crust of snow, would have gladly wiped it from their boots. They had dwelled in Russia for a century and a half and in that time the Soviet Union had treated them most poorly. They would find a more hospitable country in which to raise their children.

The word was given. Sleds pulled away from houses and farmyards along the street. They formed a long line. Anxious passengers sat tightly packed amongst their baggage on sturdy sleds pulled by stamping, snorting horses. The horses, unaccustomed to being out of their stalls at such a late hour felt the wave of suppressed emotion surging through the large entourage. Clouds of steam rose from their warm bodies and blasted from their nostrils. In the frigid air, a rime of frost immediately began to form around their muzzles and on their whiskers.

It was midnight before all of the sleighs were assembled on the street of Alexandrovka. Alexander strode to the front of the caravan. Fifty-four sleighs were lined up behind him. Two hundred and eighteen men, women and children were looking to him for their safety. Most were residents of Alexandrovka. But like the Friesens who had arrived only an hour earlier, relatives from neighboring villages had secretly been contacted and invited to join the dash for freedom. They had gladly left what they had behind for the chance to find a better future elsewhere.

Abram Siemens had approached Alexander with the request to guide the village of Alexandrovka across the river into China the day after he brought Jacob and Ludwig safely back from their reconnaissance. Alexander had at first been doubtful. It seemed impossible, a fool's errand. How could he take so many across the river without being discovered? But the notion had intrigued him. It was a challenge. And it would make him very rich. Abram had at first balked at Alexander's price, the prize horse of each family crossing the Amur to be paid when they reached Kani Fu. But Alexander had stood his ground and Abram, knowing Alexander's importance to their success, finally agreed.

And now the time had come.

The word was passed from sleigh to sleigh: absolute silence must be observed until they were safely across the river. Parents sternly warned their children—many of them excited by what appeared to be a grand nighttime adventure—to keep quiet. Having silenced their children they bowed their heads and murmured prayers pleading God for protection.

Alexander pointed the way.

Slowly the train of sleds began to follow him down the road. Southward was their direction, toward the frozen Amur River and China.

At first the going was easy. Under the cover of the dark Siberian night sky, the train of sleds followed the flat, well-packed road southward.

Jacob rode beside the sleigh carrying his and Ludwig's families. It was piled so tightly Jacob wondered that the two horses pulling it could manage the weight. He could see the shadowy figures of Rachel and Ruth, with Joseph tucked between them. Across from them huddled Anna Hostetler clutching Peter. The toddler was sound asleep, wrapped cocoon-like in a thick woolen blanket. Anna was fond of saying her son could sleep through a thunderstorm, Jacob remembered. He smiled; this night it would be a virtue to sleep and wake when it was done. On either side of Anna, Margaret and Judith pressed tightly against the protective figure of their mother. Beneath and around them all were stored the things they would need to begin their lives in a new land. Ludwig sat awkwardly amongst some baggage tied securely on the front seat. He held the reins softly, flicking them now and then, encouraging the horses in their arduous task. He held a whip in his hand, but would not use it except when forced to.

It was very cold. Someone had said it was -50. Jacob spat and heard the water from his mouth crackle as it hit the snow. He jumped at a sound like a gunshot off to the right in the woods beside the road. There had been no flash of light; he knew it must be the bark of a tree exploding as its sap froze and expanded. Jacob pulled the wool scarf that covered his cheeks, nose and mouth tighter around his face.

Except for the monotonous whisper of the sleds' runners and the soft plodding steps of the straining horses, all was eerily silent. Noticing the imposing silence, Jacob thought this could be a funeral procession. He pushed the ominous thought away even as he considered the unknowns that lay ahead of them. So many people attempting what seemed impossible. And if they made it to China, what then? Would they be welcomed? Or would they be kicked around from place to place, as had been their lot in Russia? Would they ever actually achieve their dream of freedom in North America?

The train of sleds ground to a halt. Jacob could not see beyond the sled in front of the one he rode beside. He knew its occupants' vision was also limited by the cold darkness. They were all completely dependent upon the ones going before them. If we were being led over a cliff, thought Jacob, we wouldn't know it until we were plunging through the air. Nudging his horse with his heels, he rode ahead to see the reason for the delay.

To this point, the road had been level and well traveled; the going had been easy for those who walked and for the horses doing the work of pulling. But now, Jacob saw, Alexander was leading the train of sleds onto the fields of the open steppe. The train had paused as workhorses, hesitant at the illogical change in direction, were guided off of the flat, hard road into soft snow that reached up to their bellies.

Judging they'd traveled less than two kilometers on the road, Jacob decided they had perhaps sixteen kilometers through the fields before the ice of the river. He watched as the horses pulling the sleigh at first floundered in the deep snow before finding their legs. "God help us," he murmured.

Jacob remained where he was, watching the sleds turn into the field until the last one made its way onto the track that had been left by those going before it. He looked at the passengers in the sleds. He saw the white sheen of frost on scarves and coats where moisture from breathing froze as soon as it was expelled. He saw beards and mustaches growing small icicles. With his mittened hand, he rubbed his nose and cheeks. His scarf helped, but he realized his skin was still becoming numb from the cold. His body, too, was becoming chilled. He wiggled his toes to restore feeling in them.

Jacob watched the last sled disappear into the darkness. It was time he began his assignment to patrol the rear of the caravan. With the wide trail they were leaving behind and given their slow progress, it would be easy for anyone to find and catch them. Jacob hoped he would not discover anyone following them. Although he knew what he should do if the fleeing villagers were discovered, he was not at all sure what he would do. He remembered the pistol in his pocket and noticed its weight against his thigh. It was foreign, a newly grown and unwanted appendage. Jacob could no longer hear the muffled noises coming from the train of sleds. He was alone with his thoughts and his fears. With a click of his tongue and a nudging of his heels, he slowly followed the broad trail in the snow.

And so the heavy sledding began. The powerful horses in the vanguard broke the trail, doing double duty plowing through the snow while pulling the sleigh with their strong legs. Every so often, the first sled would pull aside so that the next might take a turn at the heavy work. Progress slowed to a crawl as the train fought its way toward the Amur River. Soon a few riders were called to the front to break the trail, making it a little easier for the horses pulling sleds behind them.

The train of sleds had traveled perhaps three kilometers over the rolling fields before it neared the Russian village of Voykovo. Voykovo was the first outpost of the Soviet border guards. Two outriders had approached the town while the convoy made its way through the fields half a kilometer from its outskirts. They rode back to report that all was quiet and after a short, tense pause, the train of sleds made as much haste as it could to put the village behind it.

The gently rolling fields of the steppe gave way to more unforgiving terrain. Steep slopes of gullies and deep ravines, some without snow, tested horse and driver to the limit. Sleds broke and had to be repaired on the spot. In the severe cold, fingers froze quickly, making it difficult to repair torn leather or splintered wood. The men worked frantically until all feeling left their fingers. Fingers were rubbed with snow to restore circulation. Feeling restored, work quickly resumed.

The sled following Ludwig's carried a family and the whole carcass of a freshly slaughtered beef. Barely controlled, it careened down a slope. The team of horses pulling it was jostled and only just managing to prevent having its hind legs clipped. When the sled hit the bottom of the ravine both of its runners were shattered. While other sleds maneuvered around the wreckage, a decision was quickly reached. It was judged too badly damaged to be salvaged. The family was loaded onto other sleds; the beef would have to stay. As they looked mournfully at the food being left behind, the father said sadly, "Let the wolves have it. Or the border guards."

Another sled broke down right where the border guards were known to patrol. Men worked frantically to repair it while others passed them by.

The train moved painfully slowly. Sleds were constantly being delayed. Tree stumps hidden under the snow wreaked havoc, sometimes entangling horses, at other times upending sleds. In the darkness, drivers never knew what to expect in the terrain they encountered. Dips hidden by snowdrifts could break the tongue of the sled. A rearing horse struggling to drag a sled up a steep embankment bare of snow could tear a harness or splinter a tongue. Multiple sleds were being repaired by desperate men with freezing fingers, faces and toes—six, seven sleds at a time—bringing the whole convoy again and again to a halt.

Those who waited shivered in the cold, their hearts beating in growing fear at the difficulty and slowness of the journey. Men working together on broken sleds and mothers with their children sitting and inactive in their places looked carefully at each other to see the telltale signs of frostbite and hypothermia: pale, bluish-gray, waxy, rubbery skin, excessive shivering, poor judgment, clumsy movements.

The sleds repaired, the train moved painfully onward. Everyone was determined that nothing should stop its progress to the Amur. Under their breath, drivers cursed and cajoled their teams. When their horses balked and refused to move forward, drivers ruefully but fiercely brought their whips down upon the backs of their teams. This was not a time for courtesy or kindness. The elements were conspiring to keep them from their goal and they would not be denied.

The sky was beginning to turn grey in the east as the train of sleds neared the Amur River. But first, it had to bypass the Russian village of Orlovka. Here a company of twenty border guards was stationed and equipped with a heavy machine-gun. Would the guards be extra vigilant today? The silent convoy heard the crowing of roosters in the distance. Sound traveled far in the still air. Would sounds of their passing be heard?

There was no sign of the border patrol.

The train of sleds haltingly passed by Orlovka. As the blackness of night gave way to the deep shadows of early morning, the villagers' sense of vulnerability grew. Willing the horses to pull harder, the sleds to move faster, the train left Orlovka behind them. But ever as they went, the terrified people of Alexandrovka wondered whether the explosive rattle of the machine gun might begin to mow them down.

Still there was no sign of the border patrol.

The convoy moved slowly onward.

At last the vanguard came upon the banks of the Amur River. Those who came upon its edge looked down the steep embankment. Their hearts fainted and they wondered how they would ever bring themselves safely to the river's icy surface.

"We have come this far and now we are faced with an almost vertical drop the height of a two storey house," muttered Abram Siemens as he peered down the slope.

Nevertheless, they were not to be deterred. A group of men gathered around the first sled. After a short discussion they arranged themselves to manhandle both horses and sled over the cliff. Passengers disembarked and were helped down the slope. Then came the sled and horses. The horses reared back and wished to refuse the commands of the men who pulled them over the brink. Fearfully they obeyed and stumbled over the edge and down the embankment. Other men managed the sled, initially by pushing it and then by holding it back lest it tumble down too quickly. The task was slow and strenuous, with great danger for all. But in the end, sled and horses stood safely on the river's icy surface.

Not all sleds survived the descent intact, but at last, all made it down to the surface of the river. The men, heated and sweaty from their exertion, had taken off their coats. Now, shivering, they wrapped themselves again in their furs against the fierce cold. Broken sleds were repaired and reloaded. Their guide, Alexander, looked on, impatient to begin the trek across the frozen river.

And still there was no sign of the border patrol.

In the graying light, an icy mist could be seen here and there floating above the ice. "Good," said Abram, "perhaps it will hide us somewhat in the growing light of day."

When all were finally ready, Alexander pointed the way. The train set out for the opposite shore and China.

From the top of the bank, Jacob watched the last of the sleds disappear into the crystal clouds. He shivered and realized he'd been inactive for too long. He needed to move his body to restore circulation. Climbing off of his horse, he vigorously stamped his feet on the ground and swung his arms across his chest, running around in a small circle. After a few minutes of strenuous movement, he began to feel warmth seeping into his hands and feet. He no longer shivered and knew he should stop. Breaking a sweat would only cause him to become chilled again more quickly.

Jacob mounted his horse. He looked back along the trail of flattened snow left by the train of sleds. Pulling on the reins, he directed his horse to retrace its steps along the trail. After about a hundred meters he came to the last ravine the convoy had had to traverse. Its banks clearly showed the destruction of the convoy's passing. Trampled bushes lay askew as if crushed by the feet of a giant. A multitude of deep ruts were cut into the snow. Loose dirt showed through in places where the howling winds had reduced the snow to a mere skiff.

Jacob stroked his horse's neck and listened carefully. He heard nothing. No birds sang. There was no crackling of snow-laden branches, no exploding bark. He took a final look around. The dormant, frosted pines and bare birch and larch trees along the ridge and in the ravine stretched their frozen branches toward the charcoal sky. "Amazing," Jacob thought, "so much space, such a beautiful place, and not a sound to be heard. It's as if there is no living thing here at all."

Satisfied there was no sign of the border patrol, Jacob turned his horse's head and headed back toward the Amur River. Coming to the familiar embankment, his horse refused to descend the steep incline. Jacob nudged it, encouraging it until it acquiesced and plunged over the edge. The horse slid down on its haunches, Jacob hanging on for dear life. Once at the bottom, Jacob patted its neck to settle it down before heading out onto the ice. It would not be difficult to find his way; the train of sleds had made sure of that.

From the top of the embankment a short distance away, Colonel Yevchenko watched as the man on the ice patted his horse and kicked it into a steady walking pace onto the river. The colonel had not been out on patrol for very long, but was already feeling the effects of the cold. "This is not a night to be out hunting," he had told himself. Thinking he might call it a night, Yevchenko was about to turn back toward his home in Konstantinovka when he espied movement on the riverbank. His heart leaped at the sight. "At last!" he exulted. He had watched as the rider and his horse slid down the bank. Good riding, he had thought absentmindedly.

Yevchenko pulled his rifle from its case. Removing the mitten covering his right hand, he lifted his gun and sighted along the barrel. He carefully moved the bolt and pushed a cartridge into the breech. The steel of the gun felt unbearably cold. His fingers immediately began to go numb. He could feel the moisture on his index finger freeze onto the trigger. He hoped it wouldn't affect his shot. Yevchenko silently cursed the cold that gripped the Amur basin like an iron fist. Knowing he had only a small window of opportunity before he would need to put his mitten back on, the colonel concentrated on his target. The moving horse and rider were clearly in view. Knowing it would not be long before the icy fog that drifted above the river might obscure them, he aimed fractionally in front of the rider and gently squeezed the trigger. CRACK! Almost immediately, horse and rider collapsed onto the ice. "Got him!" the colonel muttered confidently.

Yevchenko urged his horse down the slippery slope of the riverbank.

Jacob felt his horse collapse beneath him before he heard the gunshot. Everything happened so quickly he had no time to react. His horse fell forward as its front legs lost strength and then toppled over on its side. Its legs thrashed about for a few moments. It gave a shuddering cough and lay still.

Jacob lay on his side on the snow-covered ice of the river. When he was finally able to collect his wits, he found that his right leg was pinned beneath his dying horse. He had not had time even to take his foot out of the stirrup before the horse fell. Fortunately, there was a cushion of snow beneath him. He tried to work his leg. It felt fine. He started to tug at it, but the weight of the horse was making it difficult for him to free it.

As he lay in the snow wondering at what had happened, Jacob became aware of movement coming toward him. Craning his neck to look over his horse's body, he saw a horse and rider slide down the riverbank. He lost sight of them as they came to the bottom of the embankment. All suddenly became clear. His heart rose to his throat. "Border patrol," he groaned. He began to pull his leg more vigorously. His heart beat faster and faster. "I must get free," he told himself with each lunge.

Finally, Jacob's leg pulled free. Without thinking he stood up. Realizing his foolishness, he immediately crouched down. To his relief, Jacob felt no pain. "The bullet must only have hit the horse," flitted through his mind.

Jacob kneeled behind his dead horse. He reached into his pocket and took out the Webley revolver. Shaking from fear and cold, he was unaware that he had still got his mitten on. He lifted the gun and pointed it in the direction of the rider who was trotting toward him.

Colonel Yevchenko saw the rider stand and then quickly kneel down. He was not concerned that he had only hit the horse. "I have him," was his only thought. He had put his mitten back on and carried his rifle outstretched for the descent down the riverbank. Rather than stopping for another shot, he decided he would take the man alive and then decide what to do with him. At the thought of the sport to come his heart hammered with adrenaline rushing through his veins.

In his hurry, Colonel Yevchenko did not notice the bowl-shaped indentation in the ice. Nor did his horse. By some trick of the current, a small area of the river's surface had not frozen solid. The snow had collected above it and formed a thin, hard crust; not hard enough to be stepped upon by a man let alone a horse.

Jacob watched the approaching gunman with icy terror. Bundled in his furs as he was, Jacob did not know the man. As the colonel urged his horse forward, the horse stepped on the thin crust of snow and fell through into the river. The colonel cried out in surprise as his horse went down. His left hand held the reins. His right hand holding the rifle flailed to maintain balance. The rifle flew out of his hand and disappeared in the snow. Only Yevchenko's superb horsemanship allowed him to remain in his saddle.

Fortunately, being close to the shore, the water was only a meter or so deep. The horse heaved and lunged in water halfway up its chest. The colonel's legs were covered in water above his knees. His right mitten and hand were soaked from striking the water. The horse reared and scrabbled with its front hooves to find a grip on the ice.

Jacob stood. He recognized the man struggling in the water. "You!" he shouted, surprised and suddenly enraged. "You!" he shouted again in disbelief. Jacob pointed his pistol at the colonel.

Colonel Yevchenko took no notice. He leaped from his horse and landed on the firm ice. Coming around to the horse's head, he tested the ice. It held. He leaned in and grabbed the reins. Pulling on them, he helped the struggling horse as its front hooves fought for a grip on the ice. Its iron shoes finally gave it purchase and it clambered out of the river. The horse shook itself to shed the icy water, but soon began to tremble as the water on its hair and skin immediately began to freeze.

Yevchenko looked his horse over for a moment, checking its legs for damage. Satisfied that it was okay, he turned his attention to Jacob. "Well, if it isn't our little office clerk," he sneered, pulling at his rapidly freezing mitten. Staring at Jacob holding his pistol outstretched in his mittened hand, he laughed. "You ain't gonna shoot anybody with that mitten on."

Without taking his eyes off of Yevchenko, Jacob quickly removed his mitten. It dropped onto the snow at his feet. He pointed the gun at the colonel. His arm trembled with the effort of holding the heavy pistol outstretched. Fear seemed to melt whatever strength his muscles had. The pistol wavered in front of him. He brought up his left hand to support the gun in his right.

"Clerk," Colonel Yevchenko stuttered, beginning to shiver, "What do you think you're going to do with that gun?" He looked down at his legs. His pants were freezing solid. He flexed his legs to break the ice at his knees.

Jacob said nothing. He felt again the terrible pain of Naomi's loss; he smelled and felt the warm, sticky blood seeping from her wound. Caught in the memory, he recognized the great evil of violence and, in a moment of clarity, realized that in taking his revenge he would be perpetuating it vicious cycle. The implications of what he intended swept over him like a tidal wave. He swayed, fighting to maintain his balance.

The colonel saw Jacob's hesitation. "Are you planning on shooting me, clerk? 'Cause if you are, I'd suggest you get on with it."

Jacob said nothing. His breath was coming in gasps. The pistol wavered in his hand.

"Well?" said the colonel. He had meant it as a show of bravado, but there had been no strength behind the word. He was beginning to shiver violently. Seeing the indecision in Jacob's eyes, he spat, "I didn't think so."

"You killed my wife!" shouted Jacob, anger welling up inside him, hot magma bursting into the open.

"What?"

"You killed my wife!" Jacob screamed in anguish.

"What are you talking about?" said Yevchenko, his teeth beginning to chatter. "How did I kill your wife? She died in the Ukraine, you said."

"You killed my wife!" Jacob sobbed, tears beginning to freeze his eyelids, threatening to stick them shut. He blinked furiously and quickly rubbed the back of his mitten across his eyes and nose. He stood rooted behind the carcass of his horse. "At the river! You were in a boat! You shot her! You killed my wife!"

But Yevchenko was no longer paying attention to Jacob. The colonel's face fell as he realized the fingers of his right hand were already past becoming numb. He could feel nothing. His fingers were already refusing to bend. His legs were burning with cold. He was rapidly losing feeling in his toes and feet.

The colonel knew he needed to make a fire. He did not have time for this clerk and his grief. He knew that if he did not warm his body soon, he would suffer irreparable damage. He might lose fingers or toes. No, not or. Fingers and toes. Not probably. For sure. In fact, he thought with a shock, he could lose his life. He imagined the freezing temperatures slowly creeping along his limbs and torso, gradually turning all his organs, his flesh and his blood into stone.

"Help me build a fire, clerk," the colonel said, "I'm freezing."

"Why should I help you?" shouted Jacob. "You killed Naomi! My wife! I should let you freeze! In fact, I'm going to stand here and watch you freeze. It's what you deserve! You deserve to die, you miserable scum, you bloody, sadistic murderer!"

The colonel looked at his hand. The skin had turned a pale bluish white. "My fingers," whimpered Yevchenko. "I can't move my fingers. I won't be able to make a fire quickly enough with only one hand. You must help me." He began to stumble toward the bushes on the riverbank nearby.

Jacob fired a shot into the air. He jumped at the thunderous sound. "Stop," he shouted.

Yevchenko stopped and turned around. He took a step toward Jacob, stumbled on his freezing feet and sank to his knees. "Then shoot me now," he cried through clenched teeth. Slowly his head sank to his chest. His right hand rose to his forehead, its frozen fingers and thumb curled claw-like, then his hand descended to his belly, rose to touch his right shoulder, then his left. He repeated the ritual twice, muttering with each motion, "God bless and protect." He heaved a sigh and attempted to look defiantly at Jacob. His eyes betrayed the fear that had taken hold of him.

Jacob stepped out from behind his dead horse. "What are you doing?" he shouted, recognizing the Russian Orthodox ritual of crossing oneself.

"As a child, my mother took me to Mass," mumbled Yevchenko weakly through his chattering teeth.

"But," Jacob shook his head in disbelief. "But, you're an atheist. You're a communist! You don't believe in God!" shouted Jacob, shocked to see the colonel's pathetic expression of faith.

"One does not so quickly forget the lessons of his mother." The words were soft and slurred.

"You killed the mother of my child, you son of a bitch!" cried Jacob.

Colonel Yevchenko seemed not to hear, Jacob. He struggled to his feet and began stumbling toward the bushes.

Jacob took a step forward. He lifted the pistol and sighted along the cold barrel. The man before him shuffling toward the willow bushes had lost the right to live. Jacob's pulse pounded in his ears. He was finding it difficult to catch his breath. He concentrated on shooting Yevchenko. He did not care if it would be in the man's back. He was a monster who must be stopped.

The gun was steady in Jacob's hands. But Jacob's finger refused to squeeze the trigger.

Jacob took a couple of steps toward the retreating figure. He could not allow too much distance between them. It would be too easy to miss. "Stop," he shouted again. But Yevchenko was passed listening or caring.

Jacob realized that his hand holding the gun was numb. He had lost all feeling in his fingers. He put the gun in his pocket. Taking off his other mitten, he rubbed snow on his freezing fingers. It was not long before it seemed a fire had been lit within them. Jacob welcomed the pain, knowing it signaled the return of blood flowing through the arteries and veins. He put his hand in his pocket to retrieve the gun, but in a moment of clarity he realized he did not have it in him to shoot the colonel. He took his hand out of his pocket empty.

Jacob watched Colonel Yevchenko's pitiful attempts to gather sticks to build a fire. The colonel held his right hand out like a foreign object while floundering in the deeper snow. He pulled fiercely at small dead branches with his left hand. If a branch did not break immediately, he yanked it back and forth, and twisted it. His desperation was clear to see.

"What a wretched, wretched man," thought Jacob. Jacob was at loose ends. He needed to act but was unsure of what he wanted to do. Somehow his desire avenge Naomi's death by killing Yevchenko's was fading. "Am I a coward?" he wondered. "Is that it?" Knowing he could not pull the trigger to kill a fellow human, Jacob thought, "Perhaps I should just leave him. In his condition, it will only be two or three more hours before the cold does what my conscience forbids me to do."

Unbidden, thoughts of the lessons of his faith came to Jacob's mind, teachings drilled into him since he was a child. He saw Jesus' words clearly as if they were written in the Siberian sky. He heard his mother read from the family Bible, *Blessed are the merciful, for they will be shown mercy.* Jacob shook his head. *If you forgive those who sin against you, your heavenly Father will forgive you.* "No," he said aloud. *I tell you, love your enemies and*

pray for those who persecute you. Overcome evil with good.
"Impossible!" cried Jacob.

Jacob looked again at the pathetic figure whimpering and scrambling for twigs and branches. As he watched he realized the abhorrence he had initially felt at the sight of the colonel had been replaced by pity. He felt a melancholy sadness that a human being so loved by God and made in His image could be reduced to what he saw before him, an evil man toppled and brought low to where the trappings of his power could not help him.

Without realizing it, Jacob found himself walking toward where Yevchenko fiddled madly with a small pile of twigs. His frozen right hand was useless. The fingers of his left hand were still working, but his hand was trembling violently. As hard as he tried to make a neat pile of the sticks, his shaking repeatedly scattered them. His right hand was still as stone. "Paper," he was muttering to himself, his teeth chattering uncontrollably. "I need paper. And matches. Where are my matches?"

"Where are your matches?" asked Jacob, coming close.

Yevchenko seemed not to hear.

"Where are your matches?" Jacob said again. He had spoken loudly, in a commanding voice.

"Huh?" Yevchenko looked up. "Matches? In my saddlebag. They're in my saddlebag." There was a flicker of hope in his dull eyes.

"Rub snow on your hand," Jacob commanded. "It'll help."

The colonel scooped up a handful of snow and began frantically rubbing his frozen hand and fingers.

Yevchenko's horse stood nearby. Its head hung low to the ground. Tremors racked its body. It took no notice of Jacob as he drew near. Jacob took off his gloves to better grab what was needed. The cold immediately attacked his fingers, nipping and licking them like a hungry dog. He rifled through the saddlebags and quickly found a box of matches. He also found some documents. Somehow both matches and papers had remained dry.

Bringing what he'd found to where Yevchenko knelt in the snow, Jacob got down beside him. Looking about to make sure there were no snow-laden branches above where he planned to make the fire, Jacob crumpled the paper up into a ball and arranged a few small twigs around and over it.

"H-h-hurry," stuttered the colonel bleakly. "H-h-hurry. My hands are balls of ice. I can't feel my fingers." After a moment, he added, "I can't feel my feet."

Jacob struck a match. It flared weakly and went out. He took another from the box and struck it. It flared and then caught. He held the flame next to an edge of the paper. The paper slowly began to char. A wisp of smoke tickled his nose. A tiny flame appeared and grew. Grey smoke began to billow from the paper ball. Carefully, Jacob fed the growing flames, first with tiny twigs and then with slightly bigger ones. Yevchenko yelped with relief. He dove toward the flames, his hands outstretched. Jacob pushed him aside. "Wait!" was all he said.

The fire grew bigger. Jacob stood and split some dry branches over his knee. Tenderly, so he would not crush the small flaming tinders and kill them, he placed thicker pieces of wood on the fire. Slowly they took up the cause, flames licking their sides before engulfing them. Jacob stood up. He stepped away from the fire. As he stepped back, the colonel crawled close to the fire. Reverently, he held his hands over the flames, bringing them as close to the heat as he could without burning them.

Knowing the colonel's feet were also frozen, Jacob realized Yevchenko needed to sit, not kneel. He looked around for something suitable. He spied a lump in the snow by a fallen tree. Scrapping off the snow, he found a piece of the trunk that had rotted and broken away. It was not very big, but would have to do. Jacob carried the piece of wood and laid it close to the fire. Yevchenko was having trouble controlling his movements, so Jacob helped him to sit on it. "Put your feet close to the fire," Jacob said. "Your boots are frozen solid. We need to get them off."

Jacob heard movement to his left. With sudden realization, he remembered where he was and the danger he was in. He was making a fire. Fires make smoke. Smoke can be seen from a distance. Border guards were patrolling the area. He looked up. What he had heard was Yevchenko's horse moving nearer to the fire. It stood as close as it dared. He saw it was trembling with cold. Jacob sighed with relief.

Yevchenko sat close to the fire, awkwardly keeping his feet near its base while holding his hands above it. If the situation hadn't been so serious, Jacob would have laughed at the sight of him. The colonel looked crumpled and defeated. Jacob noticed Yevchenko's boots were beginning to steam and soften. They were losing the glassy sheen that had coated them. Yevchenko gritted his teeth with pain as his hands began to thaw.

Leaving the colonel where he was, Jacob went about collecting as much dry wood as he could. Every so often, he stopped and searched the top of the riverbank, scanning it slowly. Had the shots been heard by others? In the dim morning light, he could see no sign of any border guards. He knew if they should appear, he would be a dead man.

Jacob threw the dry branches he'd found onto a growing heap close to the fire. When the pile was large and he judged there to be enough, he turned to Yevchenko. "Here," he said, "let me help you with your boots. We should be able to get them off by now."

Together, one pulling one way, the other pulling the other way, Jacob and Yevchenko slowly removed the colonel's sopping boots and socks. "You'll need to dry these completely before you go anywhere," said Jacob needlessly. He looked at Yevchenko's feet. They were white and as hard as ivory.

The colonel looked at Jacob quizzically. "Why are you helping me?" he asked, gritting his teeth at the pain coming from his thawing limbs.

Jacob did not answer. He scanned the embankment one more time looking for the border patrol. All was still.

With a last look at Yevchenko sitting by the fire Jacob turned his back on him. He walked out onto the ice of the Amur River. As he followed the broken trail of snow and ice left by the train of sleds, he set his face toward China. For a while, as he walked southward Jacob could hear the colonel's howls as the pain of the feeling returning to his frozen hands and feet became unbearable. Gradually the cries became quieter until eventually

Jacob heard only the crunching of his winter boots upon the crusted snow.

"Why did I help him?" Jacob asked himself. He put the question away, knowing one day he would need to answer it. For now, he did not have the strength or will to consider it. His one concern was to follow the tracks left by the train of sleds and to find his family.

As he walked upon the frozen river, Jacob felt a wave of relief. After the shock of meeting Yevchenko and after the storm of emotions the confrontation had unleashed, he suspected he was leaving more than the crippled man by the fire behind him. Jacob's steps became lighter as he hurried toward the far shore.

In the grey light of morning, the train of sleds fought its way across the broken ice on the Amur River. Wherever possible, Alexander led the fleeing villagers around the jagged block piles. In some places, though, there were so many ice jams the sleds were forced to go over them. Passengers were unloaded to reduce the risk of injury, and men and horses worked together to wrangle the sleds over the uneven crags. While the rest if the train waited impatiently, sleds that overturned were quickly righted, their baggage and passengers reloaded. More sleds broke down. If they could not be moved aside to let other sleds by, the train halted again while repairs were made.

With agonizing slowness, fifty-four sleds clawed their way toward China. And ever as they went, Abram Siemens would stand up on his sled and look back, scanning the receding shore. He knew it was impossible to see a man hidden amongst the trees now almost a kilometer away—even had the light been brighter—though he thought he might see the flash of the rising sun's reflected rays on the glass of binoculars. He could not help himself. He had to look back.

The train came upon a collection of small islands in the river. The drivers urged their tired teams around and between them. As the sleds passed the last island and found open ice before them, Abram, together with other drivers and passengers, began to crane his neck for the first view of the distant Chinese shoreline where the village of Kani Fu awaited their arrival.

Seeing the faint smug of smoke from the Kani Fu's fires, Rachel nudged Joseph. "See," she said pointing. "China. That's where we're going."

And even as she spoke, Rachel wondered where her husband, Jacob, was. She knew he was part of the rearguard. He was patrolling behind the train, watching for enemies who might try to stop them. Her mind grasped onto that word, "Enemies."

"Enemies," Rachel thought. "I've never considered the communists as my enemies before. But I guess that's what they are. That's what the border patrol really is. The communists have persecuted us relentlessly for years. The border patrol who are the servants of the communist leaders will certainly not hesitate to shoot at us if they find us." Silently she prayed for the border patrol. "May they neglect their duty and stay close to their fires on this cold, cold night. And may they drink their vodka until they cannot stand up straight." She smiled at impertinence of her prayer. Becoming more serious, she prayed for Jacob's safety, "And, if some of the guards are more diligent in their duty this day, hide my dear husband from their eyes, oh Lord." Rachel considered the brutal cold and the fact Jacob was traveling alone. She prayed no accident would befall him and that he would be strong in the face of the cruel weather.

Now that the islands were between the train of sleds and the Russian shoreline, one would think the anxieties and fears of the villagers would be lessened. After all, they could no longer be seen from the Russian side. They had traveled more than one and a half kilometers of ice from the Russian shore, but still no one felt safe. They knew they had left a clearly visible trail on the ice. It could be followed by the dullest of soldiers. And as the light of day grew stronger, more than a few imagined a posse of horsemen flying across the river to stop them. Many glanced fearfully backward to see what demons came behind them. The closer they drew to the Chinese shore creeping slowly toward them, the greater was their fear that they might never reach it.

As the smoke from Kani Fu's fires grew darker in the sky and as the trees on its shoreline grew more distinct, those riding in the last sleds noted a walking figure following them in the distance. They looked closely at it to divine who it might be, but could not make out if it were a friend or a foe.

At last, to the welcoming chorus of Kani Fu's roosters, the train of sleds reached the little bay with the wide road that led straight into the heart of the Chinese village. The exhausted horses slowly pulled their sleds one by one up the gentle incline and passed the first house at which Jacob had seen the old, suspicious crone.

As the refugees from Alexandrovka entered the village, the residents of Kani Fu gathered in a large crowd to greet them.

Strangers greeted one another with silent stares and shy nods of the head, the steam of their breath mingling in the cold morning air.

In the excitement, a lone figure walked purposefully by the last sled, making its way through the convoy with determined steps. The hoar frost and ice that had formed on his beard and the clothing tucked closely to his face hid the exhaustion he felt and the distracted look in his eyes.

Jacob wound his way through the throng gathered in Kani Fu's narrow road until he found his family. He almost wept with relief when he saw Rachel and Joseph standing amongst a group of people beside the sled that had carried them across the river. Despite the ordeal they had been through, his first impression was that they both appeared to be in good health.

As he came near, Jacob saw that Rachel and Joseph were struggling to unload some baggage from the sled. Ruth stood atop the sled, handing down the heavy bundles. Beside them, Anna looked on as a Chinese man was earnestly speaking with her husband. It was clear that Ludwig did not understand a word the man was saying. The man began gesticulating to make clear what he meant. Ludwig finally caught his meaning when the man pointed the way to his home, gesturing that they should follow him to it.

Jacob came up beside Rachel and touched her shoulder. Turning, to see whom it was, Rachel gasped with relief. She looked at Jacob with shining eyes; her husband had finally rejoined them. Jacob tried to smile but the ice covering his frozen mustache and beard held his lips firmly in a grim line. Only his eyes showed how welcome was the sight of his beloved family to him.

Sleds began to disappear down side alleys as families were led to the homes that would host them. Weary horses gave a last effort; somehow they knew their journey was coming to an end. It wasn't long before it became obvious there simply were not enough homes in Kani Fu to house so many refugees. Those who remained on the road when all the hosts had left with their guests were sent to another village nearby.

The Hostetlers together with Jacob, Rachel, Joseph and Ruth followed their Chinese host to a small dwelling off the main road. He bowed and opened the door for them. Shyly they stepped across the threshold. After so many hours in the extreme cold, the warmth inside the home embraced them like a hot bath. A smiling Chinese woman welcomed them, showing them where they could put down their few belongings. As the ladies removed their coats and boots, she indicated the stovetop and began to fill bowls with hot millet gruel.

Jacob and Ludwig were bringing into the house the last of their bedding when, from the corner of the *kang* where she was unwrapping the blankets with which she had protected Peter from the cold, Anna wailed, "My baby! My baby!" And she broke down with cries of utter grief.

Ludwig was first by her side. His little son lay still on the blankets. His skin was grey. Ludwig touched his face. It was cold. The little eyes were closed, as if in sleep. Panicking, Ludwig placed his fingers under Peter's small nose. No warmth came from inside them; Peter was not breathing. Ludwig picked up the still form and hugged it to him. He began weeping loudly for it was clear Peter was dead.

Anna was inconsolable. She took Peter from her husband. Sobs wracked her body. Still holding her son, she threw herself down upon the *kang* moaning in despair. Her daughters, Judith and Margaret quickly joined her, weeping to see their mother's grief.

Rachel quickly joined Anna and her daughters on the *kang*. Somehow her arms were able to tightly encompass them all as together they wept over the tragedy that had befallen them.

After awhile, Anna began to moan, "I have smothered my baby! I should not have wrapped him so tightly!" Rocking her son she wailed, "I should have checked on him as we went! It is my fault he is dead! My son is dead!"

As their tears mingled, Rachel did not try to convince Anna that Peter's death had not been her fault. She knew that to be the truth, but that was a conversation to be had another day. Nor did she suggest that God was in control of what had happened and that there was a good reason why Anna's little son had been taken from her. She knew such notions, though often expressed in distressing times by well-meaning people, were false.

Swept into the miasma of grief and despair, Joseph standing in the center of the room began to cry softly. He reached up to his father who was standing numbly beside him. Jacob picked up his son and hugged him, trying to calm him and bring him comfort even as he sought to contain his own grief.

As the heartbroken families wept their sorrow, their Chinese host quietly slipped outside on the excuse of seeing to Ludwig's horses. His wife busied herself with small tasks in her house, trying to be inconspicuous in her own home, wishing somehow to bring comfort but unable to communicate her heartfelt sympathy to the distraught foreigners. Eventually, she thought to boil water for tea, to be ready for offering when the time was right.

And so, the families mourned their devastating loss. The harrowing, painful hours they had just spent crossing the Amur River in -50 degree temperatures were all but forgotten. They became as nothing to them for nothing could compare to the pain brought about by the death of a young child.

The next day, Ludwig and Jacob carried a borrowed pick ax and shovel to a place shown to them by their Chinese host. It was the village's graveyard. On a barren hillside they broke through the frozen soil. They dug a grave in the unyielding, rocky ground that was just large enough to hold a child who had not yet seen his third birthday. Anna had wrapped Peter's pale little body in a warm comforter. Bending his knees, Ludwig kissed his child's forehead and laid him down in the cold earth. Standing again, he took his wife in his arms. In unison they shook their heads in disbelief at the horror they were experiencing while their tears froze upon their cheeks. Even as the grave was filled with stones and dirt, they prayed they would awaken from such a bad dream.

Theirs was a nightmare, but it was no dream.

Friends who had fled the Soviet Union with the Hostetlers gathered with Ludwig, Anna, Judith and Margaret around the small grave. Abram Siemens read a passage of comfort from the Bible. From memory they sang hymns that for years now they had been forbidden, on threat of imprisonment, to sing aloud in public. To some the reaffirmations of their faith brought comfort. To others, it was the solidarity they felt standing in the open air with their fellow believers rather than the songs that were sung or the prayers that were uttered that brought them a sense of hope for the future. For, while the community lamented the

Hostetlers' loss using the traditions of their faith, it did so freely without fear of reprisal.

Anna wept all the harder at the pressing reality of the funeral; as it ended she began pulling at her hair. The thought of being forced to leave her son buried in a place she would likely not ever again be able to visit was more than she could bear.

As the refugees of Alexandrovka left the graveyard to return to the warmth of their hosts' simple homes, Jacob's thoughts turned again toward the north and the icy bank of the Amur River. He wondered if danger approached from that direction. He had left alive a man there who could send others in pursuit of them.

What Have I Done?

It was not Jacob only who worried about a Russian pursuit. A Chinese host spoke to his guests of raids by the Soviet border patrol in which they took prisoner people who had escaped across the river, forcibly returning them to the Soviet Union. Word quickly spread among the refugees that it was not unusual for the Russians to cross the river looking for escapees. The euphoria that had suffused them after their escape was replaced by the biting fear of recapture. With travel arrangements still to be made, the refugees were trapped in Kani Fu. They had nowhere to go. There was nowhere to hide.

In the darkness of their second night in the village, Jacob and Rachel lay in their soft bedding upon the warm *kang*. His lips close to her ear, Jacob whispered to Rachel what had happened on the north shore of the Amur River. He told her of his fear of what might come as a result. Though he could not see her eyes for the darkness, they grew wide in fear of what could have happened and at the thought of what might still come of it.

"Do you think he will send the patrol after us?" Rachel squeaked, her mind racing. "Perhaps he didn't make it back to Konstantinovka. Do you think he will have survived?"

"I don't know," Jacob said in answer to all of her questions, "though I'd have thought if he were going to send the patrol after us, he'd have done so already. They would have come yesterday or today."

"Do you really think so?" Rachel asked, wanting to believe in the possibility that there would be no pursuit.

Remembering the condition in which he had left the colonel, Jacob said, "His feet were badly frozen, but if he took the time to warm them and to dry his socks and boots thoroughly, he had a good chance of surviving." As an afterthought he added, "His horse was still with him when I left."

"I'm glad you left him living," Rachel murmured. "You could not have lived with yourself had you done otherwise." Then, after a moment's reflection she asked, "Should we not tell the others?"

After discussing it awhile, Rachel and Jacob decided they would tell no one of what had happened. If the Soviets came there was nothing anyone could do about it. They were stuck in this village until they had permission to travel and the means to do so. Adding fuel to the fire of everyone's fears would serve no purpose.

A meeting was held the next day at which the refugees affirmed Abram Siemens' leadership. His skills would be needed now more than ever as their representatives met with government leaders and organized travel arrangements. Other leaders were chosen to help Abram. Jacob declined when asked to serve; his place now, he said, was with his family.

The meeting was hardly over when a squad of Chinese policemen arrived from the nearby town of Chikade. They immediately confiscated all of the refugees' firearms. When they knocked on the door of the home in which he was staying, Jacob happily handed over his Webley pistol. Taking the gun from his coat pocket, he felt its weight and looked at its dull gleam. As he put it into the Chinese officer's palm, he felt a huge burden being taken from him, as if he had just rolled a stone away from the mouth of an empty tomb.

Jacob knew now that he could never use a gun against an enemy, even in defense of his own life. In his quiet moments of reflection he no longer questioned whether his inability to shoot the colonel meant he was a coward. Rather, he felt that his actions in saving Yevchenko's life were the bravest he had ever done. And, as a Christian, were they not also the most Christ-like, he wondered. He had shown mercy to a man who, humanly speaking, had merited none, a man who, if he had been able, would have killed him.

At night before he fell asleep, when Jacob relived his experience on the river, he thought again of Jesus' impossible command to love your enemy and to pray for him. He was sure he had felt no love for the colonel and he had yet to pray for him. As for forgiveness, he had no idea of whether he was capable of such an act let alone how to go about doing it. But, he wondered, had not his actions in saving Yevchenko's life been a higher form of love? Had he, in that act—while not feeling able to forgive—had he not shown forgiveness? What could be more forgiving than to save the life of your enemy? In all of his uncertainty, he was certain of one thing, that he had done the right thing.

The Chikade police demanded import duties, claiming the cost of bringing horses into their country was five rubles per horse. Various other taxes were also levied, seemingly at random. More than one of the refugees wondered if the police weren't simply taking the opportunity presented by the newcomers' arrival to spread jam on their own bread. Begrudgingly, they paid what was required.

While the police collected their taxes, traders from surrounding villages began to arrive in Kani Fu. Some insistently pestered the refugees, trying to sell their wares. Others looked at the Russian horses of the refugees and hounded their owners with offers to buy. When the traders discovered that many of the refugee women had brought sewing machines with them, their eyes lit up. Good sewing machines were expensive and hard to come by in their isolated part of China. But no matter how hard they haggled they could find no one willing to part with their machine. Eventually the traders left, disgruntled and disappointed.

From that night on, though, the refugees from Alexandrovka placed guards in the stables in which their horses rested. They knew their animals might prove to be too much of a temptation for some of the Chinese peasants.

Abram Siemens and two other men traveled to Zakholian, eighty kilometers away to obtain visas for the refugees' stay in China. They also needed to arrange buses for the journey to Qiqihar, 580 kilometers to the southwest. Qiqihar was the regional capital of the Amur District. There, the refugees could catch a train to Harbin where many countries' consulates were located. There they could apply for permission to immigrate to Canada and the United States.

Jacob was happy to let others do the work of the inner circle. For him now the welfare of his family was all that mattered. After helping with any necessary chores, his days were spent talking with Rachel and playing with his son. He found some pieces of wood and whittled tiny figures for Joseph's amusement, though time with Joseph was sometimes scarce; he had become Judith and Margaret's center of motherly attention.

Abram Siemens and his helpers returned after a few days with the news a Chinese visa for each adult would cost ten rubles per month. The refugees gladly opened their wallets.

The matter of the buses was not so easily managed. Eight buses were needed to carry all 217 of the refugees. The charge was 8000 Chinese dollars. The refugees were shocked at the exorbitant fee. All must share the cost, though some had not the money to pay their portion of such a huge amount. Those who could loaned money for the payment to those who needed it. The buses were secured.

Christmas came and went unnoticed as the refugees from Alexandrovka languished in Kani Fu waiting for their transportation to Qiqihar to arrive. Jacob and Rachel thought that the date on which they celebrated the birth of Christ must be near. Or had it passed? Who had a calendar that they could check? The days ran into each other and became a long ambivalent blur. Time had slowed and become somnolent as they sat or lay on the warm *kang* in the hut of their hosts.

With little else to do, they found themselves becoming acquainted with the Chinese lice. The insects did not distinguish between the hosts they preferred. Jacob and Rachel muttered in disgust, scratching and giving blood to the vermin at night and searching the seams of their clothing for the pests during the half-light of day. Anna and Ludwig grudgingly matched them in their mission to eliminate the itchy plague. Their Chinese hosts smiled apologetically while doing the same.

Finally word came that eight buses would pick up the refugees in Kochurikho, a village a few kilometers away. The road to Kani Fu was too decrepit for a bus to manage. The day of the buses' arrival was uncertain so the refugees would need to wait for them in Kochurikho.

The refugees harnessed up the horses that were left to them after the payment made to their guide, Alexander. Knowing they would still need their horses, Abram Siemens had made a new bargain with Alexander. Small families could go together in their payment. Alexander settled on taking from the people of Alexandrovka only twenty of their best horses. Jacob's horse was one of them. When the horses were collected and stood together in a herd, Alexander smiled the smile of a wealthy man and promised to lead the refugees to their next destination.

The refugees loaded their sleds with their children and their belongings and made the trip to Kochurikho on narrow icy roads that wound through the hilly Chinese countryside. Hope grew in their hearts for they were leaving the Russian border further behind. In front of them was the promise of transport to the Chinese interior where no Soviet border patrol could venture to find them.

Listening to the swish of the runners on ice and snow and bundled in their coats and furs, not a few of the refugees could hold back memories of their hazardous trip across the Amur ten days earlier. It lay still fresh and heavy in their minds.

Anna Hostetler sobbed as she left the village of Kani Fu and its graveyard behind. Ludwig walked beside the sled in which his wife rode. His head was bowed; he gritted his teeth in his grief and stared at the snowy ground as it appeared step by step in front of his winter boots.

Walking beside Rachel, Joseph, and Ruth riding in the sled, Jacob Enns looked straight ahead. What the future held, he hoped, must surely be better than what lay behind.

Through the Blue Mountains of China

December 27, 1930

The town of Kochurikho was a ramshackle collection of huts and businesses on the main road to Qiqihar. The train of sleds carrying the refugees from Alexandrovka arrived in the town in the early afternoon. Groups of sleds split off to find accommodation in the inns that hugged the road and nearby alleyways.

Jacob and Rachel found the townspeople to be unfriendly and suspicious of the refugees' presence. Perhaps they had seen too many German Russian migrants fleeing over their roads and through their fields. Indeed, Jacob was surprised to find there were several other refugee groups already in the town that had also recently escaped into China. It seemed the people in other villages near the Alexandrovka collective had had the same dream as had the people of his village. As the groups mingled there were many merry meetings of relatives and old friends who hadn't known of each other's plans. Chinese guests at the inns responded by stealing from the refugees what was not hidden or locked away and by making the refugee women uncomfortable with their lascivious stares.

After three days the hoped-for buses arrived. Looking at their dilapidated condition, Jacob wondered if they were sound enough to make the long drive. He asked Ludwig Hostetler for his opinion. Ludwig shrugged pessimistically. He'd been listening to the noisy engine of the bus he'd been assigned to. There was something about it that worried him, a faint sound that should not have been there.

Jacob helped the driver of his bus tie the passengers' luggage to the bus's running boards. When all was ready, the refugees crowded themselves into the bus like chickens in a small crate. When he was finally seated, Joseph on his lap and Rachel pushed up against his side, Jacob wondered how the overloaded old bus would manage to carry so much weight over the mountain passes that lay between Kochurikho and Qiqihar.

Looking through the window, Jacob saw Ludwig and his family climb aboard their bus. He smiled and waved. Though Ludwig glanced in his direction, he seemed preoccupied and did not respond.

Without a word from its driver, Jacob's bus rumbled out of town. It became quickly obvious the road was filled with ruts and potholes. Sitting cheek to jowl, the refugees grunted and mumbled apologies for the rocking bumps and swaying shoves they gave each other in time with the rhythm of their creaking bus's grinding gears and howling engine.

Coming to an icy hill, the bus quickly lost traction. The men piled out and pushed. Reaching the top, they climbed back aboard, only to repeat the procedure at the next icy stretch on a rise in the road.

The road was long and weary. Climbing out of the valley, the bus took them through mountain passes, along narrow roads hanging above deep gorges with ice-encrusted waterfalls and rivers rushing over their stony beds far below. They creaked over rickety one-lane bridges that trembled as they drove over them. For a time they traveled over the high barren Mongolian plateau before climbing again over the last passes through the mountain range to the lowlands beyond.

Through the frosted window beside them, Jacob and Rachel stared at the passing countryside, draped in the ragged white cloak of winter. They reminded each other that these mountains with their rounded, flat peaks were the same ones they had seen shining blue in the distance from Alexandrovka.

Finally the bus left the mountains behind and traveled over the wide, empty steppe of northern China. The vast grasslands stretched beyond view around them. Little moved upon the steppe, though once or twice along the road they came upon lonely collections of low, circular tents huddled beside corrals in which flocks of sheep crowded together for warmth. Outside of one village, they saw a man leading a string of camels along the road.

With stops for the night at wayside inns, Jacob counted the days until finally they arrived in Qiqihar. The road began to widen and became smoother. His body, exhausted and vibrating from the interminably rough ride, sagged with relief. He looked out his window at large buildings blocking the sky. After the long trip over the vast, open steppe, he felt a little claustrophobic entering the man-made canyon.

The bus drove through the arched gate in the tall crenellated castle wall of the city and came to a stop in front of a two-storey inn with a covered veranda hanging from its façade. Locals eyed the *laowai*, the pale foreigners, as they tottered off the bus onto the paving stones of the sidewalk. Seeing nothing of interest, they turned away and continued with their business. Jacob joined the refugees brushing away the crust of dirt and snow from their belongings before untying them from the bus's running board.

The End of One Road and the Beginning of Others

It would be two weeks before all of the refugees from Alexandrovka arrived in Qiqihar. The old buses staggered into the city one by one like blistered and worn out marathoners. Worried friends in the city waited together, commiserating and wondering at the delays, rejoicing when one more rattletrap creaked to a stop in front of their gathering place.

When asked about their trip, passengers in one bus spoke of stopping along the road and standing out on the frozen wind-blown steppe for hours while a new mother aboard the bus struggled to give birth to her child. Another bus was delayed so that a family could bury their elderly father who had died as they bumped and jostled on the rough mountain road. Still another bus was accosted by a gang of thieves that rummaged through the refugees belongings looking for anything worth taking.

Ludwig and Anna's bus was last to arrive. Jacob saw immediately that it was not the same bus as the one in which they had left Kochurikho. The pinched, haggard faces of each member of the Hostetler family reflected the exhaustion they all felt.

After they were all settled in their rooms, Jacob asked Ludwig what had happened. He told stories of their bus crashing into a ditch on an icy hill and then later, of a mechanical breakdown. "I knew there was something wrong with that motor the moment I first heard it," he grumbled. He spoke of a group of men, he among them, wandering over the steppe in a blizzard looking for shelter when the engine of their bus died. He talked of painful frostbite on the fingers and toes of some of the children, and of the kindness of a Chinese peasant who somehow managed to accommodate them all until a replacement bus arrived.

"What kept us going," said Ludwig as he warmed himself by a hot stove, "was the dream that we will finally arrive at a better place. When it seemed we were being stretched beyond our ability to endure, we simply refused to give up." He looked fiercely at Jacob. "There was always the hope that with God's help we will one day be able to provide a better future for our children. We would not give in to circumstances that would deny us that chance."

Jacob found it difficult to imagine the ordeal the Hostetlers had endured while he and his family waited impatiently for them to arrive at the inn in Qiqihar. But he knew the hope Ludwig spoke of. It was the same hope that had led him and Naomi on their disastrous attempts to first go to Moscow and then to cross the Amur River by boat. It was the same hope that had propelled the entire village of Alexandrovka to leave everything behind and cross the Amur River into China. It was the same hope that had sustained him as his family traveled on their own bus across the mountains of northern China to where they now sat by a warm stove in Qiqihar. That hope drove all of the decisions he and Rachel were making; their future, Joseph's future, must be better than was their past.

Jacob looked at Ludwig and nodded his agreement. "We're almost there," he said.

While they waited for the government's permission to proceed to Harbin the refugees languished in their rented rooms. After the many expenses along the way, they had little money left to pay for their food and lodgings. Meals were rationed. They began to trade their clothing for the necessities of life.

Jacob and Ludwig tried to find jobs by which they could earn a few dollars. However, without their guide, Alexander, to translate they could not communicate with the people they met. No one had any interest in employing them. They ate disappointment for breakfast, lunch and dinner. At night Jacob stewed over their dilemma. Without money or work, the day might come when they would be forced to beg for food. And from where would the fare for the tickets needed for his family's train ride to Harbin come?

Finally, after weeks of waiting, word arrived that permission had been granted for them to continue on to Harbin. A crowd of refugees had gathered to hear the news. When they were told that their train fares were being paid for by charitable funds raised in Harbin, Jacob's heart soared along with the others.

"We're not alone!" he shouted in amazement. "Someone is willing to help us!" he marveled. "What seemed impossible has become possible!"

The day came when Jacob, Rachel, Joseph, and Ruth were to board the train bound for Harbin. Arriving at the station the refugees gathered on the loading platform. Suddenly they heard a gasp. On the station house, a Russian flag was flying jauntily next to the Chinese flag. Were there Russians here, they wondered. Everyone looked about nervously. Would they be discovered and sent back to the Soviet Union? Someone learned the truth and passed it along through the anxious crowd: the Russians and Chinese had built the railway together, but the workers now were all Chinese. To everyone's relief, there were no Russians present.

As he received his family's tickets, Jacob noticed a calendar behind the stationmaster's counter. It read, February 12, 1931. He was amazed at the time that had passed since their flight across the Amur.

As the train chuffed out of the station Jacob thought about what lay ahead. Abram Siemens had said housing had been arranged for them all in an apartment building that had been rented and set aside for them in Harbin. Harbin's German Refugee Committee and other charities were continuing to raise money for their support. German residents in Harbin had contacts within the foreign consulates. He worried, though, about a rumor spreading among the people. They had been told Canada and the United States were not taking any refugees. Was it true? Time would tell.

"We're almost there," Jacob said, smiling at Rachel. "Next is Harbin. Then, who knows? Who knows where we'll be this time next year?"

Rachel took Jacob's hand in hers and squeezed it. "Yes," she said. "We've done it! We're free!" She poked Joseph, "You're going to have a new life. You'll go to school in a new land. You'll receive a good education." She looked brightly at Jacob, "Perhaps you'll be able to teach again."

Sitting nearby, her knitting needles fluttering, Ruth overheard the conversation. She smiled and nodded her agreement without losing concentration on the pair of socks she was making for her grandson.

Jacob and Rachel looked out the window of their railway car as the Chinese countryside began flying by and the last buildings of Qiqihar disappeared in the distance. Joseph turned in his seat to resume the game he was playing with Judith and Margaret Hostetler.

Historical Notes

This novel is a work of fiction based on actual historical events.

Encouraged by the regional government of the Amur District in 1927, Mennonite pioneers from Slavgorod established the village of Shumanovka in southeast Siberia, about twenty kilometers from the Amur River. They were trying to escape the oppressive policies of communist government by distancing themselves from Moscow. As experienced farmers, their community flourished. Many other villages in the region were established around the same time. One year after Shumanovka was established, the government forcibly collectivized the villages. Four villages, Shumanovka, Kleefeld, Friedensfeld and New York, were grouped together to become the Shumanovka Collective.

In southeast Siberia, the Amur River forms the border between Russia and China. In the summer of 1930, the leaders of the Shumanovka Collective concocted a plan to escape from the Soviet Union. Under the watchful eye of the GPU, the Soviet Secret Police, they pretended to prepare for a trip to cut firewood in the forests of Khabarovsk, 800 kilometers away. Instead, when the time was right, they intended to cross the frozen Amur River into China. Led by Jakob Siemens, the manager of the collective, they invited the residents of the three other villages in the collective to join them.

The village of New York agreed to participate in the plan, but at the last moment its leaders asked for a delay. They needed extra time to sell their flour. Threatened by the leaders of New York with exposure if he did not comply, Siemens agreed. On the night of December 16, 1930, afraid of the increasing danger of discovery by the police, the people of the Shumanovka village decided to make their escape alone. Together with a few close friends and relatives from other villages who had come to join them, 218 people in 54 sleds successfully crossed the river in -50 degree temperatures.

Guided by Alexander, a local, trusted Chinese smuggler, the refugees reached the Chinese village of Kani Fu in the early morning hours of December 17, 1930. While arrangements were made for the next leg of the journey, the refugees were forced to stay in Kani Fu for ten days, ever anxious about the possibility of a Russian border patrol raid.

After many setbacks, on February 12, 1931, the refugees from Shumanovka arrived in Harbin, China, an international city where many western governments had consulates. The refugees lived and worked in the city for a year while the Mennonite Central Committee lobbied foreign governments to allow them into their countries. All favored going to Canada or the United States, but neither country would accept them. In the end, only Paraguay offered them a home. The entire group left Harbin on February 22, 1932, for the long journey to the Paraguayan Chako, a region already settled by other German Mennonite emigrants from Russia.

Woven into the narrative of this novel are other documented escape attempts. They include the Moscow migration in the fall of 1929, the mother who sent her children to play on the ice of the Amur until the time was right that they could run across to China, the abortive attempt by a young couple to take a boat across the river during which the wife was shot dead, and the attempt to cross the river by a group of families from Shumanovka that failed when their guide failed to show up as promised.

There are many other accounts of the brave attempts to escape the Soviet Union by crossing the Amur River into China. Many of those attempts were successful. As a result of the evacuation of whole villages in the winter of 1930-1931, those who remained in the villages of the Mennonite collectives were eventually moved far away from the river by the authorities.

For more information, check out these resources that I found most helpful.

Escape Across the Amur River: A Mennonite Village Flees (1930) from Soviet Siberia to Chinese Manchuria, by Abram Friesen and Abram J. Loewen, Translated by Victor G. Doerksen,

Echo Historical Series, Published by CMBC Publications, Winnipeg, Manitoba, 2001

Events and People: Events in Russian Mennonite History and the People That Made Them Happen, by Helmut T. Huber, Springfield Publishers, Winnipeg, Canada 1999

The Odyssey of Escapes From Russia: The Saga of Anna K., by Wilmer A. Harms, Hearth Publishing, Hillsboro, Kansas, 1998

River of Glass, by Wilfred Martens, Herald Press, Scottdale, USA, 1980

"Harbin (Heilongjiang, China) Refugees," article by Robert L. Klassen, Gameo, 2009

51748393R00141

Made in the USA
Middletown, DE
13 November 2017